The Shadow Beyond the Hills

EMMA LAWSON

Emma Lawson has asserted her right to be identified as the author of this work.
This book is a work of fiction. Names, characters, businesses, organisations, places and events other than those clearly in the public domain, are either the product of the author's imagination or are used fictitiously. Any resemblance to actual persons, living or dead, is entirely coincidental.

Copyright © 2023 Emma Lawson
All rights reserved.
ISBN: 9798868206870

For Micah, Zach and Ava

Prologue

Marie lay on a rough, grainy bedsheet and blinked at the IV drip hooked to her hand. She tried to lift her fingers, but they were too heavy. A lady in a white uniform brought a bottle of water to her lips. She choked. It was like she'd forgotten how to swallow. The window was open a little and a light breeze blew through the room, lifting a sheet of paper on a clipboard at the end of her bed. Where was she? A ghostly choir of faint groaning surrounded her. She could barely move. When she turned her head, she was bludgeoned with pain, every nerve screaming for release. A row of beds partially hidden by mint green curtains flanked the room and stretched down further than she could possibly see. How did she get here? She closed her eyes in exhaustion and lost herself to specks of white light floating in the darkness behind her eyes.

'I'm here, don't worry, I'm here. Komera.'

Marie forced her eyes open. Kevine's familiar

outline became clearer and filled her with comfort.

'Oh, my sister.' Kevine took Marie's hand and held it with both of hers.

Marie formed words in her mind, but as soon as she tried to speak, they were gone. It was too hard. She was too tired.

'Shh, rest now.'

With Kevine by her side, she succumbed to sleep again.

She woke up to a stinging pain shooting through the back of her head as a lady in a green uniform began to unwrap her dressing. She still had no idea where she was or why she was there.

A woman with skin as pale as the walls appeared at Marie's side. She sank to her knees, closed her eyes and started whispering. Marie looked at Kevine, who was sitting on the opposite side of her.

Kevine lifted her hands, palms facing the ceiling. 'Yes, Lord. Amen,' she kept repeating as the white woman paused between laboured whispers.

Marie had no idea what the woman was saying. It was all just a string of meaningless sound.

When she finally stopped, Kevine said, 'Marie, can you tell me who is kneeling next to you?'

The walls started closing in. The room shook and nausea rose up from her belly. All she saw was darkness. Then the little orbs of white light appeared again.

PART ONE

CHAPTER ONE
BEAUTY FROM ASHES

They weren't how she imagined they'd be. She'd pictured Tim as a big, bulky man with sandy-coloured hair, and Anna a short, petite woman with hair the colour of the sun. How different real life was from the things she imagined. Would she be what they had imagined? What if they decided they didn't want her? Were they going to come and go like all the other visitors to the centre, bringing with them the energy of the wind that comes just before a downpour in rainy season, and petering out just as quickly? Abazungu were as pale as the moon, but their presence was as rich and fruitful as the dark volcanic soil in the countryside around her. They made things grow. New buildings would spring up. There would be a few more cows for the farm, books for the school, clothes that spoke another story from another country.

'Right, Miss, how about you go and freshen up.

Emma Lawson

Splash a bit of water on your face and change your clothes, yes?' said Mama. Her white face was etched with lines on her brow and creases around her eyes and mouth. 'First impressions count for a lot.' The lines and creases softened and smoothed out as she stroked Marie's hair. 'Go on, off you go.'

Marie didn't freshen up; she wanted to see the abazungu as soon as they got out of the car. She snuck out of her dormitory and made her way along a path lined by neatly cut hedges, past the court where Paul was playing basketball, to Mama's cottage near the entrance to the compound. The scorched air of dry season pricked the inside of her mouth and orange dust swirled in her wake.

Once inside the dim light of Mama's cottage, safe from prying eyes, she followed the narrow corridor to the bedroom at the end of the cottage, shut the door and settled herself on the bed by the window. She rested her head against the windowpane and waited, drumming her fingers against her thighs. The room was immaculately made up with the usual flourishes that Mama made sure the staff added when there were visitors. Hand sanitiser, a King James Bible, and a pot of Bougainvillea with a single lily erupting through the centre stood on the table by the bed.

Emmanuel cranked open the gates. An old Toyota Hilux crawled up the drive, coming to a stop beside the flame tree. Mama said its deep red flowers reminded her of the fall in Pennsylvania, where she lived before starting Beauty from Ashes.

Tim got out of the car first and walked toward Emmanuel, his face breaking into a wide smile. He greeted Emmanuel with an outstretched arm white as

The Shadow Beyond the Hills

bone.

Tim was as skinny as a stalk of corn. They couldn't have been American – Americans usually looked healthier and better fed. Marie had overhead other girls talking about this. Americans can drive anywhere to get meat, eat in their cars and then drive home where they have more meat. Europeans can do this too, but they don't want to be fat because white women in magazines and movies look like they don't eat anything other than a few beans. The richer you are, the poorer and sicker you look. The girls had laughed about this.

Thick, dark-brown hair framed Tim's narrow face. Anna followed him, her steps measured and calm. Her willowy figure was wrapped in cream trousers and a sky-blue blouse which buttoned up close to her neck, concealing her milky skin.

She could see them mouth Kinyarwanda greetings – this much they knew. They even understood something of what Emmanuel was saying. They must have been in the country for some time.

Emmanuel beckoned them towards the cottage. Tim took Anna by the hand, whispered something in her ear and walked ahead of her. Did she flinch slightly? Marie couldn't be sure. His steps were sure and confident. Anna followed, as if walking on stepping-stones in a stream.

They would be going to meet Mama, most likely in her cottage where there was only one entrance – the one Marie had come in by. She'd not thought this through in her giddy urgency to see the abazungu who wanted to adopt her.

'Don't get too excited too soon, dear,' Mama had said. 'These things take time.'

Emma Lawson

Marie was about to head back to her dormitory when heavy footfall and voices flooded the corridor.

'Welcome to Beauty from Ashes! I'll give you a tour of the centre once you've put your bags in your room,' Mama said. 'Here, let me show you.'

Marie slid under the bed as a door creaked open. She needn't have worried; the voices were coming through the thin wall between her and the bedroom next door.

'I hope it suits your needs,' said Mama. 'We like to keep things simple here.'

'Absolutely, no problem at all. That's the thing with all our modern, hurried living isn't it? Everyone's hustling and bustling around, got to have it all right now. And where does it get us, hey?'

'Right.'

'We don't want to get in your way. Just do whatever you usually do,' said Anna. 'We just want to see Marie and Kevine. Get to know them a little bit. We don't want them to feel like this is an interview or anything like that.'

Tim laughed. 'We haven't picked them out of a mail-order catalogue. We prayed about this for ages, going back and forth, praying some more, thinking some more, talking about it some more … At some point you've just got to trust you're doing the right thing. The Lord confirmed to us that they were the ones as soon as you told us about them. And who are the sheep to doubt the Shepherd's voice? We're just clay in the Potter's hands, after all.' The floor thudded with the force of their bags. 'So, tell me, what do they know about us?'

'That you're here today because you're applying to adopt them, that's all. Let me give you a tour of the

The Shadow Beyond the Hills

place. Then we'll head on over to the girls' dorms so you can meet the little lady in question. Well, she's not so little. She turned thirteen last week. And oh my, does she know it! You'll see that in her. She's precocious,' said Mama, laughing. 'We'll start with the sewing centre. Kevine's up there, I think. I hope it'll be a great income-generator for some of our girls.'

'You have a sewing centre now? You're a force of nature, Mama! How you get so much done in so little time is beyond me,' said Anna.

'I never had time for people who say they're going to do this and they're going to do that. Quit talking about it and get it done.'

The door clicked shut and their voices faded away. In the silence, the weight of this knowledge – that Marie was 'the one' – pressed down on her. Why her? How could she even question it if God had told them? And what if they were wrong?

Once they were over the crest of the hill, Marie headed to the girls' dorms. The grass had long turned a mustard shade of yellow.

'Hey!' Paul was still playing basketball in the late afternoon sun.

'Sup, dude?' Marie had learned this phrase from an umuzungu called Will who'd visited from a church in Florida. 'I've got to get back to the dorms. Mama and the abazungu are coming to see me soon.' Marie crunched through the grass to the concrete court. It radiated heat through her feet and up through her body. She snatched the ball from Paul's hands, ran up to the hoop and shot it straight through. 'I just had to do that first.'

'Complete fluke.' He grabbed the ball and returned

to Marie's side, a space he slotted into with ease. In the swirling eddies of life at Beauty from Ashes, where visitors came and went every few weeks, Kevine and Paul were her constants. Somehow, Paul managed to both calm and excite her at the same time. Her tummy trembled as she remembered him sneaking into her room at lights out, when the guards had fallen asleep to the buzz and crackle of their radios.

'What's this about?' He wiped a bead of sweat from his brow.

'Mama says they want to adopt me.' Marie stared at the concrete. She still couldn't believe it.

'Really?' He tilted his head towards her. 'Does this mean you'll go to America?'

'No. I mean, I don't know where they're from. They could be from England or somewhere else in Europe. Anyway, they probably won't want to once Mama tells them about me.'

She shoved her hands into her pockets and glanced in the direction of the primary school.

'That's them! I've got to go. See you later.' She gave him a sly grin and left him on the court.

Paul returned to his game.

Marie returned to the dormitory. There was still time to freshen up. Mama would call her when it was time to meet the guests. Her life was measured in segments of time spent waiting – waiting for breakfast, lunch, dinner. Waiting for her teachers to let her loose from lessons. For the arrival of visitors and the gifts they would bring.

She inspected her face in the small square mirror above the sink, worked her fingers over the skin on her neck to scratch out any scabs or rough patches and

The Shadow Beyond the Hills

applied body oil.

'Come on in. She should be in her room.' Mama's cool voice crept around the corridor and through her door. 'Marie? Where are you, honey?'

Marie walked into the gloom of the living room and was met by the faces she'd studied through the window in Mama's cottage. The three adults stood in a line facing her, a wall that could not be passed.

'Marie, I'd like you to meet Tim and Anna.'

Tim made the first move and offered his bony-looking hand. A fuzz of dark hair poked out from under his sleeves. She would have to get used to the hair.

'I'm so happy to meet you, Marie. Mama's told us so much about you,' said Tim, his voice light and breezy.

Marie stepped forward and took his clammy hand. She smiled but wasn't sure what her face looked like or whether she'd made the right impression. She tensed and tried to loosen her muscles. *What do you think about me? Am I what you were expecting?*

Anna came forward as Tim retreated in what looked like an awkward dance.

'We've waited a long time for this moment, Marie,' said Anna. She swept her hair aside and took Marie's hand. Her hand was warm and delicate.

'Take a seat.' Mama gestured to the faded red couch.

Tim perched on the edge of the couch and leaned forward. 'We know you don't know much about us, Marie, and that's why we're here over the next few days. I understand that it must be very daunting. Please don't feel daunted. We're alright really!'

His aftershave reminded her of woodsmoke and pinecones.

Emma Lawson

'And please understand that we feel the same. We all just need to take the time to get to know one another,' said Anna. A gentle smile framed her mouth but didn't reach her eyes. 'We'd like to understand your world, see what life is like for you here and what you enjoy doing. Understand what school is like and how you're getting on. Just to get to know you better.' Her hands were folded in her lap as if in silent prayer.

Marie fingered the crust of skin on her neck.

'Marie, have you been scratching again? Here let me get that.' Mama pulled out a handkerchief from a pocket in her caramel-coloured caftan, wet it with her tongue and wiped the bloodied skin on Marie's collarbone.

Marie looked away.

'What are your favourite subjects at school, Marie?' asked Tim.

'I don't really have a favourite subject,' Marie replied, looking first at Mama and then at Tim. 'I enjoy reading. But I guess biology would be what I'm most interested in.'

Tim nodded, his eyebrows inching up into his forehead.

'We share 99 per cent of our DNA with the gorillas over there.' Marie pointed to the volcanoes beyond the window.

'Your English is brilliant, Marie,' said Anna.

'We don't speak Rwandese here,' said Mama, her voice sharp and angular. 'All of our children are brought up speaking English. That's what's going to help them in the future.'

No one speaks Rwandese here, Mama; we speak Kinyarwanda.

'That'll be why then,' said Tim.

The Shadow Beyond the Hills

Tim once again took Anna's hand. She looked at him with a tight smile.

They passed the next hour in small talk – what her hobbies were, what she enjoyed reading, what sports she played. It would have felt like a test had it not been for their smiles. Tim looked at her too long, but something about Anna put her at ease.

Cassava and roasted sweet potato wafted through the vents above the window and snaked around the room.

'We ought to get going,' said Mama. 'Francine and the kitchen crew will have knocked up something delightful for us, I'm sure.' She pulled herself up with an exaggerated sigh. 'Marie, would you go ahead of us and let Francine know that we're coming soon? I'm just going to give these two a tour of the animal stalls.' Mama turned to Tim. 'The milk from our cows goes to the kids during recess. Every bit of nutrition helps.'

'See you in a minute, Marie,' Anna called after her, as if in reassurance.

It *was* reassuring. Marie stepped out into the cool air of early evening, savouring its fading light. It was a relief to be out of that stale room. The hum of the day's routine was winding down. It was her favourite part of the day – a time when she could breathe deeply and know that a stash of books awaited her in bed. Or Paul. Her skin tingled. As she rounded the corner of the dormitory, a child's screams pierced the air.

CHAPTER TWO
POSSIBILITY

She turned and froze. Roberti lay writhing in agony, his body twisting and arching as he sucked in huge gulps of air to fuel his next barrage of screaming. A steady flow of thick, bubbling liquid poured along the floor and out of the door of the outbuilding. Marie peered through the steam and into the murk of the room. Beside Roberti's body a cooking pot was turned on its side, its liquid innards still spilling across the floor. For a boy of three, his cries were haunting. The pitch of his screams tore through her eardrums. He pleaded for his mother. She didn't know what to do first.

'Imana We!' A flurry of footsteps and a sound that drowned out Roberti's sent a shock through her. Immaculate pushed Marie aside, picked Roberti up and whisked him out of the room.

His body was a quivering wreck. Immaculate held him gently and shouted for help.

Mama appeared. 'What happened here?' Her voice was shrill with panic. She looked Roberti over and

The Shadow Beyond the Hills

squinted into the outbuilding room. 'That boy needs cold water, and he needs it now. Immaculate, take him to the bathroom in the boys' dormitory, put him under the tap and just keep that water running all over him.'

Roberti's screams gave way to pitiful whimpers, which trailed behind him as Immaculate carried him away.

'My God. Mama, what can I do?' Anna gripped Tim's arm as he mouthed silently in prayer, his chin tucked into his chest.

'I don't know, but I need to call Dr Claude. There's a clinic just ten minutes from here,' said Mama. 'I've tried to drum it into them so many times. They *do not* cook porridge on the floor with young children around to trip and fall into. It's not rocket science!' Mama turned the palms of her hands up toward the sky and shook her arms, her thin, saggy skin wobbling underneath. 'Marie, I don't know why you're just standing there staring into space, but you need to go and get Francine right now!'

'I did some First Aid training recently for work so I can help in the meantime,' said Anna.

'Sure, that would be ... Marie? Marie!'

'Sorry, Mama.' Marie jolted into life and sped along the path to the kitchen. Other kids were filing past, wanting to see for themselves what all the shouting was about.

She bounded through the door to find Francine bent over a chopping board laden with tomatoes and peppers.

'Francine, it's Roberti. You must come.'

'Jesu we.' Francine spun around and barrelled out of the building.

Marie stood idly, belonging everywhere and nowhere. Unsure what to do with herself, she wandered back to find Mama and the others.

She found them in the boys' dormitory bathroom, Francine kneeling in front of Roberti, holding his shoulders. 'My boy, my angel, my darling boy,' she kept saying.

Anna was peering into a First Aid kit, pulling out creams, gauze, and ointments, while Tim rubbed her back. She didn't seem to notice.

'It should be pretty comprehensive. One of our volunteers re-stocked it a few weeks ago,' said Mama.

'I can see. I've got everything I need here.' Anna's smile broke the static of the room. 'Sweetheart, I need you to come to me so I can help make it better. Is that alright? Ngwino hano. Ndashaka kugufasha.'

He whimpered and looked at Anna in fear, his tear-stained face streaked with mucus.

'You need to let her help you, mate,' said Tim.

When Roberti refused to move, Anna walked over to him.

'Mama, just so you can tell Dr Claude what I've done, I'm going to put some lidocaine gel on his legs. They look like the most badly affected area. It's an anaesthetic, so it's going to take the edge off the pain.'

Mama nodded. 'He said he'll be here in fifteen minutes or thereabouts, but who knows – that could mean an hour or two. He's just finishing up with a patient.'

Marie watched the delicate way Anna applied gel to Roberti's plump, wet little body. Anna wasn't distracted by the agony in his face; her single-minded focus was on his leg and the gels and ointments at her disposal.

The Shadow Beyond the Hills

'Tim, can you crush up this Ibuprofen and put it in some water for him?'

'Sure.'

Mama paced up and down. She wasn't used to being rendered redundant like this.

Anna squeezed some light-green gel from a tube onto her gloved hand and placed it carefully over Roberti's raw skin. 'This is Aloe Vera. It's going to soothe the burns.'

He shrieked as the pain hit him again.

'Roberti, take this.' Immaculate brought a small bottle of cloudy water to his lips. He grimaced but swallowed it without question.

'And this is an antibiotic ointment to prevent infection.' Anna applied a pure white paste over Roberti's legs, arms, and the side of his abdomen, working over the areas with the skilful care of a doctor. She knew exactly what she was doing. Marie was impressed. What Marie most admired was the way that she took each area of his body, each limb, like they were separate things, somehow detached from him. This was how she could get on with it like it was a commonplace chore, unmoved by the sharp cries that burst out of Roberti.

Mama turned and faced the crowd of kids clamouring outside the door. 'Go away! Your staring isn't helping the situation.' She sighed and continued pacing. By now, visitors would have seen not just the sewing centre and the farm, but also the nursery, schools – both primary and secondary – and the on-site carpentry; instead, they were standing under the sterile glare of fluorescent strip lights while Anna wrapped Roberti's arms and legs in dressing.

Emma Lawson

'Right, that'll do until he gets checked out by the doctor,' said Anna, standing up and taking a deep breath.

'You've probably done all that the doctor would have done,' said Mama.

'What's that?'

'Oh, just saying that Dr Claude's only a rural doctor and I have no idea where he went to medical school.' Mama sucked in a tense breath of air. 'Still, we need to get him checked out. He's going to need more medicine.'

'There, little man, all done,' said Tim.

Roberti and his mother looked like they were waiting for someone to tell them what to do next. When no one indicated otherwise, she rushed forward and held him with caution, as if he might break in her arms.

'Thanks for stepping in there, Anna,' said Mama with a grudging smile. 'I'm going to take Francine and Robert up to my cottage to wait for Dr Claude. I'm sorry you two, but you'll have to have dinner without me while I attend to this.'

'Oh, don't be sorry,' replied Tim. 'You do what you need to do. Don't mind us.'

'Immaculate will show you to the canteen. Marie, you'll go with them and keep them company for me, okay?'

The canteen was quiet, emptied of the usual chatter and commotion of mealtimes. They sat at one of the glossy, varnished tables to a meal of roasted sweet potato, cassava, chips, plantain, and fried Tilapia. This was a special meal – a visitor meal.

'Well, that wasn't a great start to the day.' Tim had his hand on Anna's shoulder. 'But that was a stellar response back there, Genie.'

'We covered burns on our First Aid training at work a few months ago. It's still fresh in my mind,' replied Anna.

'The poor kid was lucky you were around, hey?' Tim's voice bounced off the bare walls.

'Why do you call her Genie?' asked Marie. With Mama elsewhere, Marie felt free to ask what she wanted.

'She makes my every wish come true,' said Tim, smiling. This was obviously an inside joke, but he relished the explanation. 'She's an absolute gem this one.'

Anna glanced at Marie and gave her a wry smile.

'Mm, this is top notch stuff,' said Tim, in between mouthfuls of tilapia. He looked at Anna. 'We're loving this meal, aren't we, hun?' He focused again on his food without waiting for a reply. 'I expect this was freshly caught as well. I'm never sure about eating fish in the city restaurants. You don't know how many times it's been frozen and defrosted. I don't suppose you get a dodgy tummy like us muzungus, do you?'

Marie recalled the explosion of her bowels only a few days before they'd arrived. She was about to challenge him, but she looked at Anna and softened. She wanted to please her not for what would come from it, but because she liked her. She'd never felt this way about any other umuzungu before.

Even though Mama wasn't there, she stuck to the script. 'Not very much, no.'

Satisfied, Tim tucked a forkful of chips into his

mouth.

'Why do you live in Rwanda?' Marie asked, looking at Anna.

'Well, it's a beautiful country full of wonderful people. It's a privilege to be here.' She looked like she was going to say more but slipped into silence, laying aside her knife and fork and leaving only the dark green stain of cassava on her plate.

Why do you want to adopt me? What is it about me? The questions kept swinging back and forth in Marie's mind. She wished she felt brave enough to ask them.

'Where are you from?' asked Marie.

'The UK,' replied Anna. 'We're from a very green and quiet part of the country, with lots of fields and dogs and people who love dogs. It's actually very boring to be honest. None of the colour and craziness of Africa.'

'People love dogs? Why?' asked Marie, thinking of the growling, salivating brutes that guarded so many compounds.

'They're usually considered family pets rather than guard dogs. People often joke that in Britain we care more about dogs than people. Sometimes, I think they're right. Lonely people who crave affection get it from animals. Animals can be easier than people; people come with lots of issues …'

'It's nice to go for a walk here and just meet people, and the odd goat of course, rather than having someone's labrador come bounding up to you,' said Tim, not picking up on the smoke from the conversation Anna had just snuffed out. 'It's cruel how animals are treated in many countries, but I think we've gone overboard in the UK. We need to reconnect more

The Shadow Beyond the Hills

with people than with our pets. That's what I love about this country – your social fabric is so much stronger than ours.' He laced his fingers together and tried to pull them apart. 'It's all about community here. I love that.'

'Anyway, enough about labradors and loneliness. Marie, I think I'd better go to bed and get some rest for tomorrow but thank you so much for sitting with us and keeping us company,' said Anna.

'Nta kibazo,' said Marie. She knew Anna would understand this. Besides, Mama wasn't there.

Tim yawned and rested his hand on Anna's leg. 'Yep, let's go, Genie.'

Marie headed through the compound to the girls' dorms. Apart from the incident with poor Roberti, today had been a success. She'd managed not to say anything that made the visitors raise their eyebrows and laugh awkwardly.

But how could they know they wanted to adopt her? She didn't know them and, other than her favourite subject at school, they didn't know her. None of it made sense.

'Sss, hey!'

Marie warmed to the voice – just who she needed. 'What are you still doing out?'

Paul sidled up to her with a playful shove. 'Just bored. Wanted to see if you were around.'

'Yes, I'm around, but I'm going to bed. I have a book to read.' She threw him a teasing look.

'You and your books. I'm going to be a banker in Kigali. I'm going to drive a VIP car and take you places. You'll see,' said Paul. 'We'll go to the best places to eat in the city and stay in fancy hotels. All the girls will look at you.'

'Big boss man, hey?' Marie laughed and planted a delicate kiss on his lips, pressing her body against his.

A spreading warmth grew from her legs up to her chest. Their bodies became entwined, entangled, his hands exploring her. Guided by childhood whispers, goaded by the warnings of adults and swimming in sumptuous guilt from Mama Judy, excitement bubbled up in her belly. Mama even frowned at boys and girls holding hands. What would she think about him reaching under her top or his hands slipping under the seams of her knickers? Everyone made decisions for her. Her life was drawn in strictly measured lines she had to follow, from sunrise to lights out. Nothing was hers. Except Paul – in this moment, he was all hers. It had never gone further than a quick fumble in the dark. Now, delicious possibilities tempted her more than ever before. And Mama would never know.

CHAPTER THREE
BLOOD

An auburn sun slid over the horizon as Marie got dressed for school. Her hips had filled out, curving and rounding her body, and her breasts were budding more than ever. Being flat chested was something the boys had teased her about. It never hurt her, this facile frenzy to become a woman, but it had annoyed her. Perhaps now they would get off her case. It didn't bother her when her monthly bleed hadn't started by her twelfth birthday, as it had with some of the girls. They talked about it in hushed tones, and there was a tacit understanding among teachers and students that when so-and-so wasn't in class that day due to some mystery illness, that it was because of cramps. She'd discovered her own shortly before her thirteenth birthday, by way of Sylvestre. She'd stood up to go to the toilet during class when he pointed at the stain with a sharp burst of laughter that ricocheted around the classroom. A ripple of snide comments from her classmates made her sit back down on the chair as if it were a magnet, and she a stick of iron melting in a hot mess of scarlet shame in her underwear. She'd sat there for the rest of the class, prickling with embarrassment and the horrifying sensation of release that couldn't be stopped. It was typical of Sylvester to shame and humiliate her. He'd always taken every opportunity to make her feel small, and she had no idea why. But she hated it. She hated him.

She buttoned up her shirt, tucked it into her grey pleated skirt, and pulled on her blue jumper with the Beauty from Ashes logo emblazoned on the right-hand side. The morning air was already parched from the sun's fierce rays as Marie walked down to Mama's cottage to report for duty. It was an unspoken expectation that she would come to Mama and be told what she needed to do and where she needed to be while Tim and Anna were visiting. Porridge and cooking smoke floated through the air, and a hum of activity was beginning to animate the compound as children made their way from the dormitories to the school over the hill.

Mama was sitting in her office, lit by the sun streaming through the window behind her. 'Good morning, dear.'

'Good morning, Mama.'

'They should be here soon. I think they're just finishing their breakfast.' Mama squinted at her laptop screen and pushed down at the keys. It was a slow and painful exercise watching her stubby fingers type.

Mama always woke early and went straight to her desk every day for her morning ritual of 'quiet time' with a Bible and a cup of coffee. No one was to disturb her during this time.

Hung on her wall were photos of her family in

The Shadow Beyond the Hills

America; babies with gummy grins held in strong, porcelain arms; happy white faces with rows of straight, dazzling teeth; children, some chubby and some gangly-limbed, crossing lines and clutching medals; golden, shaggy-haired dogs with tongues lolling out on lush green lawns – all of them emblems of success. Above these photos was a large, rectangular frame, with the words: 'For I know the plans I have for you; to give you a hope and future – Jeremiah 29:11', in silver, spidery script.

Pierre was the first to breeze into her office in his navy overalls and boots, reeking of manure, urine and grass. 'Mwaramutse, Mama.'

'English please, Pierre. Oh, and you might want to knock before you come in.'

'Ah, yes, sorry. Good morning. She's still not producing much milk.'

'And is her calf in the stall with her?'

'No, we put her in another stall.'

'Well, that'll be why. The calf needs to be with the mother at first or she won't produce milk. I've had five of my own, Pierre, I know what I'm talking about. Close physical proximity is so important. You just can't separate them and expect her to keep up her milk production.' Mama stiffened with irritation. 'Now, go and get that calf in with the mother.'

Pierre charged out of the door, leaving the stench of manure hanging thickly in the air.

No sooner had Pierre left than Felix came in. He was a newbie in the admin office – a 'risk', as Mama put it.

'Good morning, Mama.' He paused for a reply that never came. 'The RSSB say they need to know staff numbers to renew the medical insurance.' He was pleased to mention office business with her. He beamed, looking proud in his new job.

'So? What do you expect me to do about it?'

His face fell. 'I don't know exactly. Sorry.'

Mama Judy glanced over at Marie and turned her attention to Felix again with a look that bordered on apology. She raised the mug of coffee to her thin lips. 'I've got a lot on today, Felix. I've got a ton of paperwork to get done, I've got visitors to show around, I've got people pestering me for this, that and the other, and to top it off the district commissioner is asking me ridiculous questions. As if I need to prove what this place is about after *all* this time.' She rolled her eyes and sipped her coffee.

As Marie waited for Tim and Anna, staff continued to file in and out of the office to speak with Mama, chief umuzungu, the queen bee in her colony.

'And here they are! Did you sleep well?' Mama stopped typing and looked up from her screen.

Tim appeared in the room with Anna a hair's breadth behind him. 'Marvellously, thank you! Once I'd managed to zap the mozzie that was buzzing round my ear in the early hours of the morning.'

Anna shifted on her feet and turned to Marie. 'How are you today, Marie?'

Marie stood up, feeling unsteady on her legs. 'Fine, thank you.' It was a new experience to feel this way with anyone. It unsettled her. No matter how much she tried to view them as she did any other visitor to the centre, the knowledge that this couple wanted to adopt her was lodged in her brain.

Mama looked at the clock on the opposite wall.

The Shadow Beyond the Hills

'Shoot, we've got to get going. Marie starts class in five minutes.' She rose from her desk and led the way.

Marie studied Tim and Anna as they walked to her class. Tim had Anna's hand clasped in his, a knot of knuckles and stretched pastel skin. Every time they slowed to let Marie join them in conversation, she slowed her pace, keeping a comfortable distance behind them.

'What class are we going to now, Marie?' asked Tim, looking over his shoulder.

'Religious studies.'

'Excellent.'

The conversation stalled for a little while.

Anna broke the silence. 'We follow the Montessori method in our preschool.'

'Monty-who?' said Mama.

'Maria Montessori. She encouraged independence and child-led learning.'

'Uh-huh. And is that child-led as in teachers wrapped around their little fingers?' Mama threw Anna a sideways glance and let out a dry laugh. 'At Beauty from Ashes, we follow a robust curriculum and instil values of integrity, honesty and concern for others.'

'Sounds good,' replied Anna.

They walked on again in silence.

The classroom was a throbbing mass of bustling bodies and scraping chairs. Mama left Tim and Anna sitting at the back of the class while she went on with her work.

Everyone was looking at Tim and Anna, no doubt expecting them to come to the front and introduce themselves like visitors usually did.

'Good morning, P6. Let's quieten down now please.

Come on, attention this way.' Ms Celine was a tall tower of timidity, always pleading rather than commanding. 'Today, we're continuing our study of the Pentateuch in the Hebrew scriptures. I hope you read the passages that we're looking at today?'

Murmurs of grudging consent rolled around the room and up into the steel rafters.

Ms Celine had seven students take turns reading the passage, a tedious exercise she had drawn out especially for Tim and Anna.

She drew a Venn diagram on the blackboard while the students craned their necks to look at the resident abazungu. Marie glanced back at them too. Tim was looking at the Venn diagram, its circles of Abrahamic promise piquing his interest. Anna smiled at Marie, who promptly turned back to the blackboard.

'So ... Marie, who did God save, can you tell us?'

'The fish?'

A spurt of laughter erupted from the class and caused Ms Celine's face to become pinched and rigid.

'Marie, I don't think you are taking this seriously!'

'Miss, it's Noah and his family,' said Calixte, puffing out his chest.

'Good, Calixte. And what divine promise does this relate to? Think about the meta-narrative of the scriptures ...'

Everything became muted and blurred as Marie's mind took her to dark places – to lungs choking, spluttering; to bloated bodies in stormy seas. A scarily real picture in her old Children's Illustrated Bible floated to the surface of her mind: men, women and children banging on solid wooden doors, eternally shut out.

A pencil case clattered on the floor and jarred Marie into reality. Ms Celine moved around the classroom handing out papers, by turns eliciting sighs, groans, and surprised shouts of laughter. She slapped Marie's paper on her desk, an A+ circled in red ink in the top-right corner of the page.

'Would you look at that!' Tim's hand fell on her shoulder and made her jump. 'Sorry to sneak up on you there. Do you get these sorts of grades often?'

'Yes.'

'Good work, my friend. Keep it up.' Tim beckoned Anna over to the desk, motioning to the paper with a jerk of his head. 'Check out Miss Genius over here!'

Anna weaved through lines of students, who all took the opportunity to smile at her and initiate conversation.

'Did you like our class, Miss?'

'Are you from America?'

Anna returned their smiles but filtered past them towards Marie. 'Your teachers must be very proud of you.'

Marie gave Anna a shy smile and zipped up her bag.

'Very interesting class there,' said Tim, reaching out to shake Ms Celine's hand. 'It's really important to get the word of God into kids these days. In our Western culture, education is eroding every trace of Christianity. Our culture is in crisis.' He shook his head. 'It's a mess.'

Anna looked down at Marie's paper. 'And I see Marie is doing really well.'

'Too smart for her own good, I think,' said Ms Celine.

While Tim joined the boys in a game of football in the courtyard and Anna chatted to some teachers in the break between classes, Marie wandered the courtyard with Paul. Girls huddled together in constellations of gossip and chitchat.

Some of the boys broke away from their game and ran down to the entrance of the compound. Behind their laughter, Marie could hear high-pitched squeals, as if some something was being tormented – animal this time, rather than human. This was enough to drag some of the girls away from their chatter. Not much usually happened in the day-to-day routine at the centre, especially when there weren't any foreign teams visiting.

'Come on, we've got to see this.' Paul edged forward, pulling Marie along with him.

The screeching reached a crescendo as children spilled through the open gate and onto the main road. Marie peered through the crowd that was now beginning to form outside the compound gates and got just enough of a glimpse to see what was happening. Beatrice and Emmanuel were trying to herd eight waddling piglets back through the gates. Ripples of laughter rang out from the Beauty from Ashes kids.

Pierre crouched down by the side of the road, but what he was shielding couldn't be seen. A gust of wind from one of the big white buses hurtling by lifted the back of his navy-blue work coat and jostled a few brown paper bags on the side of the road.

'What on earth is happening now?' Mama Judy parted the crowd. As she came forward, Pierre moved aside to reveal a red stream trickling by his legs toward the pavement, as well as a half-pulverized piglet mashed to the tarmac.

'Give me strength.' Mama held her head in her hands.

The Shadow Beyond the Hills

'Mama, I—'

'Just get a sack and shovel, Pierre.'

Some of the girls pretended to retch while others roared with laughter as Pierre came back with a shovel and lifted what was left of the piglet into the sack, a loop of entrails snagging on the frayed opening. The squealing piglets raced by as Emmanuel and Beatrice channelled them back into the compound.

'Pierre,' said Mama. 'How did this happen?'

'I don't know, Mama. I had the gate open for a short time while I unloaded the truck, and they just ran past and out the gate. Beatrice was trying to catch them. The door to the pig pen was open when I was up at the stalls earlier, so I shut it.'

Pierre heaved the bloodied sack over his shoulder and walked away, reluctant to say anything else.

'Right. I think I know what happened here.' Mama sighed, her chalky face lit by bright noon sun. She looked up at the conifer trees lining the opposite side of the road. Fruit bats stirred in their branches.

Now that the piglets were safely on the compound side of the gate, Emmanuel and Beatrice tried to gather the animals as they dispersed among the crowd.

Mama spun around to face Beatrice, who was hobbling around trying to herd the piglets back into a group.

'Honey, I thought we'd said that you were cultivating the vegetable gardens ...' She looked at Beatrice with an open, suggestive face. '... that you weren't helping with the animals anymore.' She raised her eyebrows, a gentleness flowing into the lines in her forehead and softening her gaze.

Emmanuel translated for Mama, since Beatrice

didn't speak a word of English.

She looked confused at first, as if she was wondering how she got to be standing there with piglets dashing about her legs. As Mama talked about her tending the spinach, carrots, peas and cabbages, and how gathering grasses for the animals was no longer her responsibility, her face fell in resignation.

Marie often saw Beatrice go back and forth about her jobs, absent-minded, unproductive. She must have been one of the ones begging outside the gate whom Mama had taken pity on and made a job for. She was dressed in a faded green t-shirt, which said 'Eagle Hills Spring Break '98' on the back. She blended into the background like most of the lower-level staff. A deep scar flecked her forehead, just below the hairline, and she walked with a limp.

Mama muttered a few words of quiet disapproval and walked back up to her cottage, no doubt relieved that Tim and Anna hadn't come down to witness the scene, while Beatrice continued to gather up the piglets with Emmanuel.

'No one asked for sausages for dinner, Beatrice!' said Sylvestre, prompting the cheers and whistles of the other boys.

Calixte piped up: 'Mama's going to have your bacon!'

Marie laughed along with everyone else – a tense and contagious laughter born of the blood on the road.

Beatrice spirited past with a piglet in each arm, levelling her gaze for the briefest of moments at Marie. There was no trace of malice, embarrassment or hurt in her vacant eyes. There was nothing there at all.

CHAPTER FOUR
FLASHES

'At last,' said Mama above the clicking and tapping of the sewing machines. 'It's been three years in the making, but we finally got this place up and running.'

Kevine leant over the table as Anna fed blue fabric through the Singer.

'The last time I did this was when I was at school. I definitely need to brush up my skills.' Anna looked up at Kevine for assurance, which she freely gave with a warm smile.

'It takes time, but you'll get there.' Kevine had helped Mama set up the sewing centre. She always helped. For as long as she could remember, Marie's sister had been at Mama's right hand, translating, organising, telling Mama how kids were feeling when they couldn't or wouldn't tell Mama themselves.

'Kevine is the lead Mentor for girls who want to become seamstresses,' said Mama. 'She has aspirations to be a fashion designer, don't you?' Mama held Kevine's gaze with a tenderness that Marie could never fully understand. It gave her a sick feeling in the pit of her stomach. She never got that look from Mama. She told herself she didn't care. After those momentary pangs of resentment, she couldn't stay angry with Kevine – it was Kevine who kept her world in order, kept the boundaries in place, made sure she did her homework and kept up with her chores. She was the only family Marie had.

'I won't let her go just yet; she's needed here. Oh, she'll go to college in due course, I'm sure that won't be a problem.' Mama winked at Anna.

'Are there any good college courses around that you could do?' asked Anna.

'There's this course at a college in Kigali in fashion design and the textile industry. I've looked at the prospectus. It looks amazing, and I know it would help me get a good job one day.' Kevine pushed her brown-framed glasses back up her nose, her bracelets jangling on her wrist as she did.

Mama looked concerned. 'Kevine, dear, let's see what the jobs market looks like a few years down the line. You know you'll always be welcome here.' She turned to look at Tim. 'All these college kids are graduating now but going to work where? You tell me.' She glanced at Anna, her eyebrows raised. 'There have to be jobs to go to,' she muttered.

'Well, things are changing quickly in the city. New guesthouses and restos are springing up all over the place. You should see it,' said Tim.

'I try to avoid the city whenever I can.' Mama hosted many visitors at Beauty from Ashes, but rarely graced the offices of 'big shots'– country directors and CEOs – in the city. 'Can't see the wood for the trees, that lot', she would say. 'It's all statistics, statistics, statistics, but you can't do a baseline survey on the heart of a child.'

The Shadow Beyond the Hills

Tim and Anna talked to some students and then walked with Marie and Kevine to Mama's cottage. The walls were painted a warm shade of orange, which brought a healthier glow to Anna and Tim's white faces as they sipped tea and talked about the slightly cooler weather here compared to the city. Patterned bowls and imigongo paintings hung on the wall in a bright splash of colour, and a wooden giraffe stretched up toward the bookcase in the corner of the room. Marie didn't often go in the sitting room of Mama's cottage. 'I have to have boundaries and personal space,' she'd said.

Kevine walked over to the bookcase, pulled out a cream-coloured photo album with diagonal gold stripes on the front and back covers, and placed it on the coffee table in front of Tim and Anna. 'You can see us growing up here.'

'Ah, so this is where we can really delve into the past.' Tim smiled and pulled a strange face. Marie wasn't sure what to make of it, but it made her feel uncomfortable.

The photo album was well-thumbed. Marie had seen it many times when Kevine showed her images of a childhood that came back to her in flashes of clarity. She held on to these memories fiercely, doing everything she could to make sure they wouldn't dissolve again. Kevine showed Marie the room they'd shared when they were younger – the one with painted murals of clouds and sunshine and moon and stars on the walls. She had been on the bottom bunk; Kevine on the top. Marie could only have been around four years old. There was a photo of Marie, Kevine, and some other Beauty from Ashes kids on the football pitch – the one piece of flat land in the whole compound.

'Here, let me show you this,' said Mama. She turned to a page with a photo of Marie sat astride a yellow and blue motorbike, Kevine on the back, and a metal swing set in the background. 'Can you believe how little we had back then?' She laughed. 'It's taken thousands of dollars raised by a network of generous supporters to give these kids a decent home with spaces to play and just be kids.'

'Amazing,' murmured Tim, his hand resting on Anna's.

Kevine leant toward Marie and tapped her on the arm. 'That was when Maxwell rode his motorbike into the playground and let us all have a ride on it.'

Marie thought of the old swing set, which was still there. The swings were twisted together and hung up over the top rail out of reach. The guards were meant to take it down but had never got around to it. The swings were now dwarfed by the giant slides and climbing frames that some abazungu from a church in Wyoming had raised money for.

Happiness flooded Marie when she was shown these photos. Kevine's mood always brightened, too. When she felt lost, Marie found her way by these reference points. Her recollections of childhood were as hazy as the horizon in the midst of dry season, but Kevine filled in the details for her with vivid colour.

'Look at this one.' Kevine pointed to a slightly blurry photo of a lake fringed with palm trees.

Anna craned her neck to see. 'Is that Marie there?'

'I look like I'm about to faint.' Marie laughed and Kevine joined in.

'We were telling you to get in and have a swim,' said Kevine.

The Shadow Beyond the Hills

Mama snorted into her tea. 'You weren't so keen where you, sweetie? We're raising funds for a swimming pool at the moment.'

'Do you find a lot of kids know how to swim?' asked Tim.

'It's usually only the ones who live near a lake or a river. There aren't any swimming pools other than in some of the hotels, and most parents can't afford to access those.'

When Kevine had shown her the lake photo and told her how sick she was on the bus going there, Marie's stomach twisted. It wasn't that often that she went out of town. Whenever she did, her insides would protest every bend on the road, and she would look out the window trying not to succumb to the hot waves of nausea that washed over her.

Kevine pointed to a photo of her and Marie with a group of visitors standing on a grassy plain. 'That was the group from France. They ran a holiday club and took us to Akagera before they left.'

Marie nodded. She remembered Kevine telling her about this recently. The bus had taken them out toward the east of the country, past the heat and fumes of Kigali, where the land flattens out into grassland and eucalyptus trees give way to thorny acacia. A young umuzungu called Louis had dropped his camera out of the car. He made the driver stop and got out to find it. Mama turned into a crazy woman, Kevine had said, and told him to get back in the car.

'That French boy said he always saw big cats at other national parks he'd gone to like Kruger, the Masai Mara, and the Serengeti,' said Kevine.

Marie tried to imagine Louis now. Was he still bored

with the world at his fingertips? What it would feel like to have the freedom to be disappointed by a borderless life?

They drank tea and ate some of the banana bread that Anna had baked for them. Anna said she'd like to go to the market with her and her sister, so Kevine and Marie took them to the biggest one in town. It was a place that guests always wanted to visit because they said that in their countries they could get everything in one shop, and they wanted what they called an 'authentic cultural experience'. Marie had to smile when they paid three-times the price for market staples. Not Tim and Anna though – they knew the price of a kilo of mangos, passionfruit and avocado. *They* were the ones who laughed with the fast-talking market-sellers when they tried to hawk their produce at inflated abazungu prices.

'There are lots of potatoes growing in this region. The volcanic soil is perfect for it,' said Kevine. Marie smiled at her sister, the self-appointed tour guide.

Women carrying baskets of pineapples, carrots and papaya filed past; some silently, some arguing over prices. Aside from accusations of husband-stealing, few things made the town-women madder than a market dispute.

An older man with skin as cracked as sun-baked mud thrust a small bag of peanuts at Tim, who handed him a couple of coins and shoved the nuts into his back pocket. 'We'll roast those with lashings of salt later,' said Tim, smiling.

They walked past piles of gleaming tomatoes heaped in white plastic buckets, sacks of cassava flour and scales weighed down with mounds of sambaza

The Shadow Beyond the Hills

surrounded by clouds of flies. Anna stopped to haggle with a young woman selling strips of igitenge. Kevine told her where she could find the best place to get it tailored and how much she should pay.

The stench of sambaza filled Marie's nostrils and stuck in her throat. She wanted to leave the market and head back home, but she knew that it was polite to wait for Tim and Anna to finish looking around the market – and wherever else they wanted to go.

The light was starting to fade by the time they reached the centre. Anna had gone back to her room with a headache. Marie's face had fallen at this, though she'd tried to hide it – she wanted to be with Anna. There was something reassuring about her. She didn't try to force anything. Tim went with Marie and Kevine to the canteen for dinner. The hall was filled with chatter, most of it seeming to be centred around Tim.

A few kids approached him. 'Do you have a Ronaldo shirt? How about Rooney?'

'Guys, let him have his dinner.' Kevine swatted them away like they were a swarm of mosquitos.

'It's alright,' said Tim. 'Not much of a footie fan, myself.'

Marie ripped off a lump of ubugali from her plate and dipped it in a bowl of peanut sauce. Sticky stodginess coated her fingers. She looked at Tim. What *did* interest him? What made him happy? Did he think that she would make him happy?

Paul interrupted her thoughts as he sat down beside her with a steaming bowl of beans, pasta, cooked bananas and peas, and a solitary lump of beef drenched in a brown sauce.

Her mind turned to the small birthmark on his left

buttock and how it started out patchy around the edge and became denser in the centre. It pleased her that she was the only girl who knew of its existence.

'Have you finished those math exercises yet?' Paul gave her a coy look.

'Yes.'

'I'll see you after evening devotions then?' he asked, in a quieter voice.

Kevine smirked through a mouthful of rice. Kevine had always known about her and Paul. She was the one to point out the photos of them at Beauty from Ashes, giggling to herself as she did. Kevine was like an old mama who fussed over everyone, but the immaturity that sometimes escaped from her amused Marie, especially when it came to recollections of her and Paul together.

Marie couldn't quite remember the point at which Paul not only made her laugh, but also excited her.

'You've always been close,' Kevine had said. 'Throwing mud at each other after the rains and messing about in Sunday class.'

Kevine wouldn't let her forget it, teasing her at every opportunity.

A wave of relief washed over Marie when Anna came and sat opposite her.

'Feeling better, love?' asked Tim.

'It's starting to go already. I think I'll feel better if I eat.'

Sylvestre banged a couple of bottles of orange Fanta down on the table in front of Marie and Paul. 'There's more up there for everyone,' he said, gesturing to a circular table next to the trays of food. Fanta and Coke were always on offer when visitors came.

'I don't get him. Usually he's such an idiot. Why's he being nice?' Paul pulled off the paper wrapper covering the end of the straw and sipped his Fanta. 'He's probably just scoring points for Mama while we have visitors.'

Marie watched the lump in his throat move as he swallowed. Bubbles stung her throat as she took a large swig of Fanta. It was then that the aftertaste hit her: an acrid warmth that settled on her tongue and the back of her throat. 'I'll be back in a minute.' Marie left the table and walked out of the hall into the still evening air, retching. Frothy orange liquid and remnants of dinner erupted from her mouth and splashed onto the concrete. She spat until her mouth was as dry as a husk of corn left in the sun. Should she tell Mama that Sylvestre pissed in her drink? Mama would no doubt say that although she might run Beauty from Ashes, she didn't oversee the personal lives of everyone in it; that she had no time for mini-dramas she wasn't there to witness. They would have to just grow up and sort it out between themselves. This is what Mama had said the first time Marie mentioned Sylvester's bullying, when he'd thrown her most treasured book down the guards' long drop.

Marie stared at the moon, the purity of its glow distracting her from the splash of sick pooling by her feet.

'Are you alright, Marie?' Anna came and stood beside her, her forehead wrinkled in concern.

'Yes, I just needed to get outside. I think I have a fever.'

'You do feel a bit clammy,' said Anna, putting the back of her hand to Marie's forehead. 'Why don't you go and rest. We'll be fine here.'

'How do you solve the inequality $2x + 1 > 5$?' Paul sucked air between his teeth and frowned at Marie.

'You start by rearranging the equation: subtract what is to the right of the greater than sign from both sides of the inequality.' Marie felt the heat of Paul's eyes on her. 'Pull out like factors, divide both sides by two, then add two to both sides and work out your inequality plot. You end up with $x > 2$.'

'I still don't get it, but you can show me again later,' said Paul. He closed his workbook and sat down next to Marie on the bed. 'This Tim seems like a good man.'

'You say that like you know him.'

'I can tell. I'm an excellent judge of character.' Typical Paul, always trying to sound sophisticated and impressive. He was only a year older than she was. He nibbled on her ear, making her snort with laughter.

She couldn't help feeling irritated though. Why was he so at ease with the idea of her leaving the centre, leaving each other? Why didn't he care more?

A voice came from outside the door. 'Marie? It's lights out now.' The door creaked open as Agnes stepped inside. She scanned the room briefly. 'Goodnight.'

Paul's hand grabbed her ankle from under the bed. She suppressed the urge to cry out.

'Yes, lights out, Marie,' he whispered.

The familiar length of his body slid on top of her. He was hers again now. There was nothing that Mama or anyone else could do to stop her.

CHAPTER FIVE
BLOOM

'Everything changes tomorrow.' Tim popped the cork and champagne gushed over the bottle and onto the wooden decking of their lakeside guest room. Beaming, he handed Anna a glass and sat in the wicker chair beside her.

Anna's mouth fizzed and warmed as the wine washed over it. The sun threw deep rays of pink and amber all over the lake as it sank below the surrounding hills. On the far side of the lake she could see the Democratic Republic of Congo. The Foreign Office had still not lifted travel restrictions against it. On this side of the border, she felt safe. A group of fishermen prepared their nets and gas lanterns further up shore. At night, they would use them to attract shoals of tilapia and sardines to their narrow wooden boats. They would fish for hours, a boat in the centre and two boats either side rowing in unison. The men in the outer boats would sing and whistle to keep their oars in sync. She'd been out on fishing boats like these a few years ago, after Tim suggested they get out of the city for more traditional experiences. By the time the boat came back to shore, the choppy waves and smoke fumes had made him sick. The only other time she'd seen him look so ill was when he'd eaten some suspect foie gras on the way back from Brussels.

The lake became a blinding sheet of gold as it caught the brilliance of the sun's last rays. She wasn't just adopting the girls; she was adopting a piece of all this – the culture, the landscape, the people. It would always be a part of her.

'It just doesn't seem real.' She shivered, the wind whipping round her now. Rainy season was setting in and huge grey clouds were beginning to roll in from the north.

Marie had opened up to Anna more with each visit to the Beauty from Ashes Children's Foundation. She'd been harder to get to know at first, but Kevine, the older of the two girls by five years, prompted her shy sister and gave her the cues she needed. They'd paid Kevine's tuition fees for college a few months back, when Anna and Tim had helped her move into her residence on campus in the city.

'Have you got the forms Mama Judy asked for?'

'They're in my bag. Let me just double-check.' Anna got up and went into the guest room, coughing on the insect repellent the maids had sprayed. She hated having to breathe in neurotoxins.

She rifled through her suitcase. 'Ow! Crap.'

'You okay, love?' Tim called through the fly-screen door.

'Yeah … just caught my finger on a zip.' She pulled out the transparent folder she was looking for and stared at the crisp white sheets within – signed, notarised documents, letters from the adoption agency

The Shadow Beyond the Hills

and proof of payment of administration fees, stamped letters from the Ministry, copies of their visas and passports, a letter from the British consulate – all keys to a door they had pushed at with the weight of their whole being. These flimsy pieces of paper – a trail that led to a new beginning.

It had taken endless visits to Immigration, the Ministry, and people who went incognito whenever they were called upon, to get them. Constantly chasing things up, heading over to the other side of the city through hordes of buses and motos, only to find that Mr or Ms Form-checker was once again engaged in other business and would come as soon as they could. She'd been pulled apart at the seams. Anna stuffed these frayed pieces of herself back in – if not for herself, for the children – when she went to work at Cubs International Montessori School.

She pretended to arrange the craft cupboard when it all got too much.

'Anna, will you take some tea?' Rosine would say from behind the door.

'Maybe later, thanks.'

Anna would roll lumps of lavender-scented playdough in the palms of her hands and squeeze them with her fingers. Every pipe cleaner, pom-pom and pot of glitter was a reminder of what she couldn't have. She would never sit with the warm, solid weight of a young child in her lap or make birthday cards for Grandad or Father's Day cards for Tim.

She would fix her face into a smile and walk back out to the children; none of them hers, all of them loved by someone else. She busied herself with Brio and *We're Going on a Bear Hunt*.

Emma Lawson

When she came home to their cream, bougainvillea-garlanded house, and found Tim working in the study, she'd make herself a cup of green tea and snatch a quiet moment on the veranda. After as much time as she could bear, she contacted whichever official was working on their case – it changed from week-to-week – and made a round of office visits.

'I sent that to you four weeks ago … you said you were going to see if the other department had processed it.'

'Yes, madam. We are going through a restructure and I can assure you we will process your documents. Please be patient, madam.'

Tim would push aside her hair and kiss the nape of her neck. 'The Lord will come through for us. Just wait for him to show up. He's faithful and he provides.'

God had been with her when her womb had emptied itself and she'd begged for new life to come. He'd brought them this far. He'd brought them to Marie and Kevine.

She made herself go to work every day and sit with other people's children on the polished wood floor, stunned at how any of those little people ever made it into the world when the odds were stacked against their existence. And yet, as she wandered outside with the children and inspected the vegetable gardens they'd planted, those odds shrivelled and shrank in the face of all the richness of life around her. How could the tomatoes have grown when the seeds had fallen out of the children's stumpy hands and hadn't even been planted properly? How could a seed germinate, sprout from the soil and bloom into a sunflower, bursting with yet more seeds, all of them ready to give life again? It all seemed so easy. Effortless. Why couldn't her body perform this basic action? Why did she have to be the chink in a chain stretching back to creation? She'd existed on the cold fringes of life while everything around her was fertile, teeming, filled with potency.

None of it mattered now. The girls had brought meaning and purpose to their lives. Anna would hang the story of their adoption around her like a precious jewel on a necklace. She'd let go of her desire to have their own biological child. As Tim said, a loving father and mother taking in a stranger was the most powerful mirror of uncorrupted religion. To care for an orphan in their distress and offer hope to the hopeless, pouring themselves out in sacrificial love, bringing a lost sheep into a new fold – a family – was the definition of love. Anna had imagined the lost sheep in the form of a baby, with doughy folds you could bury your face in. But in the UK, the prospects of adopting a baby were slim; plenty of older children needed loving families. And there were still plenty of older children who needed a loving family in Rwanda.

Marie and Kevine were her chance to sacrifice her desire for a baby and give two girls opportunities they would never otherwise have. It was more of a challenge. A greater sacrifice. With an infant, you could create afresh, start anew. There was no baggage to deal with – just a baby growing up with the same raw need and affection as biological parents. Anna couldn't forget the distant look in Marie's eyes, the dreamy depth of them, and how she succeeded so easily in her studies. A little bit of herself. She could help the girls achieve what they wanted in life. They would continue the legacy that Mama Judy had started when she'd taken them in. It wouldn't be a smooth transition. There would be hurdles along the way, unspoken grievances, arguments even. Marie was at a difficult age. But why should adopting an older child be easy? It would require more of them. They would be wrung out and left purer than they were before.

Tim pushed through the fly-screen door and slumped on the bed, draining the last of his wine.

Anna placed the folder back in the inner pocket of her suitcase, her head swimming from all the promise in those pages.

'Come here, you.'

She lay her head on Tim's chest. His heart thumped beneath it. Could they really adopt these two girls and do it well? Could they love them like they deserved and do them justice?

Tim cupped her chin, tilted her face towards his and kissed her, his hands searching. He gripped her with the usual urgency he'd had ever since they'd decided to adopt. Above Tim's muffled groans, crickets chirped outside, and fisherman whistled to each other on the lake.

The jarring call of an ibis pierced her ears as Tim turned over and carried on sleeping. The lake was a dark shade of blue beneath grey clouds. She rubbed the sleep from her eyes, swallowed down the nausea in her throat and pulled on a thick jumper. This was it. No more waiting.

She reached into her bag and pulled out a letter from her sister. This one didn't have a splodge of breastmilk on it. Jo said she usually wrote her letters in the middle

The Shadow Beyond the Hills

of the night in-between feeds. Her youngest, who was not yet six months old, was 'cluster feeding', and doing some other things Jo mentioned and expected her to understand. They were the perfect family. Conventional. Dull. Anna's new family would be the embodiment of diversity and embrace – an ideal personified. She swelled with happiness. She was finally who she wanted to be, and it felt wholesome and good. She was born for this.

Tim snored himself awake as she finished reading it.

'You've never sounded so attractive.'

'You know it, love.' Tim yawned and reached across the bed for a bottle of water.

Anna stuffed Jo's letter back in her bag, picked out a pair of knickers and pulled them up her thighs, smiling to herself.

'What is it?'

'It was all I could think about once.'

'What? Making love?'

'No. Making a baby.'

'Same thing.' Tim looked up at her beneath a mop of tangled hair and grinned.

Had he forgotten already? The years of planning, the cold tip of a thermometer under her tongue first thing in the morning, the charts; the slipperiness of the egg-white she syringed inside herself to make sure that the journey to new life was PH-balanced. She'd had to do this by stealth, because if Tim had seen he'd have probably zipped his trousers up straight away. She wouldn't have blamed him.

When she'd told him to come home for his lunchbreaks, his limp body had crumpled under the immensity of her expectations. He'd go back to work and Anna would lie on the cold tiles of her kitchen floor for hours, inert as stone, dead inside.

'Let's grab something to eat before we go. I need something in my stomach,' said Tim. He pulled on a pair of well-pressed chinos. No tourist shorts for him today.

'Aren't you going to deal with that before we leave?'

'Oh, sorry.' Tim removed the condom from the bedside table, wrapped it with toilet paper and put it in the bin.

Now that they were adopting, they couldn't take any chances. It was a cruel joke.

Tim led the way to the breakfast area. Plates of croissants, toast and omelettes lined the table, along with jugs of fresh pineapple and passionfruit juice.

'Are you sure you've got those documents?' Tim dropped an omelette onto his plate with a pair of tongs.

'You know I have.'

'Sorry. I can't stop overthinking everything.'

They sat in silence for the rest of breakfast and drank coffee beneath dark wooden beams.

Tim packed their things and dumped them in the boot of their beat-up old Toyota Hilux.

'Ready?' Tim gripped Anna's hand and gave it a squeeze of reassurance.

Anna forced out the only smile she could manage.

Tim turned the key in the ignition. The engine spluttered.

Please start, you useless heap of junk. The car shuddered into life. *Yes. Thank you.*

'Right, let's do this.' Tim released her hand and nudged the car into gear, driving until the lake was obscured by mist.

Cold air rushed through the windows. They sped past rows of yellow, turquoise-blue, and mint green shops, supported by pillars, like the shop fronts of old Wild West towns. They drove past a group of young men pushing crates of Coke and yellow jerrycans of banana beer on bikes. Other men carried pieces of furniture tied together with rubber strips made from old tyres, while others stacked stripy mattresses on their shoulders. Women carried plastic basins of fruit and vegetables on their heads and babies on their backs. The bulge of their little heads was visible beneath lacy white shawls.

They were finally going to collect Marie and be a family. But Anna didn't feel any different now. Maybe she'd done this to herself when she'd corralled her nerves into submission earlier that morning. They'd waited so long for this. Why did every moment she thought would change her life turn out just like every other before it? Graduating university; losing her virginity; watching her gran die. She had these peaks of expectation, and then her feelings would flatline.

They were getting closer. A belt of volcanoes jutted out of the surrounding plain, their jagged cones cloaked in thick mist. They drove past the bus park and the bar they always went to for a couple of bottles of Tusker after visiting the girls, and finally drew up to the Beauty from Ashes driveway. Tim beeped the horn a couple of times, summoning the guard. A harsh, grating sound came through the car windows as the gates ground against the concrete.

'Do you think we should give Mama Judy a quick call?' asked Tim.

'No.'

'Why not?'

'Because she's right there.'

Mama Judy opened her arms in invitation. 'Well, hello there! Come on in. The kids can't wait to see you — one in particular.'

Tim got a few things out of the car while Mama led Anna to her cottage. It was quiet around the compound. Most of the kids were in class, and staff were going about their work.

'How've you been?' asked Anna.

'Fine. Busy as usual. If you want to get something done, may as well do it yourself.' She gave Anna a hard, knowing smile.

Tim walked in with a bouquet of tulips, roses and wildflowers and handed them to Mama Judy.

'Oh my, these are gorgeous. Thank you.'

'You're very welcome. It's just a token gesture to say how much we appreciate all you've done for us. You've supported us every step of this journey. We're so grateful. And thank you for loving Marie and Kevine so well before we met them. I think what you've done in this place is amazing.'

'We've been staying at Lake Kivu for a couple of days,' said Anna. 'Tim wanted to take me away to celebrate.'

'Of course he did. You two have a lot to celebrate.' Mama Judy was loud, but her voice was already shaking with old age.

Tim sat on the edge of the couch and looked at Anna. 'Are you going to sit down, sweetheart?'

'I can't.'

They sat in bloated silence for a few tense seconds.

'Oh, right.' Mama laughed. 'Marie.' She went to her

The Shadow Beyond the Hills

office and came back with some forms for Tim and Anna to sign. 'Let me go and see her first. I'll be with you in a few minutes.'

She left Tim and Anna alone in the room. The walls were too bright a shade of orange. Anna was starting to get a headache.

'Did you bring the documents in from the car?' asked Anna.

'Right here, love.' Tim pulled out the folder from his shoulder bag and placed them on the table.

Anna filled in the forms that Mama Judy had given them. It stunned her how those wavy little marks of ink signified the permission to interlock another life with theirs.

Tim looked at his watch. 'How much time should we give them?'

'As much as they need, I guess.' She was going to need so much wisdom to nurture and guide lives that had been so different to her own. *How am I going to do this?* Her mind went blank, unable to process the questions racing through her head.

'She's been a while,' said Tim. 'I'm just going to see if there's anything she needs.'

'No, Tim, just wait—'

He left before she could stop him. She went back over the forms she'd filled in, waiting for a few minutes for him to return. He was taking too long. They both were. A white glare hit her eyes as she stepped out into Mama's courtyard. Several kids were running around shouting words that Anna couldn't catch fast enough to understand. The guard strode past her, looking down at the ground as soon as Anna looked at him.

Tim hurried back to her, thrust his hand into hers

and pulled her along the path to the girls' dormitory.

'What is it?'

He didn't say a word.

What now?

Mama Judy was waiting for them at the end of the courtyard, her face drained of colour. 'You'd better come with me.'

The corridor was darker than normal as they trailed behind Mama Judy. Their footsteps echoed on the concrete floor.

They stopped.

Anna craned her neck around Marie's door and peered inside the empty room. 'Where is she?'

Mama Judy's voice came out as a strangled whisper. 'She's gone.'

CHAPTER SIX
GONE

Mama Judy sank to the floor, her hands covering her face.

'What do you mean she's gone? What happened?' said Tim.

Her hands slid away from her face, but the blood didn't rush back. There was now a sallow translucence about her.

'She must be around.' Anna couldn't quite let herself believe anything else. 'You have guards in this place, right?'

'Oh yeah ... pretty useless most of the time.' She rubbed her forehead and moaned. 'Where *is* she? Oh Lord.'

'Shall we call the police or—'

'We'll get to that if we need to. There's no need to involve them unnecessarily. We'll keep looking first.'

Mama Judy and a band of other staff scoured the compound for well over an hour, but none of the children they asked said they'd seen her.

Tim and Anna sat in Mama's office while she directed staff, giving them names of people she knew in town who may be able to help. Jocelyn would ask around the health clinics in case Marie had ended up in any of those. Agnes would go to the cell leaders in their district and others nearby.

Tim went with Anna to search the compound – a futile effort considering no one had seen her, but it was the proactive thing to do. She couldn't just sit around and do nothing.

'Has someone called Kevine, do you think?' asked Tim.

'I'm sure Mama Judy has.'

'Hey, why don't we go and speak to that kid who's close with Marie … what's his name – Paul?'

They found him in the games room, staring at the tennis table through bloodshot eyes.

'Paul, amakuru?' Anna noticed that he'd had a growth spurt since the last time she saw him. His shoulders were broader than before.

'Fine, thank you.'

'I'm guessing you know the situation with your friend?'

He passed the table tennis ball between his hands and nodded.

'Surely someone must know where she is?' said Tim.

Paul threw the ball back on the table. It bounced off and rolled across the floor. He remained silent, staring at his shoes.

Rivets of incredulity came loose in Anna's mind, letting in a stream of reason. *Why* could this not have happened? Beauty from Ashes wasn't a high-security prison. There were no high walls topped with rings of

The Shadow Beyond the Hills

barbed wire. Was she taken, or had she run away? Anna tried to fight images of Marie stowed away in the back of a car or lorry, terrified and alone. Taken by some perverted sadist. She didn't want to think about the sort of danger she could be in. It made her sick thinking about it. And if Marie hadn't been abducted, then she must have run away. But what reason would she have for doing this? Was it them? Had they made her do this? Anna wanted to break down in a heap in the floor.

She joined a throng of children on the football pitch for prayers led by Mama Judy. Dressed in their blue and grey uniforms, they formed a circle and held hands.

'Let's lift up our petitions to the Lord,' boomed Mama Judy over the hubbub of voices. She stood in the middle of the circle. 'Father, we lift our eyes to the hills. Where does our help come from? It comes from you, oh Lord, maker of heaven and earth. We ask in your mighty name that your precious daughter be returned to us.'

The children looked sombre. Mama Judy continued in prayer, her head bowed, the palms of her hands held open toward the grey sky.

Anna looked over at Tim. His eyes were closed, his face red and strained. The veins were visible on his forehead.

When Mama and a few of the staff had finished praying, the children filed back to class. The compound was quiet again. Mama Judy went back to her office to make some more calls and follow up with the staff she'd sent on errands around town. Her hands were shaking. When would she call the local police? This was the first time Anna had seen cracks starting to appear in Mama Judy's normally cool composure. It was unsettling to see her starting to lose control. Anna had always looked to Mama Judy for reassurance.

'I'm going for a walk around town to see if I can pick up on anything,' said Tim. 'Want to come?'

'No, you're alright. I need some space.' Exhausted, Anna went to one of the rooms in Mama's cottage to try and get her head down for some rest. Thoughts of what was happening to Marie pressed in on her, making her head pound even more. She hadn't eaten since breakfast. She hadn't felt the slightest bit hungry. Tired and overwhelmed, she fell into a fitful sleep.

When she woke up, her mouth was dry, and her head throbbed. The day's light was dwindling into darkness and rain had started to pummel the window. She pulled herself out of bed, startled by shouting further down the cottage. Mama Judy's voice thundered through the walls.

Anna checked her phone to see if Tim had called. Nothing. The shouting began to die down. It seemed safe to walk to Mama Judy's office to see if any progress had been made.

'Sorry, I didn't mean to make such a racket.' A trace of embarrassment flickered over Mama Judy's face.

'Oh, you weren't, don't worry,' Anna lied.

Pierre, Felix, Immaculate, and a handful of other staff stood before Mama Judy like naughty schoolchildren awaiting their detentions.

'Has anyone heard anything?' asked Anna.

'Nope. Nothing whatsoever.' Mama Judy looked even more pale and drawn now, the lines on her face tracing out a map of stress and worry.

The staff stared at Anna in silence. The Bible verse from the book of Jeremiah – 'for I know the plans I

The Shadow Beyond the Hills

have for you …' – mocked her from the wall.

'I think it's time to call the police,' said Anna. She couldn't believe they'd left it this late.

'I know,' said Mama in defeat.

'There you are! I've been looking all over for you.' Tim's hair was wet, and his clothes stuck to his thin frame.

'Sorry, I had to rest and ended up falling asleep. I'm shattered.'

Tim walked over to Anna and squeezed her hand. 'Everything will be alright in the end, you know. And if it's not alright, it's not the end.' His face softened into a smile.

Anna wanted to believe him.

The next few days rolled into one long blur of meetings with local officials and police staff. Tim and Anna were barely at the centre. Anna paced back and forth in dingy police offices, thinking of all the places Marie could possibly be. Someone had to have seen her by now. Even if you weren't a muzungu, this was one of the most densely populated countries in the world – you couldn't go anywhere, with the exception of the open savannah in the east and the dense rainforest to the south, without seeing anyone. The country was a hill-studded stretch of mostly cultivated land rippling down terraced slopes to lush valleys. In the morning, children collected water from pipes at the bottom of the hills; women in igitenge skirts wrapped around muddy t-shirts hoed the soil; men carried stacks of firewood on their shoulders or herded cows, pigs, goats, along the road or through the fields. How could Marie become invisible like this?

'Madam, we're looking into this. We have our officers actively searching right now.'

'Uh-huh. And have you contacted the police in the Western Province?' Mama Judy sounded like she was trying to hide the alarm and desperation in her voice.

'No, not yet. There's time for that.'

'Damn it.' Mama Judy threw her hands up in the air.

'I'm going to get some air for a moment.' Anna walked outside and sat on one of the hard wooden benches by the wall. A large group of prisoners was sat cross-legged on the ground in orange jumpsuits. The suits reminded her of the scrubs that surgeons wore. Six policewomen encircled them, their AK47s casually slung over their arms. Some of the prisoners were staring into space; others were staring at Anna. One man held his handcuffed hands to his head. Anna knew that a grim future awaited them.

Mama Judy blustered outside. 'We're not getting anywhere here. Let's go. I'm needed back at the centre.' She started walking to the car.

'Tim? Are you coming?' asked Anna.

'I'm going to stay on a bit longer, actually. See if they get any leads.'

'Oh my God.' Anna began to break down. She couldn't hold back the tears any longer. 'What if something awful has happened to her? She's somewhere out there all alone. She has no one. Or she's not alone, and—'

'Anna, sweetheart.' Tim walked over to her and held her hand. 'I know this is horrible. But we have to trust that the Lord is keeping her safe. We just have to, okay?

She'll come through this. We all will.'

Laundry soap bubbles whirled around the air as Anna leant over a basin and washed her and Tim's underwear. She gave the rest of their clothes to one of the house helpers to wash. She needed to get their clothes clean and ready for another couple of days on the road, searching, asking around. The thought of going back to the city without Marie left her with a gaping emptiness.

Mama Judy busied herself with staff meetings, flitting in and out of her office and checking in on Anna occasionally. 'You're leaving tomorrow, is that right?' she'd asked.

Today was a study day so there were no classes. Several kids were milling around Mama Judy's courtyard. There was none of the usual shouting and laughter, which unnerved Anna even more. They seemed to know something she didn't. Or they were scared.

Anna hung the last of her underwear on a washing line round the side of the cottage and went back to her bedroom. She reached into her bag and pulled out another letter from Jo which she'd neglected to read. She made a mental note to reply. Right now, she couldn't figure out what to say. *Hi Jo, we're at Beauty from Ashes, but guess what? Marie has disappeared! Without a trace. And no one knows where she is. I've just washed my underwear and now I'm sat in a bedroom, still with no clue where she is or what to do.*

It was Jo and Ben who'd led them to Rwanda in the first place. Ben had told Tim about a job opportunity abroad one evening over dinner at their house.

'A friend of mine has just come back from a four-week placement with a humanitarian relief agency somewhere in Rwanda,' he'd said. 'He's a management consultant, recently split up with his wife. Hit his mid-life crisis early I think.'

'Oh Ben, stop it! You're such a gossip.'

'Anyway, he said there's a few jobs that have just opened up in their regional office. I know you've been feeling a bit shit about your job, so I just thought I'd mention it.'

Tim bristled. 'Yeah, thanks mate. I want to hear more about that. It's not project management I'm getting bored with; it's the *kind* of projects I'm managing – they're so dull and pointless, you know?'

'I'm an auditor – of course I know.'

That weekend, Tim applied for the job and prepared his notice. Anna searched for images and articles of a country she knew little about. Why did something inside her jump at the thought of being there rather than here? She didn't want the life her other sister Beth had – one that involved constantly hopping from country to country as she was commissioned for various freelance photo-journalism gigs, determinedly single and child-free. Beth was child-free, Anna childless. Anna was willing to make a life somewhere. She hadn't been able to let go of the idea.

When she'd told Jo that Tim had been successful in his interview at the charity's head office in London, Jo had hugged her tightly.

'I'm going to bloody miss you, little sis! We all will!' Jo had walked over to her handbag and pulled out a small white card. 'I want to show you something before you jet away to foreign climes.'

Anna had dreaded walking across the kitchen to look at the card Jo opened. She knew what it was.

'You're going to be an aunty again.'

She'd forced her face into a smile, hoping that it reached her eyes. 'That's wonderful news. Congratulations, Jo.'

Later came the pangs of guilt. Why couldn't she be happy for people? For her own sister? She swallowed back the bitterness and threw herself into preparing for their move, sitting at her computer every day to do more research: the common side-effects of doxycycline and malarone; the best expat-recommended health clinics; preschools she may be able to work at. She searched on expat chatrooms about whether you could get organic food in the supermarkets in town. Did they even have supermarkets? She couldn't imagine a Tesco's or Sainsbury's, but was there anything even remotely similar?

A few weeks after Tim accepted the job, they packed up and moved. When the plane lifted from the runway and the world below got smaller, so, too, did the knot of anxiety in her chest. She'd walked out onto the tarmac of Kigali Airport full of hope, blasted with hot air, as if an oven door had opened in her face. The air carried with it hints of spice and coconut – flavours of a potentially fuller life than she'd known before.

It was so long ago now.

Tim walked into the bedroom. She had no idea what the time was, or, for a brief moment, where she was. She must have dozed off again.

'I thought I'd find you in here,' he said, smiling down at her and stroking her cheek.

Anna yawned. 'Any luck?'

'Nope. The police keep saying the same thing. They don't seem to be doing anything. Mama Judy was right to come back and get on with other things.'

Francine had prepared a dinner of stewed bananas, beans, ugali and peanut sauce for them, which they ate in the dining room of Mama Judy's cottage.

'Where's Mama Judy?' asked Tim.

'I've not seen much of her.' Anna slid her plate of half-eaten food to one side.

'I just don't understand how this sort of thing can happen,' said Tim. 'Marie is here every day and then boom – she's gone. Just like that.'

Anna got up and scanned the books on Mama Judy's shelf: *Understanding Medical Surgical Nursing: 2nd Edition; Life in A War Zone: One Woman's Story; Tropical Health and Hygiene: 5th Edition; The Call to Love: Fulfilling our Purpose in a Broken World.*

'You can always tell a person by looking at their bookshelf,' said Tim.

'What does that say about you then?'

'That I'm interested in eschatology? And want to be an SAS soldier travelling the world on special ops missions?'

Anna paced the room. 'We should stay at a guesthouse for another couple of nights. I think Mama Judy needs space now. It's not as if we're helping her.'

'Don't you want to go back home first? Clear our heads a bit?'

'I've had plenty of rest. Now I want to find Marie.'

CHAPTER SEVEN
FRAGMENTS

Marie gripped the cold bars of the truck as it sped along the road. She shifted her weight as the truck pitched and swayed with every bump and bend, watching the jagged edges of Mount Sabyinyo and the smooth cone of Mount Bisoke fade from view. Her hands ached. She wouldn't be able to hold on for much longer. Her stomach ached. She'd missed her morning cup of porridge. Her legs itched from running in pitch darkness through fields of pyrethrum. As the truck slowed to a crawl and laboured up a steep incline, Marie took her chance and jumped. Her feet pounded the road and fell over each other. She stumbled onto the verge. Beyond a tangle of trees she could just make out a river, and knew that if she followed that river, it would take her far from town. It would feed into and join the Nyaborongo. The truck belched out a thick cloud of black smoke, as if to shrug Marie off and bid her a final good riddance. Fumes choked her as she ran across the road and down the embankment, fighting her way through dense knots of vegetation.

Word would have broken by now. She'd have to move fast if she didn't want to be found. Would Paul be looking for her? It hadn't been hard to escape the confines of the centre. Three in the morning was the perfect time to set out, when the buzz of the guards' radios was replaced with their snoring. She knew which branch of the jacaranda tree stretched close enough to the wall in the far end of the compound. She knew that it was going to hurt when her feet met the hard mud on the other side; they still hurt with every step. But she also knew that with every passing week, it would be harder to hide her secret.

A rush of cold wind whipped around her. The clouds were about to unleash themselves. She was wearing a green hooded jumper that an umuzungu called John had given her a few months ago, with the words 'Convinced? Reading CU Mission Week' emblazoned on the back. He was the first boy besides Paul whose lips she'd wanted to feel on hers. Did those abazungu boys know how to kiss well? His scent lingered on the soft fabric, and now it clung to her. She'd relished seeing Paul go quiet when she spoke about how John had taught her to play rummy and blackjack with the pack of cards he'd given her. She kept doing it to see his reaction.

A few fat drops of rain began to fall, jolting Marie out of her daydream. She concentrated on her steps as the rain picked up pace. It was strange to be walking outside the centre without being told how far to go, where she had to stop or who she needed to meet. It was a startling new freedom which left her breathless and light-headed.

The Shadow Beyond the Hills

A young goat bleated on the path ahead of her, dragging its tether rope behind it. It was walking with urgency. It knew where it was going.

The vegetation cleared a little and she could make out a small church further up the hill. She made a run for it, raindrops stinging her eyes. The church hall was bare except for swathes of pink and white fabric draped across the front where a long table and lectern stood. A gold-edged Bible was left open on the gospel of Luke. Marie fingered the length of its gilded pages and wished for a moment that she could absorb some wisdom and guidance. All she could hear was the rain hammering down on the corrugated iron roof. She sat on a plastic chair and pulled her jumper tight around her neck, breathing in John and trying to imagine his face now. A pale-faced Virgin Mary hung over her on the wall, as lifeless as the bricks behind her.

'Mwaramutse. Amakuru?' A tall boy around her age blustered into the church and set his leather satchel down on a chair.

'Ni meza,' replied Marie.

They sat amid the deafening roar of the rain.

Marie was glad she had a place to shelter from the downpour. What time was it? They would have had breakfast and morning devotions by now, but would Tim and Anna have arrived? She hadn't wanted to let Anna down. But as she ran her hands over the slight curve of her belly, her face burned with shame. Had Mama been looking at it? Could she have known? Would Paul have seen it? As Marie imagined each of these people in her life, her head throbbed with greater intensity. Everything went dark.

'Are you okay? Wake up!' The tall boy was gently

slapping her cheek.

His face stilled into view. She was hit by a wave of nausea and leant over, unleashing a pool of watery vomit on the concrete floor. She coughed up the last of it.

'Oh, here, sister, take this.' The boy took a plastic water bottle out of his satchel and offered it to her. These episodic bouts of darkness and nausea were happening more frequently now. At the centre, they'd assumed it was malaria and Dr Claude had given her a pre-emptive course of Coartem.

Marie swilled water around her mouth, walked outside and spat out the bitter liquid. The rain had stopped.

'My name is Mugisha. I live by the maize fields over there. Will you take some tea and bread? Please, come.'

Mugisha helped Marie walk the narrow path past the maize fields to his parents' house. 'What's your name?'

'Claudine.' Marie sat on a hard, dark brown couch in the living room.

Mugisha's mother placed a plate of bread and mug of tea next to her. 'Where are you from?'

'Mutura district.' Marie swilled milky tea around her mouth and let the sugary sweetness settle on her tongue.

'Eh, eh, eh, you've come all that way on your own?'

'I'm going to visit my aunt. She lives in Gakenke.'

'Umwana, you must eat. Take some bread. When will you visit your aunt?'

Marie bit a chunk out of the stale finger of bread and concentrated on chewing it without throwing up again. 'I'll see her in a few days.'

Marie hid in their small mud brick house for the rest of the afternoon. Mama Mugisha offered her a room to

The Shadow Beyond the Hills

sleep in for as long as she needed it. When Marie got her strength back, she helped sweep the compound and fetch water and grasses for the animals – a cow, two pigs, four chickens and a couple of rabbits. When tiredness overcame her, she rested again, but she was finding it harder to do so knowing that flesh was folding into new flesh inside her. How could life have sprung up so readily after the precautions they'd taken? She'd just finished her monthly bleed when it had happened, and the girls had said one time in the courtyard that nothing could happen then. That was after a class they were given by a couple of Peace Corps girls who'd shown them in absolute seriousness how to slide a condom over one of Mama's igitoke bananas. The rubber teat had snagged on the fibrous end of the igitoke and caused the rubber to rip, so they had to do it again. When Mama had found out that they'd taught them to do this, she sent the girls on their way and replaced them with other volunteers. She never used Peace Corps again.

Besides, Paul said he'd been careful. He was that much older than her. She trusted him. And why did life take so easily in her body when Anna must have wanted children of her own, but couldn't? She must have gone to special doctors, and they couldn't help her. Anna would have been beautiful with a pregnant belly. Marie couldn't bear to look at herself.

She spent the morning cultivating Mama Mugisha's land and joined her in a damp outbuilding room. Together, they washed, shelled and separated beans before putting them in a basin. Kevine said Marie was never happier as a baby than when she had a bucket of beans to play with. Looking at the basin of beans now, marbled in various shades of red, white, yellow and purple, she could see why. She filtered them through her fingers and let them fall into a metal cooking pot, listening as they hit the bottom with a crisp, metallic echo.

Kevine – what must she be thinking? The thought panicked her. She wished that Kevine was with her now, helping her find her way, keeping her company. She also knew Kevine would be angry with her for what she'd done. She could almost hear her sister's voice: *What were you thinking, Marie? You silly girl!*

She knew she couldn't stay here, but freshly cooked food and the guarantee of a bed to sleep in, no matter how hard the mattress was or how itchy the blankets were, made her reluctant to leave. Mugisha and his mother were kind. She didn't know where his father was and didn't ask.

Thick white smoke billowed up out of the outbuilding room and into the sky as Mama Mugisha cooked. The rain had cleared, and rays of late afternoon sunlight seared the clouds with a scarlet glow as Marie stirred a pot of beans with a long stick, while Mama Mugisha added some more oil, tomato paste and a Maggi cube.

Marie didn't know where they would even start looking for her – she'd never known anything other than Beauty from Ashes. The few trips they'd taken with visiting groups were always out of town. They'd recently visited a genocide memorial. Mama had agonised over whether to take them there. Marie had overhead her discussing it with some staff. 'I think they're ready,' she'd said. 'They need to know their history. They need to know that they're the future of a country being rebuilt, and what it's being rebuilt from.' It was a church like the one she'd found herself in earlier, but with pockmarked walls and tattered brown clothes strewn on the ground. Dark patches still stained the walls. A few skulls – some complete, some shattered; some adult-sized and some child-sized – remained where they had been placed on the altar beneath a crucifix. A forsaken Jesus looked down at the remains of his forgotten brothers and sisters. Many of the abazungu visitors cried. 'Where were we when this happened?' they'd asked themselves. 'Why couldn't this have been stopped? Will God ever forgive us?'

Marie thought she'd have nightmares after this, as had happened with Kevine and almost everyone else. She imagined that smashed in heads and bodies ripped open by machetes would invade her dreams. They never did, even though Marie stepped closer than anyone else dared to look – through hollow eye sockets, fractured skulls and fragments of bone all lying around the altar and in-between pews. In her mind, she'd tried to collect these fragments and piece them together to re-create husbands, wives, mothers, fathers, sons and daughters; farmers, market sellers, administrators, seamstresses, shopkeepers. She'd stared at death and tried to see life where there was nothing but blood and bone.

Marie, Mama Mugisha and her son ate their meals on their laps in the living room. Mama Mugisha ate her meal in silence while Marie and Mugisha talked, her movements small, restricted.

Marie could see photos of what she guessed were family members adorning the walls in thick plastic frames, as well as religious blessings stitched on beige fabric backgrounds. A calendar from several years ago, a Tottenham Hotspur poster and a picture of a blonde-haired, anaemic-looking Jesus hung on the wall opposite in a pink plastic frame.

'What class are you in at school?' asked Mugisha.

'P6.'

'I thought you were older than that.' Mugisha slid a fork of rice into his mouth. 'How many times a day do they use the stick in your school?'

'When visitors are around, or Mama, none.' Marie pictured her teachers in their white coats, pacing classrooms and clutching canes behind their backs. They didn't need to use it that often – it was a silent admonishment. She remembered Calixte squealing like a piglet when he was beaten for failing to write the correct answers to an algebra test. Somehow, she'd always managed to avoid it.

Marie and Mugisha took the cutlery and plates to the back of the compound and washed them with a small jerrycan of water and bar of soap. His mother had fallen asleep while they were talking.

As they stacked the plates to dry, a door slammed shut.

Mugisha grabbed Marie's hand and pulled her back into the house and into his room. 'Get under the bed, now!'

A man's voice bellowed through the walls. Mama Mugisha was awake now, her voice desperate, pleading. There was more banging and thudding, things being thrown around.

Silence fell for a moment. Then Mugisha's bedroom door flew open.

The Shadow Beyond the Hills

'You pathetic boy, and his pathetic mother!' A harsh slapping sound shot across the room, followed by a sharp intake of breath.

Mama Mugisha sobbed. All Marie could see were her shaking legs.

The man's legs swayed as he shouted. 'Do you also think a man should come home to a cold dinner?' A few spots of spittle landed on the floor. 'And yet I see three bottles of Coke on the table! Who has dined in my house without me? Were you going to tell me?'

'Papa, I am sorry, I—'

'Shut up! Get out of my house, both of you. Go, now!'

Mama Mugisha and her son ran out of the room, leaving the heady aroma of urwagwa hanging thickly in the room.

A bottle smashed on the floor, sending shards flying as the man turned and stumbled out of the room, grunting and muttering to himself.

Marie could barely breathe or swallow. She noticed a trickle of blood running down her cheek. She felt it with her hand and caught her finger on a small shard of glass puncturing her skin.

Marie lay stunned, unable to move, waiting for the lingering silence that would signal her chance to escape. She prayed for Mama Mugisha and her son. She pictured them sheltering in a neighbour's house, safe, unharmed and holding each other. The image was enough to make her slide out from under the bed and peer around the open door. She could hear ugly snoring coming from the living room. This was her moment to sneak out. The only light in the house came from a kerosene lamp in the living room, which had filled the air with dirty smoke. She picked her way through broken glass on the floor, crunching on a few shards, freezing, waiting until she knew it was safe to move again.

She bumped into the bike in the hallway, cried out as she stumbled over the back tyre, pushed the metal frame to the floor. She didn't register the pain as she pulled herself up straight away and ran out the back door. Heavy footsteps were getting closer.

'You thief!'

Marie screamed. She ran, heavy rain lashing down on her and stalks of maize scratching her face, arms and legs. Had she finally lost him? She collapsed to the ground. Her cheek was throbbing, the glass still embedded beneath the skin. The slurred voice and whispery brushing of maize stalks rushed at her. She ran again, pushing through her aching stitch.

She reached the end of the field and raced through a clearing. A flash of lightning lit up the river she'd seen earlier from the road. She looked behind her to check that she wasn't being followed. She shivered. It looked like she'd lost him, but she still wanted to be on the other side of the river. A clap of thunder tore through her as she made her way over the makeshift bridge. Everything was soaked: her hair, her clothes, the tree trunks that formed the bridge beneath her feet. There was no rail to grip on to as her legs gave out from underneath her. Only the inky chill of a swollen river.

CHAPTER EIGHT
WAITING

Everyone she approached shrugged and looked at her with vacant expressions. Anna held out the pocket-sized photo of Marie, searching for glimmers of recognition. None came. They'd left early in the morning when the air was cool and people were going about their business, to the fields, to the market, to town. Mama Judy had told them they should go back to their house in the city and get some rest; that she was going to do everything in her power to find Marie, *even if the damn police were incapable*. But Anna couldn't give up or let go. Anything could be happening to her. Marie needed them.

The midday sun sweltered behind a thick band of grey clouds. Anna's body prickled with heat and beads of sweat began to form on her temples. They took refuge in a street shop selling the usual things: bars of laundry soap, tins of sardines, mandazi, meat sambusas, cheap alcohol, matches, cases of Fanta – the same things in every shop. Anna ignored the shiny glint of a cockroach scuttling around the meat sambusas and opted for a bag of mandazi. They reminded her of the little bags of doughnuts her dad would buy them at the seaside as a child. They weren't freshly baked, but the sweet dough was delicious. She washed it down with a lukewarm Coke. In villages like these, it was believed that cold drinks made you ill, and in any case, there was no refrigerator. A few other customers sat around the low table drinking mugs of milky tea out of large plastic beakers.

'We'll find her. She *is* out there,' said Tim, running his fingers over his wedding ring.

Where was God in all this? Where did Tim see all of this fitting into God's plan exactly? Where was the missing piece of this neat celestial puzzle? Tim was always so sure of everything.

She couldn't deny that when they'd first met, this was what had attracted her to him. They'd met on an Indian summer evening on the Brighton sea front. It was Freshers' Week: nerves, hormones and alcohol intoxicated everyone except Anna. She wasn't even sure if she'd chosen the right degree course. She was sat in Jongleurs listening to a stand-up telling jokes about knowing when girls were up for it or not. A pitcher of bright-blue liquid filled with glowing straws stood in the centre of the long table, while the strangers she was meant to call her new best friends pretended they were having a good time, roaring with nervous laughter. She walked out after a joke about date rape and listened to the waves beat against the sea wall. That's when she smelt it: the faint hint of bonfire mixed with salty sea air. She turned to see a guy with a mop of thick, dark brown hair holding a flask of steaming liquid in his hands.

He looked at her and smiled. 'What am I drinking? Is that what you want to know?'

'Well, I just—'

'Lapsang souchong. A liquid bonfire on your tongue. It's lush. Want to try?'

'No, thanks.'

'No worries. Better than the stuff they're serving in there. Are you tired of the forced hilarity, too?'

Anna couldn't help thinking how strange he was. But she was drawn to him – the way he talked so confidently and held himself. She would know what lapsang souchong tasted like later.

They finished their mandazis and Coke and walked the dirt road through the village, stopping now and again to show Marie's photo and ask if anyone had seen her. Anna struggled to process the speed of the language. She felt like the classic 'stupid foreigner'. She never thought she'd have to use her language skills for this; money and numbers – yes; directions, times and places – yes; asking where her newly adopted child was – not so much. She nearly didn't have language lessons at all. Most of the expats she knew in Kigali said not to bother if you knew a bit of French, and everyone was learning English now anyway. Learning a new language was slow and clunky, like being a child again and feeling utterly helpless.

Tim flinched at something and looked away.

Anna turned and saw a woman stumbling across the dirt road wearing only a bandana around her head. The woman didn't appear to realise she was naked, nor that she was in the path of oncoming moto drivers zipping around the village. A few villagers laughed but did nothing.

'Tim. What should we do?' Anna whispered.

'I don't think there's anything we *can* do.'

'She's vulnerable. We can't just leave her like that. Either she's drunk or she has mental health problems – either way, we need to get her off the road.'

Tim stared at the ground and pulled his lips into an awkward grimace.

'Fine then.' Why was Tim being so unhelpful? Sure, the woman was naked, but did he have to be so useless? Anna walked up to a woman selling pineapples and jackfruit on the side of the road. 'Do you speak English? Do you know what has happened to that woman?'

'Ah, that one is an umusazi,' she said, laughing.

'What does that mean?'

The fruit seller tapped her head. 'She's crazy.'

Anna walked up to the naked woman. She spoke slowly and deliberately to her in Kinyarwanda, introducing herself and asking where she lived. She was met with a blank look. Anna took her gently by the hand and led her off the road. She then crumpled a wad of notes into the fruit seller's hand and told her to buy the woman some clothes and take her to the clinic in town. It was all she could think to do.

Tim watched a pair of harrier hawks circle the sky. 'Is she alright?'

'What do you think?'

Back at the guesthouse, Anna took out a letter of Jo's and lay on the bed. She knew she should reply, but how would she share the news? Jo would be devastated for

The Shadow Beyond the Hills

her. She didn't want to feel any more devastation. She'd never wanted to be the childless couple, impotent and sterile. Objects of pity. She should probably contact her mother, too, and tick off a ton of other items on her mounting to-do list, but while Marie was out there, none of them were important.

'Who were you speaking to?' asked Anna.

'Mama Judy. I was reporting on our progress ... or lack thereof.' Tim took a book from his bag then pulled the mosquito net down, stretching it over the corners of the bed and tucking it underneath the mattress. 'But I've got to tell you, when I was doing my prayer meditation earlier, I had this keen sense that everything was going to turn out fine; that Marie would be found, and we'd know peace again.' He rested his hand on Anna's thigh.

She shirked his touch.

'I guess I'll have to believe it for the both of us then.' Tim opened his book.

Why hadn't Tim been so sure and full of faith when it had come to making a baby in the first place? After a year of trying, Anna had suggested they go to a doctor to explore their options. It was hard enough trying to convince him to get a sperm count. 'It's no more playing God than a fifteen year old having a wet dream,' Anna had said. He'd balked at this, as if such a thing had never happened to him. She'd given him photos of herself so that he wouldn't be tempted to look at any of the other images provided.

She hadn't told Tim about her own private investigations. Perhaps Tim didn't want to know why they weren't conceiving, but that didn't mean she didn't. It had been a bitter January morning when she'd gone

Emma Lawson

to the hospital for a pelvic ultrasound, her bladder uncomfortably full. Once a cold smear of jelly had been rubbed on and the scanner passed over her belly, the dark masses in her uterus were revealed for what they were: fibroids. Now there was a name for the lower-back and abdominal pain that she'd been suffering with. 'At least it's not cancer,' the technician had said. *No, at least it's not cancer. But it is a potential lifetime without something I'll always ache for.* When would she get through 'at-least-happiness' and find something worth getting out of bed for?

At Wednesday night Life Group, Tim had asked for prayer for their situation.

All Anna asked for was for Tim to consider that modern medicine could be a vessel that wasn't beyond the Almighty's reach; that just like when organ donors are used and people have transplants, or doctors use pacemakers to help faltering hearts, it's part of God's plan to create and sustain life. God didn't always have to work in mysterious ways.

Later that night in their kitchen, Tim had explained to Anna that there's a time for everything, and that it's the Lord who opens and closes the womb. How could he allow embryos – humans – to be created and then tossed aside like any other expendable thing in favour of 'more viable ones'? No, they would wait and see what happened.

So, she'd waited. She'd waited for Tim to finish inside her. She'd waited for morning to come so that she could stop trying to sleep. She'd waited for life to bloom in her and for some semblance of joy to bleed colour through the black days. Because if it didn't, she was terrified of what it would mean.

The Shadow Beyond the Hills

She woke the next morning to the call of the ibis, a bird that followed her wherever she went. Tim packed their bags and got the Hilux ready for the drive back to the city. Anna stood on the balcony and scanned the hills. Marie was out there somewhere. Anna shivered. She noticed a stream that cut through the valley below, a ribbon of light tapering away around the next large hill. She could see and hear little figures shouting and splashing about in the water. One of them ran and jumped off a little jetty. She remembered Mama Judy telling her that they were going to build a swimming pool at Beauty from Ashes. 'Perhaps you can bring Marie back here for swim lessons,' she'd said. 'Of course, they've got the Milles des Colline pool in the city. You can take her there as well.'

'Can she swim now?' Tim had asked.

'Oh, no.' She'd laughed. 'Not at all.'

CHAPTER NINE
RISE

'Claudine! Rise from your sleep, precious girl.' Mama Mugisha pressed her cheek against Marie's chest.

Marie shivered. She felt cold and wet, even though she was dressed in dry clothes and lying on a bed.

Mama Mugisha's kind eyes looked her over with concern. She held her hand to Marie's forehead and left it there for a moment.

'You have a fever. Mugisha, bring more water.' Mama Mugisha's voice was hoarse. Patches of skin on her face and arms were badly bruised.

When Mugisha came in with a plastic beaker of water, his skin was also blemished, his lips swollen, with a deep cut down the bottom lip.

They were in a room with turquoise blue walls, riven with huge cracks stretching from floor to ceiling.

Marie ran her hand over the curve of her belly. Was there still life in there? She held her hand over it for a while, waiting to feel a flutter. Waiting to feel anything. She coughed and it felt as if there was still water in her lungs, threatening to bubble up and drown her.

'How am I alive?' The sentence came out raspier than she expected. She cleared her throat and said it again.

'By God's grace. They found you washed up on the riverbank by a big tree root. I think you must have gotten caught on it and managed to pull yourself out. You're lucky it was one of the smaller rivers. It would've been very different if you'd fallen into the Nyaborongo – you'd have been pulled under and carried away.'

Marie had no recollection of pulling herself out of the river; only of being pushed under the freezing water by overpoweringly strong hands holding her head down, the pain of unspent breath burning away inside her.

'Where is he? Your husband – where is he?' Marie searched Mama Mugisha's eyes for traces of fear.

Mugisha and his mother had tended to her every need. They clearly hadn't had the compassion or empathy beaten out of them.

'He can't hurt us anymore,' said Mama Mugisha. 'The cell leader has dealt with him.' Her voice wavered a little as she spoke, as if she didn't quite believe herself. 'We'll stay here until you're well enough to go.'

They were at Mugisha's grandmother's house. She was a frail lady of at least fifty years and her skin was as wrinkled as old brown paper. She brought Marie medicinal herbs for healing. The day would start with a cup of tangawizi chai. She would spill some of it as she passed it to Marie, her hands as unsteady as her feet. Then she would grind some igisura to a dark green paste. It tasted bitter and stung Marie's throat, so she added some honey to it to help it go down. There were flours and juices and teas that Marie took, none of which she'd tasted before, but she knew she could trust the mother of Mama Mugisha. She swung between peaceful sleep and sweat-drenched wakefulness.

Mugisha read to her from his schoolbooks, trying to impress with his patchy pidgin English. He had a tattered copy of *Tintin* under his bed that he brought out in the evenings and would read to Marie by the light of a kerosene lamp. They laughed at the Belgian umuzungu in the Congolese jungle with his small white dog. Were the Congolese that much darker? They were the blackest faces she'd ever seen, much darker than her and anyone she knew. For the first time since she'd left Beauty from Ashes, Marie felt less burdened. She looked forward to their evening sessions of *Tintin* – it was something to think about as she fought down the various pastes and juices that Mugisha's grandmother concocted for her.

Mama Mugisha brought Marie a cup of sorghum porridge and sat down next to her. 'You need to see your aunty. She must be worried about you.'

'I know. I'll leave tomorrow,' said Marie, a feeling of dread building in her. She knew she couldn't stay. She needed to get further away. She helped Mama Mugisha prepare one final meal, even though a dull but persistent ache pulsed through the lower part of her back. They sat in silence and peeled cassava, neither one wanting to talk about what had happened back at their house. Marie loved cooking almost as much as she loved books. She loved pressing her hands into warm dough and stretching it, or stirring a thick, bubbling sauce. She loved the sound of garlic and dodo sizzling in oil, and moulding ugali with her hands.

The Shadow Beyond the Hills

Kevine had taught her these and so many other things. She'd taught Marie that water mixed with flour and salt makes dough, and that you have to add yeast to make it rise. Marie remembered being amazed when she took the tea towel off the bowl of dough and seeing how it had risen like a thick puff of cloud. She remembered Kevine laughing when she'd tried to milk one of Mama's cows by pulling its tail. And then there were the hours of English lessons. All the words were so new and strange to her. She'd struggled, but the language soon came. Mama was surprised but told Marie how proud she was.

Having finished peeling the cassava, Marie stood up to relieve herself. A dribble of warmth run down her inner leg. Had she just wet herself?

Mama Mugisha's eyes widened. She put her knife down and stood up. 'Imana we!'

A bolt of hot pain struck Marie in between her hips. She doubled over and cried out. The watery dribble running down her inner leg turned into clots of warm, thick fluid. Her head was engulfed by dizziness and she staggered to the ground.

Mama Mugisha walked Marie steadily to the living room and helped her lie down on the couch. 'Mugisha, bring me some towels!' She grabbed them off her son when he returned and told him to get help.

He ran out of the room without a second glance.

Mama Mugisha put a layer of towels down on the couch. It was already soaked.

Bolts of pain intensified with each wave, as if someone was pulling at her middle with a ring of rope, tightening it each time. Another bout of nausea. She vomited on the woven mat, the effort of heaving producing another gush of liquid down her legs. Life drained out of her, leaching into the mud floor.

Marie drifted in and out of consciousness over the next few days. Mama Mugisha changed towels and brought food and water. Mugisha brought jerrycans up from the pipe in the valley, and Mama Mugisha gave Marie basins of water and soap to wash with. Mugisha tried reading *Harry Potter* to her in his stunted English. His grandmother peeled and ground the dried roots of the umutarishonga plant on a wide, flat piece of stone and mixed it into some tea for her to drink. Lethargy gradually left her. The thought of a baby growing inside her had been terrifying. How could she have cared for such a little one? Now the only heart beating in her body was her own. This was a hollow liberation. She was neither sad nor glad.

More than anyone, Marie wanted Kevine, even though she would have been disappointed with her. Kevine would have been right to be disappointed. How could she let herself be so stupid? She could've avoided all this. Since the Peace Corps volunteers' brief lessons about sexual health, they hadn't had any more teaching about their bodies and what they could do. They learned what they could from each other in snatched whispers and giggles. She'd believed Paul and the girls without question. She wasn't as smart as she thought.

Marie thought of Kevine again. She would know what to do. She would've taken care of her, like she always did. But she was somewhere in the city. Marie knew she had to go there as soon as her strength fully returned. She hoped Mugisha and his mother would be safe. She hoped that Mugisha would one day be able to finish reading *Harry Potter*, and that she would, too.

CHAPTER TEN
FOLLOW

Marie followed the river from a safe distance. As long as she followed its path, she would end up near the city – Mugisha had told her. She felt a dull twinge where the baby had been, as if its ghost was still taking up silent space in her. The clots had passed. Her body could bleed no more. Her strength had returned and Mama Mugisha had given her some money for a bus ticket. Where she got the money from, Marie didn't know, but she was kind down to her last franc. 'You are a daughter to me,' she'd said. 'We are all God's children. He shows us great mercy. How can I not show you mercy?' Had she known about the baby? If she had somehow known, she didn't show it. There'd been no judgement. Her hands had felt soft and gentle as she'd stroked Marie's forehead and cared for her like she was her own. Marie Uwimana: everyone's and no one's daughter.

She didn't use the money that Mama Mugisha had given her for the bus – it wasn't enough anyway – and she needn't worry about leopards at night. Marie knew that leopards lived only in the far east of the country now, in the national park. A group of abazungu had once been talking about their final days in Rwanda and how they'd already seen the gorillas on their previous summer trip, so they wanted to spot leopards in the national park. The gorilla permits had cost them a fortune, but it was worth it, they'd said. Gorillas were one of the most famous things about her country, and most of her people had never and would never see one. She'd only seen them in photos and books or seen them carved from the wood of the musave and jacaranda tree by local carpenters whom Mama hired to make custom gifts for visitors to take back to their home countries.

Marie no longer ran her fingers over her belly. She tried to work out whether she was relieved. She was just numb. She found respite in the steady rhythm of her footsteps as she picked her way through tall reeds and tough grasses scratching at her heels. She passed women carrying hoes and men carrying machetes, and older girls carrying their baby brother or sister on their backs collecting water in jerrycans.

It started to drizzle with rain. Marie decided to head into a thicket of eucalyptus trees, taking a narrow path which cut through the middle of it. She ripped a leaf from its branch and rubbed it between her fingers, revealing a lighter shade of green and leaving a waxy residue on her fingertips. As she walked, she held her hands to her face and breathed deeply. She'd never smelt anything so refreshing.

Thoughts of Paul sneaked up on her as she wound her way through the trees. How would he have felt if he'd known what had happened, and what would he have thought to do about it?

Emma Lawson

The light was starting to fade. She'd been walking for hours and her knees and feet ached. Crickets and frogs were starting to vibrate and croak into life, and the delicious scent of brochette and chips cooking nearby was carried on the wind from a restaurant further up the hill. It made her stomach growl with hunger. The thought of skewered chunks of goat willed her on despite her aching. She slipped slightly as she climbed the last terrace of land, grabbing on to a clump of grass to pull herself up. A single light bulb hanging on a bare wire on someone's house flashed on and off, but she used the light to follow a thin alleyway past some houses to the hard mud road that cut through the village. She would have to eat something soon; the stick of sugarcane she'd been chewing on all afternoon had done nothing to soothe her hunger.

Light drops of rain started to lick her skin. She ducked inside a small shop where an old man wearing a leather hat hobbled over his wooden staff and smiled at her. He sat at a plastic table, chewing tobacco, pausing only to cough now and then. Marie ordered a mug of steaming milky tea and a bag of bread rolls. She felt the unmistakeable prick of a mosquito on her elbow and tried to slap it away. She'd experienced malaria several times in her life, the last attack happening less than a year ago. Mama had stayed with her in the clinic, leaving only to bring her avocados, tree tomatoes and passionfruit – 'nature's tonic,' she'd called it. It was the worst fever she'd ever had. Nurses marched in and out of her room to check on her, while Mama stroked her forehead with a wet, cool strip of cloth and told stories of her nursing days.

'You had to forget about yourself. No time for

The Shadow Beyond the Hills

anything but looking after others,' Mama had said as she'd mopped Marie's brow. 'Oh, I never stopped! I was always on my feet. You had to be you see.' Mama told Marie of war veterans who couldn't sleep and collapsed at loud noises and men who'd worked at the furnace who came in with hot metal in their eyes.

'There was this one man – handsome devil he was, but you didn't hear that – and oh my goodness, did he howl when he had to have his shots. I'd never heard anything like it, not from a grown man, anyway.' Mama had laid her hand on Marie's arm. 'I'm telling you, honey, you're being so brave. I'm super proud of you.' Her eyes watered, but she sniffed and straightened up in her chair.

'I'd get the kids ready for school, get my make-up and uniform on and be out from morning until night. Jim had to make his own dinner. But I wouldn't have changed it for the world, dear. It was my calling, just as Beauty from Ashes is now. I was needed in that hospital. There was no arguing with me!'

Marie could well believe it.

When she'd finished her bread and the last dregs of tea, Marie went back out into the street. The rain had stopped but she could see a flash of lightning over the far hills. She had no idea where she was going to sleep for the night. Dread surged through her. She looked for any churches she could sneak into and take shelter in, but they were guarded by night watchmen in thick jumpers, coats and woolly hats who were still awake listening to their radios.

She began to feel desperate. Tears pricked her eyes. As she blinked them away, she saw an open gate to her left. The mud road tapered into a single path, so she was nearly at the end of the village. The gate was bordered by a couple of large concrete pillars, and a Heineken sign hung beneath a hook on one of them. She couldn't hear any music coming from inside, nor could she see any lights or a night watchman.

She treaded with caution up to the gate and peered inside – she wanted to check that a dog wasn't going to come out to bite her. It was empty. She walked inside the gate and saw a run-down old house standing in front of her, its windows cracked, shards of glass still speckling the ground. As another flash of lightning lit everything up in bright white light, she could see that the garden must have been well kept at some point but had now become overgrown. A few mango trees dotted the border of the compound, and a large banana tree waved its frilled leaves in one corner.

Her eyes adjusted to the lack of light as she wandered around the side of the building, coming out to a large lawn behind the back of the house and another shabby building to her right. She took some steps down to another level of concrete and saw a large thatched building with an open front filled with bar stools. The walls on either side were draped with ripped velvety fabric, revealing bamboo walls behind it. She saw a broken mirror stood behind the bar, and empty bottles of Mutzig on rubber beer mats.

She ran her finger across the bar and collected a thick layer of dust. It wasn't going to be cosy, but this place had clearly been abandoned. She wouldn't be disturbed.

Around the side of the bar were some steps that led up to a room. The cracked glass door creaked open as she pushed it aside. In the far back corner, she saw some

The Shadow Beyond the Hills

cardboard on the floor as well as a woven mat. This must have been where a guard had slept. This was where she would sleep. She pulled up the hood of her green jumper and managed to sleep for several hours, disturbed only by the shuffling and scuttling of rats in the rafters.

She woke up hearing Kevine calling her name in her head. The grey light of dawn crept over the courtyard and into the echoey room. She chewed a piece of stale bread roll and looked at herself in a broken piece of mirror. It was the first time she'd seen herself since leaving Beauty from Ashes. Her hair was a mess of frizz and curls, so she pulled on the woolly bobbled hat she'd found on the floor and tucked as much hair as she could underneath. Her lips were dry and chapped, and a splinter of scabby skin stretched across her chin.

She searched every dusty, crumbling room in each of the buildings in the compound, and collected a hair comb, a water bottle, an old white sack and a small pot of Vaseline, which she spread on her skin straight away.

'Eh, eh, eh, umwana!' A large lady in a navy-blue uniform and black boots appeared behind her.

Startled, Marie hid the pot of Vaseline in her pocket. 'Sorry, I'm going now.'

The lady smiled and laughed. Her fringe was stuck to her forehead with a generous amount of gel.

'How did you get in here?'

'The gate was open. I didn't think anyone was here. I'm on my way to visit my aunty.'

The security lady laughed again. She laughed at everything Marie said, even though Marie didn't see how it was funny. She spoke simple Kinyarwanda, making a confused face when Marie spoke. Marie repeated herself. Exaggerated movement accompanied her every sentence. She danced as she talked, lost in her own little world. There must have been a reason why she'd had been sent to guard a derelict building.

Marie shared a roll of bread with her and talked to her for a little while longer, but she was getting restless. She wanted to get out of the village.

A few shafts of sunlight broke through the clouds as she made her way through the village. She passed a couple of men sitting cross-legged playing igisiro. They looked elegant and pure in their white robes and brimless, rounded white caps.

Mama had sometimes spoken to her and other students about Islam in morning devotions. Apparently, the Moslems, as she called them, were going to take over the world and establish an Islamic Caliphate. Mama encouraged all the staff and kids to pray for God to do something about it. It was only a matter of time before they would all be living under Sharia law, walking ten paces behind men and wearing hijabs. She spoke about how American families had gotten smaller. Not them though – they'd had five children, she'd said with pride. When Mama was out in her courtyard and the call to prayer could be heard from the mosque by the bakery, Marie would see her bristle. Marie thought the singing sounded strange and beautiful.

The men concentrated on their game of igisiro, dropping pebbles into small wells dotted around a long slab of wood. Marie didn't know how to play; she only knew how to play Uno, rummy and blackjack.

Marie paid a bike taxi to take her to the main road. She needed to make faster progress than she could on foot. Even though holding on to the back of a truck

The Shadow Beyond the Hills

terrified and exhausted her, she still waited on the verge part-way up a hill for a truck as it inevitably slowed. It was all about timing. Paul had shown her how to jump on a moving truck when they were out on a trip one time, before Mama put an abrupt stop to it – 'You'll get yourself killed doing that! You do make me worry, you lot.' Mama had a way of laughing while also being totally serious. It was unnerving, but effective.

A white Mercedes truck drew up the hill and slowed to a crawl, revealing a young boy wearing a faded Coca-Cola t-shirt. He was holding on to the back rails. The truck pumped out dense clouds of black smoke. Marie held her breath, ran up behind it and jumped onto a ledge above the exhaust. Panic gripped her. Was she going in the right direction?

She shouted to the boy over the chugging of the engine. 'Where are you headed to?'

'Nemba!'

She was going in the right direction. Her arm muscles burned as the truck rounded corners and momentum pulled on them. As the truck lurched to a stop, the boy jumped onto the road and sprinted towards a building on the opposite side of the road. That's when the driver finally noticed them, but before he could get out and threaten her with a stick, Marie jumped and ran toward a tangle of vegetation.

She hid from view as the driver got out and urinated behind a tree. She needed a rest before jumping on another truck, so she found a quiet, wooded area not too far from the road. She laid down the empty white sack she'd found in the abandoned restaurant and curled up on top of it, trying to get as comfortable as she could on the uneven ground.

Emma Lawson

Had Tim and Anna given up on finding her yet? Were they even trying to find her? Her chest tightened as she thought about Anna and their conversations. Would Anna feel angry with her? There was no way she was going to come out of this without disappointing someone. A sense of failure overwhelmed her. She picked at the crust of scab on her chin and felt the air reach the raw skin underneath. She tried to rest but her mind was racing. She headed back out to the road and waited for another truck.

CHAPTER ELEVEN
KIGALI

The city lights twinkled like a carpet of stars rolled out over the hills. Marie was wedged between a truckload of bulging sacks, which provided some shelter against the biting rush of wind that buffeted her as the old Toyota truck flew round corners and jerked down steep slopes. She'd snuck onto it as the driver was loading a few extra sacks in the passenger seat. She was scared. She'd never been in the city on her own. She'd never been anywhere on her own. She guessed that there were still a few hours until dawn. The driver slowed down as the truck's headlights lit up the burnt-out metal carcass of an overturned bus, which must have veered off the road and smashed into the barriers separating the road from the sheer drop below. It wasn't the first accident she'd seen on the way – not long after the truck left Nemba, she'd watched as a couple of men lifted a motorbike off a young man. The man's lifeless body lay in a red pool,

Emma Lawson

his legs and arms twisted at unnatural angles. Her eyes had lingered on the scene for as long as they could; she'd seen dead bodies in open caskets at funerals, but she'd never seen the newly dead – minutes dead.

The city loomed large now, and the air was already thicker and smokier. The truck lurched to a stop at some traffic lights. It was quiet except for a few drunkards swaggering around or stretched out on the ground. Marie grabbed her bag, jumped and ran.

Where would she go now? Panic gathered in her chest. She ran further down the road towards a line of warehouses, all of which were locked and bolted. In front of the very last building on the stretch of road, she noticed some beat-up old cars gleaming in the streetlights. She coughed from petrol fumes and grease as she ventured closer. Rusting car parts were strewn all over the front of the garage, and a night watchman was sat on a chair, arms dangling either side and a baseball cap pulled down over his face.

Further round the side of the building, Marie tried the doors of another car resting on four flat tyres. The driver and passenger doors wouldn't budge, but one of the rear doors yawned open effortlessly. She slinked into the back seats and lay down.

Sleep eluded her for the remaining hours of night. She crept out of the car as soon as the first rays of sunlight came. The city was beginning to come to life: cars, motos and buses were winding through the streets in greater number and street hawkers were setting up stalls selling chapatis, newspapers and leather belts. Marie used her dwindling supply of money to buy a chapati from a teenage boy selling them from a clear plastic bucket. She held it in a greasy paper napkin and sat on a low wall on the side of the road, her back warmed by the morning sun. She sat there for a few hours, traffic filtering through the city, throngs of people filing past her, all of them with places to go and things to do. Occasionally an umuzungu would traipse around looking confused, as if they'd wandered into the wrong part of the city. Street hawkers would thrust *Time Magazine*, *The Economist* or *The New African* into their faces and bark prices at them, smiling and laughing. The umuzungu would politely decline and hurry past or give them some francs but leave without the magazine and then rush off.

The sun burnt the clouds away and was now bearing down on her. Beads of sweat tickled her cheeks as she walked through a market rammed with a bewildering display of plastic toys and trinkets. There were heaps of Nike and Adidas trainers and stacks of Levi jeans, as well as the usual things: oils, creams, deodorants, packets of matches and tins of sardines.

There were too many things and too many people crammed into small spaces. It made Marie's head throb. She had to get away. She left the mass of market sellers and walked the cobble road up a hill towards the hub of the city.

She turned and saw a man dressed in a shirt, tie and jacket dragging himself along the ground, two little stumps where his legs should have been. He stopped for a moment and looked up at her with yellowed eyes. Perhaps he was going to hold out his hand to beg. But then, how could he think she had anything to offer, looking the way she did? She couldn't give him her last few coins. She needed them now as much as he did. She shuffled away guiltily. He must drag himself to the same spot every day and take what he could get from the hands of strangers. He'd be extra lucky if the abazungu saw him. A few of the abazungu she'd accompanied on day trips to the city had what they called a 'beggar budget'. They carried money in little bags they called 'fanny packs' or 'bum bags' attached to the front of their waists to give to beggars. They would say 'God bless you' and carry on down the street with smiles on their faces. Marie guessed that the beggars came back to the same spot the next day, as they did outside the gates of Beauty from Ashes whenever visiting teams came.

Hours passed and the clouds were closing in again, soaking the city air with a stifling humidity. She homed in on a street hawker selling city maps, language dictionaries and phrasebooks to tourists. 'Where is the College of Higher Education?'

He ignored her at first, so she asked again more loudly.

'Over there.' He waved his arm in a vague direction, sounding irritated. 'In Nyarugenge district.'

Marie didn't know where that was. She would have to ask, but she would ask someone else. Trips in the city were always with Mama and groups of abazungu visitors. They insisted on sampling all the markets for strips of igitenge, and Mama would arrange for a driver to take them around the city hotspots for the day, windows open and boxes of Source du Nil in the back of the car. They also bought woven bowls, postcards, wooden giraffe statues and dark wooden masks made by the Congolese.

The Shadow Beyond the Hills

Usually, they wanted to go to the Genocide Memorial. Mama would solemnly tell Marie and the other kids, who all took it in turns to accompany visitors on these trips, what they were about to see. Marie had only been twice but guessed that Mama always went through the same routine.

They would wander slowly around the dark corridors and rooms of the inner building, reading the backlit information boards and peering with sober eyes at individual photographs hung on the wall with small pegs. Marie remembered a teenage umuzungu called Annabelle who'd burst into tears after the photo wall. Mama had put a hand on the top of her back and said, 'I know, dear. I know.'

At the end of the exhibits, a lady with a curt city accent thanked them for coming and explained that they were all architects of a new Rwanda. She told them how the RPF had stopped the killing and saved Tutsis from the genocide. 'Although we were forgotten by the West, we are a country on the rise again. Africa is rising up and the world cannot stop her.' She paused to look at a photo of the President staring down at them from the centre of the wall. 'We are moving forward. Never again will our President allow this to happen. Never again will we suffer the indignity and pain of the past.'

Marie had been too young to remember what had happened. Still, the ghost of genocide haunted almost everyone she knew in some way. She was old enough now to realise the grief and fear that rumbled through every conversation the adults had, especially around April. The radio, as well as the papers she sometimes read in Mama's office, reported those who'd recently been brought before the gacaca courts or sentenced in the International Criminal Tribunal in Arusha. Every April, there would be reports of newly discovered and exhumed graves, and the secrets of the dead would be laid bare yet again.

Mama attended the memorial talks with some of her students, her face grave, head bowed. Government representatives gave talks about Banyarwanda and how there was no longer any Hutu or Tutsi ... apart from when they spoke of the Genocide against the Tutsi. Then they could be named. They listened in silence. The speaker would report on how poverty levels in each sector had fallen and were projected to fall further. 'Are any of you walking barefoot?' The representative would look around the hall with raised eyebrows and let silence settle the matter.

Marie finished the last of her water as she drew near to a man selling watches in front of a parade of shops. He was wearing a multi-coloured shirt, as if someone had thrown buckets of paint at him.

'Do you know where Nyarugenge district is?' Music blared from the two loudspeakers either side of the watch seller's stall.

'You're standing in it!'

'Oh. Do you know where the College of Higher Education is?'

'I sell stolen watches,' he said, grinning. 'Do I look like I know where such a place is? Hey, you want to go bring abazungu to me? I pay you well.'

Marie walked on through the wet heat as sweat trickled down the nape of her neck. She took a minute to rest and sat under a palm tree outside an Asian store, breathing in the heavy scent of turmeric and coriander wafting through its door. A twinge of hunger seized her.

The Shadow Beyond the Hills

Her stomach cramped and she half-expected a stream of blood to run down her leg. She distracted herself by watching taxis ferrying people back and forth: men in smart business suits and crisp white shirts and women dressed in the most exquisite clothes – some in finely tailored igitenge and others wearing the sorts of blouses and trousers that abazungu wore. They all looked so beautiful and elegant.

Surely a taxi driver would know where the college was? She walked over to a taxi parked on the side of the road.

A slightly drunk-sounding driver leaned out the window. 'Follow KN 2 Avenue past the prison and keep going where the road forks into two. When you see the mosque, keep going for another ten minutes,' he said.

Marie tried to remember his directions, but they were slipping from her mind already. She was sticky and cold, sweat now cooling on her skin as the sky darkened. The air was thick with fumes and spices, brochette and chips. The startling glare of light from the roadside stores illuminated tins of powdered milk, packets of porridge, foil strips of condoms, and bottles of soda standing on wonky shelves. There was still no sign of the college she needed to find. No Kevine.

A man who looked to be in his thirties or forties approached her. 'You look thirsty. Let me get you a drink.' He was mature, bland and ageless. He smiled and motioned for her to sit at a plastic chair in the bar they were about to walk past. He had a thin moustache and was wearing thick-rimmed glasses, and his pin-striped trousers were held up by a Dolce & Gabbana belt.

Marie was thirsty. She wasn't going to object if

Emma Lawson

someone wanted to buy her a drink.

'What would you like? Skol? Mutzig?' he asked.

'Coke.' She couldn't bring herself to drink Fanta.

'My name is Vincent.' He went to the bar and returned with a bottle of Coke for her and a Mutzig for himself.

Marie sipped her drink while Vincent looked at her.

'What's your name?'

'Ennistine.'

'And where are you from?'

Her mind went blank. She couldn't think of a sector. 'The other side of the city.'

'I work in KCB. I'm a financial advisor.' He sounded proud, arrogant even.

Why was he trying to impress her? She looked like a street kid rather than a high-class city girl.

He talked about the type of house he lived in, his furnishings and his 50-inch flat-screen TV.

A waiter brought them a plate of chips.

'I guessed you were hungry, too.' He talked about growing up in Kiyovu and going to school at Ecole Belge. He talked only about himself.

Marie thought about how she was going to find Kevine in the dark bowels of the city.

'So, anyway, after completing my Master's at Imperial College in London, I moved back here. Now I work at the bank. I just bought a new Landcruiser. I can help, you know.'

Marie finished the last of her Coke.

'Do you want to study or live somewhere better? Or both? I can help you. I'm a man who makes things happen.' He winked at her.

'I don't think anyone can help me.'

The Shadow Beyond the Hills

'Oh, come now! Don't speak such falsehoods. I wouldn't be where I am today if I hadn't accepted help.'

Marie stared at her bottle, trying to ignore his eyes on her.

'Let me buy you another drink.'

A tight feeling began to spread over her chest.

Vincent returned with another Coke and a bottle of Waragi. 'You need to relax. I can tell you're uptight.' Without asking if she wanted any, he poured some of the clear, strong-smelling Waragi into a glass, topped it up with Coke and slid it across the table to her. 'That's better. Now, where were we?'

Marie didn't feel like he would accept her not having the Waragi and Coke.

'Ah yes, you were telling me that you cannot be helped. Bullshit. You're a beautiful girl, and I'll make sure you succeed in life. You can have whatever you want, baby.' He leaned over as he said this, his sour breath hot in her face. 'I have connections in this city.'

He didn't wait for her to speak. He wasn't interested in her voice. He spoke again of himself and his connections: some men he knew in the police and the military, as well as a good friend of his who was the Vice-Chancellor of the national university.

As he spoke, she could feel his hand under the table, grabbing, clawing, pulling. She felt sick.

'I'm just going to the bathroom.'

She could feel his eyes on her as she walked over and pushed the door open.

A couple of women were applying lipstick and talking about which club they would go to next. 'I'm not dressed for Pata-Pata. I'll be refused entry!' said a woman in a tight leopard-print dress.

Marie pushed the door back open slightly. Vincent's back was turned. Perhaps he was checking his phone. She walked back out to the street, her steps as controlled and brisk as she could manage without breaking into a run. The street was a blur of neon green, red and purple lights. Heart-shuddering bass reverberated through the air.

A heavy hand landed on her shoulder. 'Why did you leave? I thought we were having a nice time?'

Marie pulled away from his firm grip and tried to run, but he slid his hand down to her sleeve and held fast. She let the hoodie slip over her arms and shoulders and freed herself, running until her legs cramped and her lungs burned.

He gave up easily. He was looking for easy prey.

A stitch stabbed her side. She stopped to gulp down more air.

'Hey, are you okay?'

Marie straightened up and saw a pencil-thin woman in a trouser suit, with long hair held up in a swirl of braids. Marie shivered. She was wearing only a strappy top over her jeans now.

'My name is Speciose. I work with an NGO and am here to help vulnerable girls and women find a safe space.' She showed Marie a badge that said New Beginnings International in bold, red print, held in place on her neck by a loop made of plain red fabric.

Behind her stood a tall, broad-shouldered man wearing a New Beginnings International polo shirt.

'Will you come with us and take some tea?'

They all walked down the street until they came to a large white building bordered by bright red gates. She was taken to a small room. There were posters filled

The Shadow Beyond the Hills

with symbols and numbers on the wall.

Speciose returned with a blanket, a mug of tea, and a lady called Brenda. Speciose draped the blanket around her shoulders.

'Thank you,' Marie croaked.

Brenda's face was framed with long mousy brown hair, a mess of curls that bounced around her face when she talked. She had an American accent, but not quite the same as Mama's, and she wore a shirt that said, 'There is no force equal to a woman determined to rise'.

'How long have you been on the streets, sweetheart?' Brenda looked at her with concerned eyes.

Marie's mind froze. She didn't know what or who to be. She was completely drained of energy – physical and mental – as if her body was allowing all the fatigue of the past few days to catch up with her.

'It's okay, you don't need to talk right now. We can offer you a room for the night and take it from there. Do you have any other belongings with you?'

Marie shook her head.

'No? That's alright.'

No one asked to lay hands and pray over her as they took her down a long corridor and showed to her room, which contained a single bed and bedside table. A bottle of Source Du Nil and a pack of biscuits were waiting for her. On her bed was a laminated sheet of information about New Beginnings International – who they worked with and what they offered. She would read it properly tomorrow. Now, she needed to sleep.

CHAPTER TWELVE
SUNBIRD

Anna and Tim left before the morning rush hour traffic could clog the road past the bus park out of the city. They'd been driving for almost an hour, barely speaking. She sensed something beginning to unravel in him. If he'd bothered to take notice, perhaps he'd have sensed the same in her over the years.

'I'm never going to get that grant proposal sent off before Friday.' Tim gripped the steering wheel and stared straight ahead. 'Alice expected it to be done by now. I'll have to call her later and have *that* conversation. How fun.'

Anna pushed her hair out of her face. 'Well, sorry to inconvenience her. Life happens sometimes … not that she'd know what an actual life looks like.'

Tim forced a laugh. 'You know, for all the annual leave she gets, I don't think she's taken even one week of holiday.'

The Shadow Beyond the Hills

'And that's why Alice went for the regional director job and you didn't.'

The hills rippled endlessly around them as they drove north, the foliage becoming more alpine the further they went. She remembered a holiday to northern Italy she and Tim had taken to celebrate their second anniversary. They'd enjoyed time together as a couple, and had planned to start trying for a baby, even in their log cabin in the Dolomites. They had a routine: they would make love in the morning followed by a breakfast of fruit and granola, hike in the mountains, read and then have dinner. They would talk about the future; about what their family would be like, the traditions they would have at Christmas and Easter, and how often they would take the kids to see their grandparents. It had all seemed so certain then, as inevitable and effortless as falling asleep and waking up.

Now, they were far from the pristine waters of the lake outside their log cabin and the icy air of the Dolomites. They weren't talking about the future. They weren't really talking much at all. Whenever she thought about their future it misted up in front of her. All she could think about was Marie and where she could be.

They pulled up under the flame tree at Beauty from Ashes and stepped out of the car onto a mushy carpet of orange, red and brown petals. The centre was so full of promise when she'd visited in the early days of their adoption journey. It had filled her with nervous excitement. Now, she was free-falling down an endless tunnel.

'How are you doing?' said Tim as Mama Judy walked towards them with her translator.

'I've been better.' Mama Judy gave Tim and Anna a

brief hug and then dumped a raffia bag onto the rear passenger seat, pushing her sunglasses onto the top of her forehead.

They were going to explore a few villages just out of town, not having had any success in the town itself. Mama Judy insisted on coming with them now. Since the police were being useless, they'd just have to take matters into their own hands and keep searching themselves, she'd said to Anna.

They sat in silence for a few minutes, staring at passers-by on the way to the market.

'I got a letter yesterday from my youngest son,' Mama Judy said, her voice loud even in the back of the truck. 'His divorce papers came through last week. That makes three out of five separated.'

'I'm sorry to hear that,' said Tim. 'Have they got kids?'

'Oh yeah. They all do. They've got so many between them I thought they were having some sort of competition.'

'What a shame. It doesn't seem like many families stick together these days … most important unit of society as well.'

'If Satan's going to break up society, he'll start with families.'

The truck pitched and swayed down a steep mud track that cut through a banana plantation. Anna surveyed the scenery around her, an undulating patchwork of lush green and dark brown dotted with small mud brick houses. They were in the thick of a rural village.

A mob of children descended on them, the older ones pointing the muzungus out to the younger ones:

'Reba, abazungu!' The younger children stared in silence, but the older children giggled and peered in through the truck windows, running their hands along the metal panels.

Smiling, Mama Judy shook hands with a few children and walked with her translator up a path that wound around the hill. Tim and Anna followed. They passed a coffee plantation and reached a row of shops. Mama's translator, Jean-Paul, approached farmers, shopkeepers and moto drivers. Anna and Mama Judy held out their photos of Marie. Tim hung back in silence. His moping was annoying her. Why wasn't he getting involved?

They did this until the heat of the day forced them to retreat below the thatched parasol of a bar, where they shared goat brochettes. A thunderstorm broke the humidity of the air.

Back at the centre, Mama Judy ran straight to her office, shouting instructions at Emmanuel over the rain.

Tim and Anna went to the guest room in Mama Judy's cottage. She'd said they could stay the night and go out to another village the next morning.

Anna laid her bag down on the end of the bed and shut the window, which had been left slightly ajar and had let in a spray of rain. She flumped on the bed, not having a clue what to do for the coming hours.

Tim went to sit at the long oval table in the dining room to do some work on his laptop. She could tell when he was worried about a project when the usual pleasantries of a kiss on the cheek as he left the room were forgotten. New lines of worry etched his face.

Jo's letter flashed in her mind. *Don't forget to contact Mum*, she'd said. Their mother: raised to immortality in her childhood, now forgetting her keys and burning the toast.

She'd have to say that they'd still not heard anything about Marie's whereabouts. She wasn't sure how many times she could bring herself to do this; she'd tried to avoid her family, but they were persistent. She knew how the conversation would go if she called:

'Hi, Mum.'

'Oh, hi, darling.' That sound of surprise again. 'How are you doing out there?'

'I know what you're going to ask, and the answer is no. I told you I'd let you know as soon as we heard anything.'

A pause, the line crackling slightly.

'Sorry. It's been another day of nothing. I'm just really tired,' Anna would say.

'I can imagine, sweetheart. Jo rang. She was just concerned because she hadn't heard from you recently. We're all worried about you, that's all.'

'I know. I'm fine, really, I just—'

'And you know, what with Beth on assignment in Lebanon right now, I just want to know that all my children are safe and well!'

Beth: always on a mission, saving the world since 1983. Everything and everyone else needed saving but her – from a factory-farmed salmon in Norway to an imprisoned human rights campaigner in Yemen. She was the architect of her own destiny, the mistress of self-actualisation. Beth: the queen of contradiction. According to her, people were inherently good, and for this she would quote Jean-Jacques Rousseau and

William Blake. But they were also arseholes. Usually the religious ones, who were single-handedly responsible for all the misery and bloodshed in the world.

'Did Jo tell you that Lucy's been accepted into the National Youth Orchestra? Wonderful news, isn't?'

'Mm-hm. You mentioned it as well the last time we spoke, Mum.'

'Oh yes, sorry.'

'Anyway, I won't keep you, I know you're busy. I just wanted to check in. Your dad and I are taking the caravan to the Lake District at the weekend, so we probably won't be in touch. But ring if there's something urgent. Please.'

'I'll try. Give my love to dad. Speak soon.' Anna would hang up before her mother could press anymore.

Anna tried to focus on the book she was reading on sensory learning and experiential play. She had a week of planning meetings coming up for the next academic year and was trying to do some research, but the words kept blurring into black smudges as she re-read the same paragraph for the fifth time in a row. She finally gave up and went to make a cup of tea, peering in on Tim, who was frantically tapping away at his keyboard. *Always at his bloody laptop.*

Mama Judy's kitchen was a mess of pots and pans. There were coffee grounds all over the sink, and a few empty cans of tomato sauce lying on their side near the hob. Even her house helper had neglected the kitchen. It was still so quiet at the centre. There was a subdued air about the place. It hadn't recovered from Marie's absence. None of them had.

The thick tail of a rat disappeared into a cupboard. Anna took her tea back to her room.

Emma Lawson

That evening, when a power cut made them get into bed earlier than normal, Tim didn't hold Anna. He didn't touch her at all; not even a foot placed on hers. She rubbed his foot gently with her own. He just moved further over to his side of the bed.

'So, you're not even touching me now?'

'I'm tired, Anna. I'm sorry, I just … I don't have the energy for anything. Trying to juggle work and all this, it's just—'

'You're not the only one.' Anna's body tensed with irritation.

'I know. So how about we just go to sleep, okay? Goodnight, love.'

Anna was woken by some crows squawking and tapping the metal roof with their feet as the first rays of sunlight poured into their room. She left Tim in bed and went to sit in the wicker chair on Mama Judy's veranda to eat a small, sweet banana.

A few staff members were already out with a group of nursery children on the lawn, kicking a ball around and digging with spades in a sandpit in the corner.

'I thought you might like this.' Mama Judy appeared with a cup of coffee and hovered next to her, cupping hers with wrinkled, sun-spotted hands.

'Thanks.'

'Kevine should be here soon. I think she got one of the first buses out of the city.'

The children crept up on an ibis pecking around in the soil on the far side of the lawn, shrieking with laughter when it flew away.

The Shadow Beyond the Hills

Mama Judy smiled.

'How many children do you have?' asked Anna.

'How many *children* do I have?'

'Not here at the centre. I mean how many children of your own?'

'Oh. I have five, dear. Jim came from a large family and always wanted the same for us. I suppose I kept thinking: what's one more when you already have two. Then I thought the same after my third and fourth.'

Anna tried to imagine how anyone could juggle five children and a nursing career. But this was Mama Judy.

'I've always had room in my heart for one more. And look what happened!' She gazed down at the children tottering around on the lawn below. Her smile vanished for a moment as her eyes settled on a young member of staff, who looked like she'd barely entered her twenties. 'Alphonsine! You're with the children now. Play with them!' She sighed and looked over at Anna. 'It's such a struggle sometimes with the newer staff, getting them to actually talk and engage with the kids. How are they going to learn otherwise? We do an initial training about what's expected ... seems like the message isn't sinking in.'

A sunbird landed on the railing in front of them, its iridescent feathers shining like a splash of oil in the sun. It flew away as a child in a GAP kids jumper toddled up the steps towards Mama Judy and babbled a stream of incomprehensible words.

'What the heck are you talking about, hey?' Mama Judy scooped up the toddler and bounced her on her lap, laughing and holding her chubby hands. 'What are we going to do with you, huh?'

The little girl gave Mama Judy a gummy grin and

chuckled with delight at the attention.

Mama Judy kissed her on the cheek and placed her back down on the lawn, gave instructions to the staff and went back to her office.

Anna gathered the last of her belongings in the guest room. As she packed, the muffled strains of a heated discussion filled the corridor. Was Mama Judy having an argument with someone again? Her voice dominated the discussion.

She nudged Tim squarely in the ribs. 'Tim. Tim! What do you think's going on?'

'I don't know, but I've just had a text from Alice. I'm sorry but I'm going to have to go back home. Do you think you can get a bus back?'

'Can't it wait?'

'What – the Clinton Foundation for our funding proposal or else the project gets canned? Yeah, sure it can …'

'Fine. You work; I'll try to find our adopted child.'

'Oh, Anna. Don't be like that.'

Anna slung her rucksack over her shoulder and went to meet Mama Judy.

Kevine was with her in the office, her eyes dark and glowering. They stopped talking as soon as they saw Anna.

'Good morning, Kevine. How are you doing?' asked Anna warily. She couldn't imagine how Kevine must be feeling.

'Fine, thank you.' Kevine stared at a black and white spiral painting behind Mama Judy's desk.

They took Mama Judy's Landcruiser to another village just out of town. Kevine's hair, which was usually neatly braided and held up in a bun, was now short and

The Shadow Beyond the Hills

straight, held in place tightly with gel. She didn't look at Anna or Mama Judy the entire journey.

Was she angry with her? Did she think this was somehow Anna's fault? Anna wanted to reach out to her, take her hand and say that everything would be okay, but she couldn't. The words never left her mind and her body was too listless to move for such gestures. A deeper feeling of failure weighed Anna down and threatened to crush her entirely. The immensity of what she and Tim had decided to take on swamped her with both fear and a sense of utter foolishness. What had they done? How did they think they could do this? Mama Judy's voice echoed in her head: *With God, all things are possible*.

Jean-Paul was doubling as a translator and a driver for Mama Judy as he jammed the Landcruiser into first gear to descend a steep mud track. It had been raining heavily the night before, and the tyres were slipping. Anna tried to stop herself thumping into Kevine as the car pitched from side to side. Relieved that they hadn't ended up in an overturned car at the bottom of the hill, Anna stepped out into the muggy air. Kevine had an idea of where they should go, so they followed her lead.

They walked through a patch of eucalyptus trees, the smell reminding Anna of her mother putting vapour rub on her as a child when she had a cold. They stopped for a herd of cows walking single file on the narrow path. The cow herder hit the last one in the line with a short stick to keep them moving. Beth would have been outraged.

They passed a thick crop of maize in the valley, crossed a dubious-looking bridge, and walked up a hill to a parade of shops beside a deeply rutted mud track.

The village was largely quiet except for a small confluence of women, chickens and rabbits in a makeshift market. A woman dressed entirely in kitenge approached Anna, trying to sell several kilos of mangoes from Burundi.

Mama Judy sniggered at the price the lady wanted.

Anna bought a kilo and put them in her rucksack, even though it weighed her down even more.

They went through the usual routine, whereby Jean-Paul, joined this time by Kevine, would speak to people, while Mama Judy and Anna held out photos. And, as usual, they were met with blank looks and stares from those around them. A few locals tried to sell their produce and animals, including a woman holding an albino rabbit by the ears. She thrust it at Anna and Mama Judy as the rabbit's hind legs kicked out.

Anna's legs ached as they wandered around for hours speaking to as many people as they could. A few villagers told stories of vagrant children they'd seen, but none of them sounded like Marie.

They stopped outside a little restaurant and looked at a hand-painted sign showing pictures of rabbits, brochettes and chips.

'Not here,' said Mama Judy. 'We'll be waiting all day if we order here.'

They walked on and found another small restaurant serving a mélange of food. Jean-Paul stacked an impressive heap of everything on his plate. Kevine spooned some fried plantain, rice, and chunks of beef in an oily-looking red sauce onto hers. Anna forced down a few chips. She examined the street outside. Was it futile expecting to find Marie?

They finished their meals and walked back to the

The Shadow Beyond the Hills

street. Dark clouds were gathering overhead, and a faint peal of thunder rumbled around them.

'We should go.' Mama Judy looked around to see if anyone disagreed, but everyone was looking at the clouds. Everyone except Kevine.

'Hold on.' Kevine turned and walked into a shop on the side of the road.

Anna followed, side-stepping potholes filled with murky water.

She stood next to piles of cabbages, carrots and a few bags of charcoal and wood as Kevine talked to the shopkeeper. Anna was grateful that Kevine had joined them. She felt utterly useless.

Kevine and the shopkeeper spoke for a few minutes as sambaza cooked in a pot behind the counter filled the shop. A couple of children played with marbles and cars made out of wire on the floor.

Anna tried to read the conversation. They were talking too fast for her to understand or even get the gist.

The conversation stopped. Kevine turned towards Anna and started to walk back out to the street. Her face had fallen in dejection.

The little peak of hope in Anna fell away too.

They walked back to Mama Judy and Jean-Paul.

'Anything?' asked Mama Judy.

Kevine shook her head.

'I didn't think so.'

The afternoon rain clouds were closing in on them. They made their way down a steep bank, down towards the valley of maize.

Mama Judy clutched her shawl about her as the wind picked up and another peal of thunder tore through the air. It was getting closer.

Mama Judy's mud-splattered Landcruiser was now in sight.

'Can you drop me off in town, Mama?' asked Kevine.

'Sure.'

Shouting came from behind them. She turned to see a woman running towards them, a slight limp slowing her down. A tall boy wearing a football shirt was supporting her by the arm.

'Arrête!' Panting, the woman slowed to a brisk walk.

'What does she want?' said Mama Judy.

'She's saying stop. Let's wait for her,' said Anna.

The woman and the boy finally caught up with them. Kevine and Jean-Paul translated the woman's strenuous speech.

'Show her your photos,' said Kevine.

The woman examined the photos Mama Judy and Anna held out. Her eyes glistened. 'Imana we. Gakenke!'

'Oya, mama, oya.' The boy's voice was inflected with frustration, then excitement. Breathless, he turned to Mama Judy. 'She told me she was going to the city!'

Anna's heart shuddered and skipped.

Mama Judy dug around in her bag and pulled out her purse. 'God bless you both,' she said as she placed a bunch of notes in the woman's hand.

Anna watched the woman and her son blur into the background as streams of rain poured down the rear window.

CHAPTER THIRTEEN
FALLING

They left for the city that day. Mama Judy finally believed that Marie had ran away and that no one had taken her. Anna tried to imagine Marie in the hills on her own. Had she made it to the city? Was she somewhere safe now? *Why* had she run away from them? She thought they'd made a connection, but this couldn't be true. Anna focused her thoughts elsewhere. Mama Judy stayed at their house and went with her and Tim to the police station early next morning, waiting for well over an hour until they could speak to someone.

'We're searching for a missing girl.' Mama Judy took out a few documents and photos and handed them to the police officer – a small, squat lady with front teeth that pushed her lips out. 'We've been searching in the town where we live – where she lived – and the surrounding villages.'

'My wife was told by a couple of people in one of those villages that she was on her way to the city,' added Tim.

They gave more details to the police officer and were told that a report would be filed, and they'd be contacted again shortly. Shortly turned into the next day. And the next. Mama Judy visited a few people she knew in the city, which spared the tension and awkwardness of her being with them most of the day and trying to make conversation that none of them had the energy to make. She eventually got her driver to take her back to Beauty from Ashes, giving Anna a lacklustre wave as she pulled out of the drive.

Tim had back-to-back meetings that day, leaving Anna alone in the house. She was beginning not to care anymore; it wasn't as if they'd been talking recently anyway. She made herself a cappuccino from the fancy coffee machine she'd picked up from a yard sale the previous year and went to sit in the garden, allowing all the feelings she'd suppressed in the police station to surface. What was it about them that had made her feel that running away and leaving herself vulnerable was the better option? Anna hadn't allowed herself to feel hurt and humiliated until now. It wasn't enough that her body had failed her: now the girl they were adopting had failed her. *No – this isn't about me.* Hurt and humiliation gave way to guilt. Whatever had happened to Marie was more than anything that she'd had to bear.

Anna buried these thoughts as deeply as she could. She needed to be hopeful and believe that Marie wanted to be found. She took a moto to the market to pick up a few things for dinner; there was nothing in the pantry after their days away from home. Even the fruit flies had disappeared in search of better stocked shelves. The wind whipped around her as the moto driver weaved in and out of traffic. Riding on these bikes always felt

The Shadow Beyond the Hills

dangerous. It gave her a thrill. Jo hadn't been able to do it when she'd visited a couple of years ago – she'd heard too many horror stories of motorbike accidents from friends of hers who were doctors and nurses. Usually, thinking about Jo made her feel childless and empty; on that trip, she'd made Anna feel brave.

She made her way through rows of food-laden market stalls and haggled for fruit: a kilo of passionfruit, a couple of pineapples, a few hands of bananas. Having to understand and speak fast-paced Kinyarwanda and deciding on what they needed according to her meal plan, all while protecting her money from pickpockets in these hot, noisy markets used to overwhelm her. Now, it was still very much a chore, but one she could handle. She wandered over to lengths of kitenge hanging from wooden rails, taking her time to decide which pieces among the kaleidoscope of patterns and colours would be striking but not too garish. She settled on a piece that looked like a swirl of navy-blue and yellow teardrops.

Back home, she measured and cut the fabric to fit the kitchen table and placed a vase of sunflowers in the centre. She filled the house with the comforting smell of banana bread, diced some onions and peppers in preparation for dinner, and tidied the house, but none of these piecemeal attempts at distraction worked. She poured herself a glass of Merlot, finishing the last of it as Tim walked into the room.

'Want a glass?' asked Anna.

'Go on then. Listen, love, I know this is crap timing, but I'm going to have to make a trip back to London.'

'How long for?'

'No more than a week. I've got a ton of meetings

with donors. They want answers that we can't give them, but I'm the mug who's been roped into doing it anyway – and taking the flack when I can't. Anyway, will you be okay?'

Relief flooded her. She couldn't remember the last time Tim had touched her. They were barely speaking.

With Tim away, Anna kept busy and threw herself into doing what she could to find Marie. She'd go for a punishing morning jog just after sunrise and sit in the police station waiting room for hours. She rang Mama Judy every few days to let her know if any progress had been made. They'd talk for a few minutes before one of them made an excuse about needing to do something. Finally, Anna did have a valid excuse: Sarah had asked her if she wanted to meet up for a drink and get some dinner. Sarah wasn't the easiest of people, but Anna realised she hadn't seen any of her friends in the past few weeks. She had second thoughts about going. She barely had the energy to muster up conversation, and Sarah was bound to ask her about the girls.

They met outside The Red Cactus, but every table was either taken or had been reserved. Sarah should have booked, but she was never one to plan things. They walked down the road and stopped in a bar where you had to shout over the music. Anna ordered a couple of cocktails and brought them over to Sarah.

'Ooh, mojitos. Good choice.' Sarah took a sip and smacked her lips together. 'And there's a decent amount of mint in there.' She flipped her long honey-blonde hair behind her shoulders. 'Matt had to go to New York

The Shadow Beyond the Hills

for a few meetings at the UN, did I tell you?'

'No, I—'

'Well, a few trips to Coco Spa and I just about got over it. I said to Matt, "Fine, you can go so long as you bring me back the goods – I'm talking cranberry sauce, Easy Cheese, Oreos." Girl's gotta have her home comforts, know what I'm saying?' She laughed and took another sip of her mojito.

'Yeah, it's hard when they go away.' Anna managed a tight-lipped smile. 'How's your house coming along?'

'Oh my God, it's proving to be the bane of my life. I mean, I don't understand why it takes so long just to approve a piece of land. Like, seriously, do me a favour and stamp the stupid papers.'

'Must be frustrating,' said Anna.

'Damn straight it is.'

Sarah and Matt were in the process of building a house just outside the city. It would have grey wood clad walls and a cornflower blue kitchen with a strip of low-hanging lights above the breakfast bar. It would be their own little slice of Connecticut. Once they had a house of their own in this country, it would complete their metamorphosis from 'muzungus' to 'seriously committed muzungus'.

'And did I tell you that our house in Connecticut flooded last month?'

'No, I don't think you did.'

'Yeah, that was a real pain in the ass to deal with from here. The downstairs floor, all our furniture: ruined. Matt had to sort it out.' She paused to check her make up in a pocket mirror. 'Oh, have you been to that new coffee place downtown? I have to tell our women-on-the-move ladies about that.'

Anna stared at the menu, not remotely interested in anything it had to offer.

'Oh, shit! Sorry, I totally forgot – how are things going with your adopted girls?'

Anna looked up again and tried to string her thoughts into some kind of coherent sentence. 'She wasn't there.'

'What?'

'She ran away. We're working with the police to find her.'

'Oh my God, Anna. I'm so sorry. Does anyone know why she ran away?'

What was she supposed to say? How on earth would *she* know why Marie had disappeared? The more she thought about it, the more ridiculous the idea of adopting the girls became. There was so much she didn't know about them.

Fairy lights flickered around the trunk of a nearby palm tree. She felt weightless, uprooted. Nothing in her life made sense. There was nothing to hold her together in the shapeless void left by Marie's disappearance.

'We don't know,' Anna eventually blurted out. 'That's what we're trying to figure out. All we know is that she was on her way here. Maybe she's trying to find Kevine.'

'Does Kevine know anything?'

'No more than we do.'

Sarah blew out a long sigh and shook her head. 'You guys were so pumped for this.' Sarah gave her a look that reminded her why she'd been avoiding everyone she knew.

They ordered some food, Anna settling on grilled fish and Sarah on an avocado and steak salad.

'It'll work out, Anna. Things always do.'

Sarah brought the conversation back to herself and her dilemmas: whether she was justified in firing her house helper for stealing a necklace that had belonged to her grandmother; the best place to get the material she needed to make curtains for the upstairs bedrooms in the new house; whether antibiotics and growth hormones were routinely pumped into cows here, as they were in America. Anna indulged her.

They paid the bill and walked out to find motos.

'You know, there's this shelter for street kids which my friend runs. Might be worth reaching out and speaking to her.' Sarah shrugged. 'You never know, someone may have heard something.'

It was worth a try – every potential lead had to be investigated. And yet, Anna could already feel the bitter bite of disappointment.

Tim dumped his bags on the tiled floors of their hallway. His hair was dishevelled, and his grey-flecked stubble was noticeably longer. 'What a journey. My Heathrow flight was delayed by four hours, so I missed my connecting flight from Nairobi.' He walked up to Anna and held her tightly. 'I've missed you.'

His clothes smelt old and smoky. She hadn't missed him.

'How did it go?' asked Anna.

Tim sighed. 'Terribly. I did what I could, but it's up to the board now. Oh, Jo gave me these to pass on to you.'

Anna unwrapped the flowery wrapping paper,

revealing a mauve leather-bound notebook with the word 'Courage' embossed in wavy writing on the cover. Inside, on the front page, was a message: 'Stay strong. Our thoughts and prayers are with you always x'. She'd written a few inspirational quotes underneath about how to keep going when all seems lost.

Anna placed the notebook on the hallway table and helped Tim carry his luggage upstairs.

He took out some lacy lingerie and flashed a coy smile at Anna. 'I know I've not been easy recently. I've not been the husband you've needed.' He took Anna's hand and held it in his. 'I want that to change – whatever's going on in our lives.'

Tim took a stiff rectangle of white card out of his suitcase and gave it to Anna. 'Zanzibar. You and me. Three nights. What do you say? We need some time just for us.'

White wine sauce simmered on the stove as Anna chopped fresh chives from the garden, while Tim sat on the veranda watching the sun go down. How could they jet off on a luxury holiday when Marie was still missing? It wasn't right. And typical of Tim to come up with something like this. What was going through his head most of the time? And lingerie? Did he really think sex, of all things, was going to be the answer to their problems?

The sauce bubbled and thickened in the pan. They had been through a lot. They were stressed. She let her mind take her to a white stretch of beach and the

The Shadow Beyond the Hills

cerulean sky of the Tanzanian coast. She could almost taste the skewered fish and tamarind and coconut sauce. A luxury break felt wrong, but so did their marriage. If they weren't strong as a couple, how were they meant to hold it together for Marie? Things were falling apart. *They* were falling apart. They'd been so consumed with finding Marie, that they'd lost themselves. And while sunbathing on a beach for a couple of days wouldn't fix it all, they could at least spend time together. Away from the city. Away from Tim's work.

Anna didn't know what foundation their marriage stood on anymore. Its shaky edifice had been showing cracks for a while. She thought of those broken vases in Japanese culture, the cracks of which were filled in and sealed with gold. The vicar had spoken about this in a sermon at St Peter's, their old church in Highgate. Could their marriage ever look like that? If it did, it would have to be broken first.

'Smells delish.' Tim tried to sound upbeat as he rested his elbows on the counter, looking up at her with tired eyes.

Her conversation with Sarah came back to her. Could it lead to anything? It had to be worth a try, surely. She took a dish out of the oven and plated up the fish fillets.

'So, what do you think? Am I cancelling these flights or not?'

It wouldn't be a problem if you hadn't been so presumptuous and booked them in the first place. You didn't think to ask me what I thought beforehand.

This was the problem. This was why they were heading to a dark place if they didn't try to fix this. It may have been hasty and half-baked given what was going on in their lives, but it was his way of making an effort. His way of trying to get them out of the hole they found themselves in, at least in terms of their relationship. Maybe Tim was right – perhaps a short trip away was what they needed.

'No, don't cancel. It doesn't really feel right but …We could do with a break. We need to rest – together,' she said.

'I know. That's what I thought.' Tim smiled and took a long sip of his wine. 'You'd best get packed.'

CHAPTER FOURTEEN
DAR ES SALAAM

The plane shook over a stream of tropical air as it made its descent into Dar es Salaam. They took a choppy afternoon ferry-ride to Zanzibar and checked in at their resort by the beach. Tim insisted on small talk with her almost the whole way. Anna was wearied by it. Then again, he was making an effort.

They freshened up for dinner. The sun had dipped below the dark line of the Indian Ocean. Wearing her floral maxi-dress – the first outfit she'd worn in months that hadn't consisted of beige linen trousers or a loose fitting blouse – she and Tim walked past a sweep of thatch-roofed huts towards a kidney-shaped swimming pool, which was lit up in various shades of pink, purple, red and green. They ordered some cocktails and sat at a table by the pool, breathing in chlorine and sun lotion mingled with cooked seafood. Anna took in a delicious breath of it. But her relief was still tinged with guilt – Marie was out there somewhere, scared and alone, while they were planning on sunning themselves on the shores of Zanzibar. Had she been kidding herself about this trip?

Tim swirled a mini umbrella around his cocktail

glass. 'We're going to have a good few days here.' He smiled at Anna and touched her hand. 'You deserve it.' He had a few extra lines around the corners of his mouth as he smiled, and the lines in his brow were deeper now than they were before.

'I'm going to try and relax. I promise.' She squeezed his hand in return and placed it back around the rim of her cocktail glass.

Anna looked across at the up-lit palm fronds hanging over the pool. How different it would be if they were here when they'd first met – before all the cares of marriage, fertility and adoption had wrung them dry.

A waiter greeted them and placed a steaming bowl of coconut bean soup in front of Tim, and some sizzling skewers of fish in front of Anna. Opposite them, an older couple ate their meals, pausing for the odd sentence or two of conversation and trailing off into silence, trying to find different things to look at around the restaurant.

Anna fought the urge to envision herself and Tim in years to come. Or worse: to see their faces in the old couple's faces even now. She let the lime of her cocktail tingle on her tongue and focused her attention back to Tim, who was talking about Ben and Jo.

'How were they?' asked Anna.

'Oh, you know those two. There's always some drama.'

Anna couldn't think of any drama in their sepia-tinted lives.

'Jo asked if you wanted to try some of her placenta pills. She's got a few left over. They're meant to give you a huge boost in energy and vitality, apparently. According to the woman she paid to encapsulate and

The Shadow Beyond the Hills

bottle her afterbirth, anyway.'

Anna grimaced and drained the last of her cocktail.

'I said I'd let you know. I wasn't sure if it was appropriate,' said Tim.

'It's about as appropriate as the time I gave a 'Gin is the answer to everything' mug to my manager for Secret Santa.'

'How many years had she been sober?'

'One.'

The beach was dotted with sunshades. Sand burned Anna's feet as she and Tim made their way to a sliver of shore shaded by some overhanging palm fronds. Today was going to be a good day. Tim had assured Anna that his laptop would not be making its usual appearance. When he wasn't dealing with adoption-related matters, there was always some crisis going on with work that needed to be attended to: a donor that was threatening to pull out of a partnership or a new grant proposal that urgently needed writing.

They lay on their sun loungers in silence for a while, Tim engrossed in one of his paperback thrillers, and Anna lost to the waves lapping the shore. For lunch, they feasted on a fresh catch of seafood. The combination of food and roasting heat from the midday sun coaxed her into a light sleep.

She woke to the sensation of falling and noticed Tim smiling at her.

'You were out for the count for a few hours there.'

The sun's rays had softened into a languid warmth.

'I'm going snorkelling. Why don't you come with

me?' Tim pulled her up and thrust a snorkel at her.

Anna groaned. 'I want to drink cocktails and sunbathe.'

'Oh, come on, Genie.'

Anna shrieked and then laughed as Tim hoisted her over his shoulder and ran to the water. She couldn't remember the last time they'd laughed and had fun like this.

Tim dropped her into the ocean waves. She let herself sink for a moment, submerged and abandoned to the warm water.

They swam until the beach became a white strip in the distance fringed with palms and green scrub. The gentle currents massaged her aching muscles. She hadn't realised how much she'd been punishing her body with early morning jogs until a deep tiredness settled on her for a moment. Perhaps it was time to head back to the beach already and relax.

Tim indicated a nearby shoal of fish. Spiced rum with ice would have to wait. He took a few gulps of air and plunged under the glassy surface, raising his hand out of the water and motioning for her to join him.

Black and white striped fish darted away from her with arrow-like precision as she entered their muted world. She followed Tim towards a mound of rocks covered in coral, her hair swirling around her as she tried to take in the mad medley of colours. An oval-shaped, blood-red fish covered in electric blue spots startled her as it brushed her leg.

Tim had joked about the possibility of bull sharks in this part of the ocean. She'd given him a death stare and waved the suggestion away. Now, in this silent world, where all she could hear was her raspy breath in the

The Shadow Beyond the Hills

snorkel pipe and the occasional jet of bubbles bursting up to the surface, she saw dark figures lurking behind every rock. She tried to block out the image she'd once seen on the internet of a body torn up after a shark attack; one side of the upper torso missing, a stump of femur bone protruding from a gaping hole. How could human beings be reduced to meat? It hadn't been hard to find the images. She'd told herself that by seeing the worst of death, she could mentally prepare for it. Death was coming to all of us one way or another. *The doors are locked, and no one gets out alive* – that's how a preacher at their had church put it. If she desensitised herself, death would become another prosaic fact of life. But seeing those images didn't desensitise her; they made her sick and desperate to live. It wasn't something she dared divulge to her counsellor. Some things were just too weird to admit. Her anxiety had been at its peak when she'd had to retrieve foetal tissue out of the toilet. Pieces of her broken baby. The anxiety dipped for a while and then resurfaced after the terror attacks in New York. People plummeting to the ground. Bodies lying in a crumpled heap.

The water felt cold now. She wanted to be back on the beach. She wanted to be back home. She swam over to Tim, who was investigating a clown fish nestled in a waving clump of sea anemone and pulled on his arm. She needed to breathe.

She took a deep breath as Tim pulled off his mask and snorkel.

'Time to go back is it? Well, that was epic. Thank you, Lord! Did you spot the seahorse?' Tim was a little boy again, getting ready to tick off his finds in a dog-eared wildlife book.

'Spot the seahorse' sounded like one of the ridiculous games they played at preschool. 'No, I must have missed it.'

'Right, cocktail o'clock then. What do you reckon?'

'I thought you'd never ask.'

They swam to shore. Anna noticed a group of slender, tanned bodies in bikinis playing volleyball on the beach as she placed her feet onto the velvet-soft sand below and rose out of the water. The girls' laughter was loud and brash, and the boys in the group were showing off their sporting prowess. Perhaps this was a brief stop on a round-the-world gap year. She remembered trying to laugh like that with boys, before giving up. It was always awkward. *She* was always awkward. She turned to check that Tim was close by. A stabbing pain shot through her foot. 'Shit!' Heat and pain merged into a single sickening knot, squeezing her head in a vice-like grip as she tried to drag her herself further into shore.

Anna blinked Tim's concerned face into view. Her head was throbbing. Her foot was stinging as if it was being poked with needles. She felt nauseous, cheap aftershave and coconut-scented sunscreen tickling her throat from a small cluster of beach revellers bending over her.

'Was it a … jellyfish? Did I get s-stung by a jellyfish?' asked Anna.

'No, sweetheart. I didn't see any around.' Tim stroked her forehead, tucking a wet strand of hair behind her ears.

'Coral?'

'It was a bit murky when we got past the reef. I didn't see.'

An early twenty-something boy wearing a light-blue shirt patterned with white shells leaned over and squinted at the soles of Anna's feet. 'Do you see those?' He motioned for Tim to take a look. 'They're puncture marks. Three or four of them. They're not deep though, and she hasn't got any needles embedded in there. She was lucky.'

'Puncture marks from what?' asked Tim.

'Sea urchin, guaranteed. I got stung by one of those bastards in Bali last year. It absolutely wrecked.'

'What did you do?'

'I downed a shot of Jack Daniels for every needle that got tweezered out.'

Anna turned on her side and vomited, making the little gathering around her back away.

Tim lurched forward and scooped her hair away from her face as she retched again.

Anna moaned and wiped her mouth. 'It was when he talked about the tweezers. That pushed me over the edge.'

'Oh, my love. Let's get you back to the hut.'

Anna slept for the rest of the afternoon.

She woke to the comforting sound of Tim turning the pages of his book as he sat in the corner of the room on a wicker chair. A salty breeze blew through the open doors of the veranda, lifting the mosquito net draped over the bed. She was less groggy after a nap, but her foot still stung and ached.

'What time is it?'

'Time for another look at that foot of yours.' Tim brought over a small red bag – the one that Anna had thrown in at the last minute when packing. 'It was quite pink and swollen earlier.' He cocked his head to one side. 'Looks better now.' He ripped open a small packet of wipes, took one out and drew it carefully across the sole of her foot.

She flinched.

'Sorry, love. It's just an antibac wipe. I don't want those punctures to become infected.'

The Savlon cream he applied next soothed and cooled her foot in an instant. He applied it with caution, taking care not to work it in too hard. He looked up at Anna. There was a warmth in his eyes that melted something cold and hard in her. It was disarming. Anna was the one who usually held things together, sorting and organising their lives around work, dinner and all the other mundane tasks that made the days tick by. Now here she was, prostrate and feeble, while Tim tended to her wounds with both tenderness and authoritative care. She let him care for her.

He ordered snacks from room service. Offerings of octopus curry and mishkaki skewers were too much; all she wanted were small, sweet things. She settled on date nut bread, mandazi, and small diamond-shaped bars topped with toasted sesame seeds and honey, which the locals referred to as 'chocolate'.

Though she knew it wasn't sensible, and against Tim's better advice, she ordered a pitcher of sangria. They sat on plush orange cushions atop a wicker frame on the veranda as the sun dipped below the ocean, a chorus of crickets ushering in the coolness of night. A pillar candle burned on the large circular table in front of them.

'I hope Kevine's doing alright,' said Tim. 'She looked awful the last time we saw her. I think she's lost weight.'

Anna brought a glass of sangria to her lips, its sweet smoothness gliding down her throat. 'She busies herself with studying. I guess it's a distraction.' Kevine was independent and required so little of them. Anna didn't feel needed by anyone. She *wasn't* needed by anyone. Did Marie even want to be found? Surely she'd have turned herself into the police if she had. They'd have heard something by now. The thought stung as much as the sea urchin had earlier that day. She rested her feet on Tim's legs.

With only a slice of date nut bread, the mandazi and some sesame seeds milling about in her stomach, it didn't take long for the drink to take its pleasing effect. They talked late into the evening, slapping the odd mosquito off their skin, while Anna drank away those thoughts and feelings that had been plaguing her the past few weeks. Tim didn't make any comment about it. His gaze moved from her eyes and to her lips and down to her tanned legs as she spoke. She was letting her guard down. He was enjoying it.

The familiar bassline of 'One Love' boomed across the beach. Tim started swaying and singing in mock coolness, the way he did when he'd larked about in the kitchen in her halls of residence.

Anna gave him a playful punch on the shoulder and let out a boozy laugh. 'Stop it you loser.' For the first time in a while, Anna let herself loosen up. The tension had released its grip since her afternoon nap and Tim's confident care over her. She savoured the way he'd taken control. She was done with trying to be in control. The realisation that she never was and never would be didn't even bother her. Control was just a mirage that swam in and out of view – as was the table she tried to walk around on the way into the bedroom.

Tim grabbed her arm, stopping her face from meeting the dark-stained wooden slats of the floorboard. His grip was firm. There he was again, stopping her from falling, just like he'd been trying to do their whole marriage. Stopping her from hoping in one-in-ten chances. Stopping her from hoping in a less than forty per cent chance of her eggs being fertilised even if she did manage to ovulate. He'd stopped it before they'd had a chance to begin – he'd only been trying to save her from disappointment. Why hadn't she seen that? It was so clear now.

He led her to the bed, where she sat down and looked up at him, his tall presence both commanding and loving. She was sticky from the residue of cooled sweat and sea salt on her skin. She needed a shower. When he came into the bathroom after her, shirt unbuttoned and trouser belt loose around his waist, she didn't tell him to go back to bed. When he stood beside her, steam rising from her skin, and lathered her up with soap that smelt of lavender, his hands gentle, taking meticulous care over every curve and slope of her body, she didn't shrug him off. His body was smooth against hers. She turned to face him, her hands tracing the lines sloping down from his hips in a tempting V. She relaxed into the rhythm of him inside her and let waves of relief wash over her body and mind, her worries dissolving and floating away with the foam down the drain. A life without scheduled sex, negative signs on urine-soaked plastic sticks, and adoption meetings and paperwork unravelled before her with blissful ease. Waves of a new life for them crested and crashed over her in quaking, quivering sprays.

A hotel cleaner whistled to himself outside their veranda on the way to one of the other beach huts. Tim rested his arm loosely around her as they lay on their sides, his knees tucked under her bent legs. She nestled even closer into him as the sun's soft morning rays imbued the room with a dull pinkish glow. Hangover aside, the memory of the previous night lingered as a sweet aftertaste. More than simply a quick fumble under the covers, lights out and thoughts of the next day's errands on her mind, they had actually made love. In that moment it was enough. They were enough – with or without children, biological or adopted.

Tim stretched and yawned. 'Morning, my love.' He plumped up his pillows and pulled himself upright. 'You're incredible, you know that? You were incredible, and you are incredible.'

Anna groaned. Her voice came out as a strained whisper. 'There's no need to shout.' She turned over and kissed his stubble-covered cheek.

'Head hurting, huh?'

'If you say, "I told you so".' She gave him a teasing whack on the shoulder.

Tim's smirk softened into a broad smile.

'Can we stay in bed forever, please?' said Anna.

'Nuh uh. We're hitting up Stone Town today.

Providing you can walk for longer than a minute without hobbling.'

The alcohol, though still in her system, had stopped numbing the pain in her punctured foot.

Tim poured some water from an open plastic bottle on the bedside table into a glass and dropped a tablet in, handing it to her.

She watched as the bubbles hissed and fizzed to the surface. Traipsing around stifling hot markets didn't appeal nearly as much as spending a lazy day around the resort, snacking on delicious Tanzanian food and taking the odd dip in the pool. That was what she needed. She would work on him, which wouldn't be hard, and they would do that instead.

Tim's phone beeped. He glanced at it and placed it face down on the bedside table.

'Work?' asked Anna.

'How did you guess?' He rolled his eyes. 'It never ends, even on a mini-break. I hoped they would leave me alone for a few days. I told Alice I was going away. She knows what's happening in our lives and that we need some space.'

Thoughts of lazing by the pool with fresh pineapple juice and platters of tropical fruit fizzled out as quickly as the paracetamol in her water. She'd wondered when one of them would mention Marie – at what point their little bubble of bliss would pop, leaving them to the stark reality she'd tried to shove to the back of her mind the past couple of days. Everything had gone quiet before they'd left. Calls from Mama Judy had died down. The only potential lead they had to follow up was Sarah's mention of a centre for street kids in the city, which was a long shot considering they'd already been

The Shadow Beyond the Hills

to several and nobody was any the wiser.

Tim flung off the covers. 'Right, breakfast.' He pulled on some khaki shorts and ran a hand through his thick, dishevelled hair.

'Hold on a minute—'

'If we don't get up now, we'll still be here at lunchtime.' Tim started to make his way to the shower.

'Tim, wait ...'

He looked at her, his face open and curious.

She hadn't wanted to mention it just yet. One more day like the one they'd had yesterday, minus the sea urchin. Just one more day, that's all she'd wanted. 'When you were in London, I met up with Sarah.'

'Yeah? Have they managed to get permission for Connecticut-ville yet, or are they still battling it out with local officials?' He snorted a cynical laugh.

'She asked about Marie ... and then she mentioned this place in the city where a friend of hers works – a centre for street kids.' A note of hope twanged inside her for a brief moment. It was a dangerous feeling, but she let it resonate. She'd felt it many times before, only to have it disappear.

Tim walked around the bed and sat down next to her. 'Okay. Then we go. When we get back home, we'll go together and do everything we can to find her. Yes? We're not giving up on her, are we?' It sounded like a genuine question. He searched her face for traces of doubt.

She looked out of the double doors, past the beach to the azure waters in the distance. It made everything seem so limitless. Possibility opened and spread out before her once again, a vast expanse of potential still untapped, still open for exploring.

'No, we haven't. We're not going to fail her.'

'Good.' Tim reached for her hand and squeezed it as if they were making a binding contract. 'That's settled.' He released her hand and took the snorkel and diving mask hanging on one of the wicker chairs. 'I'm just going for a quick snorkelling session. Is that alright?'

'Of course. Go for it.' His flip flops padded down the steps leading from the veranda to the beach.

Yes: they would follow up every possible lead they could. They had to. There would be that familiar stab of pain if it didn't lead to anything, but this wasn't about her now. It wasn't about her emptiness. It wasn't about her mum's quiet disappointment in her, or Jo's beautiful children, beautiful home, perfect life. It wasn't about Beth's latest article in *The Guardian* or her highly lauded piece in *The New Statesmen*, which their father would cut out and proudly display in a frame in his study. She would carry on swimming in the shallows, and life would go on as it always did. As it must. Marie was just a child, alone and in need of love – love that they could give, her and Tim. Love they could give because it flowed from them rather than being something they depended on and needed to keep them afloat.

She pulled herself out of bed for breakfast before Tim came back. A message flashed up again on his phone. *Can't they leave him alone for just one day?* She wanted to message back and say, 'Life is about so much more than work.' She stomped over to the bedside table to turn it on mute. She saw the message: 'It was so good seeing you last week. I've missed our chats. Celia xx'

CHAPTER FIFTEEN
NEW BEGINNINGS

It was so quiet. That's what Marie had noticed. There was no shouting and running around. Everything was calm, peaceful, ordered. They were sheltered even from the blare of moto horns and traffic outside. Linde, the Dutch lady who ran the centre, led her and a small group into a shaded courtyard hemmed in by bright red railings festooned with passionflowers. Her translator followed closely behind. Most of the group spoke limited English. The city spread out in the distance, with shanty-style buildings clustered around the base of the hills and the larger commercial buildings and hotels sprinkling the tops.

The group varied from older kids to older teenagers, mostly boys. They were clean, but their clothes were tattered and old. In the brief time she'd been at the centre, she hadn't really gotten to know anyone, keeping to herself and making only obligatory small talk. 'Don't worry,' Linde had said in her guttural accent. 'You take everything at your own pace.'

They sat in a circle around Linde. A large poster was laid out in the centre of their little huddle displaying various scenes of children and adults under the title 'Know your Rights'. One picture showed a man kicking a child. Another showed a young teenage girl being offered money by an older man in a suit. Linde gave a short talk with the help of her translator, looking everyone in the eye at one point or another while everyone else's eyes focused on the poster.

She then turned the poster over, revealing a diagram of a teenage girl's body – unclothed. Mama would never have allowed posters like these at Beauty from Ashes, even if they were cartoonish pictures rather than photos. The diagram pointed out her breasts and privates, which were shaded in blurs of red. Linde's voice was toneless, seamless, as she went through a talk she'd probably given countless times before.

'You all know that these areas are out of bounds. Private. No one should touch them without your permission.' Linde flicked her long ponytail over her shoulder. Her hair was dark and flecked with subtle streaks of grey.

'What I'm going to tell you today is something you may not be aware of.' She picked up a fat marker pen and drew a circle around the whole diagram of the girl's body. 'Your body, whether here,' she said, pointing to the breasts, 'or here,' pointing now to a shoulder, 'is yours – no one else's. Yours. Whenever someone makes you feel uncomfortable, intentionally or unintentionally, you have the right to speak out. Your body matters. Your feelings matter. *You* matter.'

She used her long, slender index fingers to point to the sides of her head, which she bowed slightly so that

The Shadow Beyond the Hills

her eyes looked up at them with greater intensity. 'And here. No one should manipulate or control your mind or your emotions. Before we close our session, please ask questions. Just raise your hand.'

One of the few girls in the group raised her hand. Marie tried to figure out how old she was. She seemed mature for her age, but perhaps only because of what she'd been through, the life she'd already lived.

'Yes, Florence. Go ahead.'

'What if I need money for school fees, and a man can help me? And he doesn't touch me or kiss me?'

A short lapse followed while the translator relayed the question to Linde, who nodded and looked at Florence with piercing eyes. 'Is this man a close relation?'

'No.'

'Is he part of a registered local or international NGO, and does he communicate to you with other people around, or does he always speak to you when you're on your own?'

The translator fed these questions back to Florence.

She tugged at her necklace as she spoke. 'When we talk about money and school and other things I need, we're on our own.'

A dry, dusty breeze swept through the courtyard and lifted stray wisps of Linde's hair, which she smoothed back down. 'Then what's happening, whether or not there's physical touching at this stage, is inappropriate. You are vulnerable and he's putting himself in a position of power over you. It's a form of manipulation by which he can control you.'

Florence shrugged with acceptance.

Marie imagined her in a former life on the streets,

going back and forth collecting run-off water from the city gutters and drains in jerrycans, and using that water to cook some beans she'd collected from market floors in a dimly lit, smoky hideaway. A non-descript man brightened her future with promises of education and jobs, peppering her prospects with hope held in slick, smooth hands – hands like the man who had poured Waragi into Marie's Coke.

The group dispersed and Marie wandered back inside to the drop-in zone, a large room with lemon-yellow walls and a huge TV at the back of the room surrounded by sofas. The tiled floors had just been mopped and she nearly slipped as she made her way to one of the sofas. Brenda was talking to a couple of boys in ripped, faded jeans and brownish t-shirts. She had a look that Marie had come to know well from some of the visitors to Beauty from Ashes – a concerned look that easily turned to embarrassed discomfort.

Even from where she was sat, Marie could smell something harsh and chemical emanating from their clothes. It stung her nostrils. One of the boys had an angry-looking rash around his mouth that had spread up to the middle of his face.

'Good job, guys. I'm here if you need me.' Brenda went to talk a group of teenage girls.

The boys came and sat on the sofa next to Marie, flicking on some South African satellite channel. Marie noticed whitish-pink ridges of tender flesh on the inside of the taller boy's arms. One side of his face was wrinkled and criss-crossed in blotchy, lumpy skin. Marie's insides quivered and she looked away.

The boy laughed. He'd seen her look. 'These? Were you looking at my burns?'

'Sorry,' said Marie. It was all she could think to say.

He pulled his shirt up slightly to reveal more scar tissue on his abdomen.

Marie winced. She guessed that it was from a cooking accident, and before she could stop it, an image of little Roberti burned in her mind. His wailing assailed her ears yet again. Curiosity got the better of her. 'How did …?'

'I don't know who did it,' he said in a voice that alternated between squeaky and gravelly. 'We were hiding out in a storm drain late one evening, me and some other boys. They threw petrol bombs down at us. The only way out was through the fire.'

He gave her a vacant look and turned back to the TV screen.

Marie didn't know what to say. She tried to form words, but they never left her mouth. It was strange coming to the city and seeing evidence of this cruelty. If someone had told her before, she wouldn't have believed them. She thought that everyone had jobs in nice hotels or banks. She thought that all children here went to good schools. Now she was the one with a look of embarrassed discomfort on her face.

Marie went to her room straight after dinner and settled down with a book she'd picked up from the library. There was little she could talk about with anyone here. Her life at Beauty from Ashes made her feel like an umuzungu compared to the other kids at this centre. She felt strange and foreign, an oddity in this pocket of urban life. Kevine must surely be doing well? She was at a good college with good teachers. She would get a decent job and live the life she'd always talked about with Marie. She'd always been the smarter one, helping Marie gain her footing in life, supporting her through every wobble, and pulling her up after every stumble.

She missed her sister terribly. Part of her wanted to leave this place right now and find her, but after what she'd done, how would she face Kevine? It hadn't fully hit her when she'd run away from Beauty from Ashes. All that had been on her mind then was a sheer instinct to get away as fast as she could and get to the city, even if she didn't have any real idea of what would await her. Kevine wouldn't understand why she would have ruined her future like this and why she would run from Mama and Tim and Anna.

Was Mama still trying to find her? Were Tim and Anna with her trying to help, or had they given up? She turned the questions over in mind, staring at the same paragraph in her book, the words muddled and indistinct.

As she tried to focus the words into some semblance of order, footfall surged through the corridor – loud, well-heeled footfall. Linde's pointed voice and someone else, possibly one of the admin staff she'd met when going through some consent forms in the office, came through the door. She couldn't pin down a face. Apart from Linde and Brenda, everyone at the centre was vague and distant. She didn't have the energy to set their faces into any memorable, distinct form. She had energy only for those who decided whether she should be given a bed for the night, a classroom to study in, food to eat. She could only think survival.

The Shadow Beyond the Hills

All she could glean from the identity of the unfamiliar voice was that she was local staff – Marie could tell from her accent. She saw an unspoken order, a hierarchy of things, when it came to jobs: abazungu at the top, and black people underneath, supporting, translating, driving – doing the less important jobs, but the ones that made everything else function. It made her think of beer: white froth sitting atop the bulk of dark fluid underneath.

'Honestly, I don't know what she's doing here,' said Linde.

'I think Leonce thought she'd be a good fit.'

'A good fit? I thought she had some qualifications or training in counselling or something. I didn't know some church in Kentucky had appointed her Director of Mental Health Outreach due to her experience of putting up photos of herself with troubled African children on a projector,' said Linde.

A muffled laugh.

'Leonce knows our policy on churches and religious organisations,' said Linde.

Marie could picture Linde's peppery hair done up in a ponytail behind her back. She imagined her tucking loose strands behind her ears.

'Prayer has been shown to aid mental resilience and speed recovery from trauma. I think there was a study done at Harvard Medical School.' The unfamiliar voice was edged with a hint of appeal and apology, and it reminded Marie of the time when one of the visiting teams from America had organised a debate, with Marie on the defending side. The topic had been something to do with the use of pesticides in food.

A burst of derisive laughter shot out of Linde.

'Education is what's going to give these kids a future,' she said. 'In the meantime, if God, Thor, Ganesh or Zeus wants to come and teach the fifty-odd kids at this centre and get them through their national exams, he, she, or they are most welcome. Religion just delays progress.'

'But most of our people are religious. They go to church and believe in God.'

'It did take centuries of war and revolution to weed it out in Europe, I guess.' It sounded as if Linde shifted on her heels to carry on down the corridor.

'She didn't ask how much hazard pay she was going to get or how many paid return flights she would get every year.'

'Oh, that was just Marieke,' said Linde. 'It can't be easy coming from a UN gig in Hong Kong to an understaffed, overstretched set up like this. It's a sacrifice to work abroad under these conditions so I can understand why she left. I'm tempted to quit myself, sometimes … In any case, I want Brenda gone by the end of the week.'

Their heels clicked down the corridor.

The call to prayer floated through the morning air from a nearby mosque as Marie woke up with her book open on her chest and the covers drawn lazily over her middle. She got up and pulled on a skirt and blouse that had been put in the wardrobe for her, along with a small selection of other clothes. It had been a while since she'd put her electric blue and grey Beauty from Ashes uniform on. She didn't miss it. But she did miss Paul.

The Shadow Beyond the Hills

Shame startled her as she thought of their last night together. A night that ended her childhood as her belly expanded and, later, blood flowed.

She'd taken aptitude tests and had been put on the 'gifted and able' programme, her abilities filed neatly into their grading system. She'd scored well generally, but maths was a particular strong point.

She made her way into a classroom that didn't look too different from the ones they had at Beauty from Ashes. There were plenty of books lining the shelves, posters on the wall, and decent tables and chairs. She was in a maths class and was feeling good for the first time in a while. Numbers she could deal with. Equations needed balancing. It was simple. There were no grey areas. All they needed was to be in their place, and they always had a place. She liked these classes because there was little need for discussion: you either knew it or you didn't – no debate was needed, only clear instruction. The back of the classroom was lined with framed photos of former students and the names of the universities they'd been accepted into underneath: Cape Town; Nairobi; Ibadan; Makerere. Linde had told her of the Bachelor of Medicine degree at Makerere when Marie had said she was interested in qualifying as a doctor in the future. Scholarships were available to gifted students, Linde had said. It seemed like a distant dream. *Surgery*: even the word sounded exotic and tantalising. She would deal with people in parts.

'Good morning, class.' The teacher was a softly spoken man. He looked and sounded like he lived in a richer neighbourhood in the city. Had he studied abroad? Marie couldn't imagine a life beyond the borders of her country, but she was enticed by the

Emma Lawson

possibility.

'We're continuing in our study of linear expressions this week.' Mr Nkurunziza paced in front of the blackboard in tight-fitting beige chinos, wafting sweet aftershave throughout the room. He pointed to figures on the board. 'Is 9 a factor of $36c + 9$?'

Marie raised her hand when she saw that no one else had raised theirs. No one looked vaguely interested. 'Yes.'

'Go on.'

'I checked whether nine divides all the numbers in the expression. The numbers are thirty-six and nine, which are both divisible by nine.'

'Good. Very good.' He gave Marie a relieved smile, looking pleased that someone had been paying attention in his classes. 'You can factor out nine.' He turned to write some more equations on the board.

Marie flicked through the textbook on her desk. It was barely used, still new looking. Everything in this place had a new look to it.

The classroom door opened with a soft, unobtrusive whoosh and Linde craned her neck around its side. 'Sorry to interrupt your class.'

Mr Nkurunziza turned and gave her a quizzical look. 'Nta kibazo.'

Marie remembered being in Mama's office while waiting for Tim and Anna, and Pierre telling Mama about a cow and her calf. *English, please, Pierre.*

Linde trained her eyes on Marie. 'Ennistine, can you come to my office?'

CHAPTER SIXTEEN
HOLLOW

It wasn't hard to get into the place. Anna mentioned Sarah's friend to one of the staff and asked if she could see her. She'd been welcomed in without question. Kigali was a small world where you could make things happen if you had the right connections. Tim had been called into an urgent work meeting but said he'd come straight away if he was needed – if she was there. They'd had an argument about his needing to work weekends, especially now. 'Where are your priorities?' she'd said. She'd bitten her tongue about finding time to chat with old friends – old friends who put two kisses after their messages – and had left her still hot espresso on the kitchen counter. The warm glow of their time in Zanzibar was fading already. Sitting in the visitor's lounge with its walls covered in shiny posters adorned with words beginning with 'r' – respond, rehabilitate, re-home, restore – those seemingly innocuous little Xs surfaced again, even though she'd tried to push them down. What meaning did they carry?

Emma Lawson

She'd never been the jealous sort. She'd never had reason to be. Tim didn't really have any female friends other than work colleagues, and those relationships never ventured beyond the boardroom. Virtual kisses in themselves didn't necessarily mean anything, she told herself. Maybe he just didn't know how to express himself.

But why didn't he tell her about meeting up with this Celia when he was working in London the other week? He said it was a non-stop whirlwind of back-to-back meetings after which he collapsed into an exhausted heap in his hotel room. And yet he'd had time for long chats with old friends. Was it the same Celia she'd met on the odd occasion in their university days? She tried to remember what that Celia had looked like, but all she got was an amorphous haze – like most of the people she'd met there and had never kept in touch with.

Tim was hopeless with women, but that was one of the things that had drawn her to him. He wasn't pretentious or smooth-talking. He didn't think he was something he wasn't. He did, however, know his own mind, and to an insecure young woman who didn't know her place in the world and was afraid to assume it, that was attractive. The thought of him talking late into the night with another woman was ridiculous. But it had happened, and she didn't know where or when, or what they had talked about, or why he hadn't mentioned it. Maybe that's because it wasn't worth mentioning. Still ... What other sins of omission had he neglected to tell her? Her mind was tense, a coiled thing ready to spring. Suspicion nested in dark crevices she didn't think she had in her. She sat on this new, thorny feeling while her second coffee of the morning turned cold.

'Sorry to keep you waiting.' A svelte lady with a hard, German accent greeted her.

'Not at all – I turned up without an appointment.'

'I'm Heidi … And you are?'

'Oh, sorry. I'm Anna.'

'And who was it you wanted to see?'

'Joanna, if it's possible.'

'Right. Come with me.'

They walked up a corridor and then out to a courtyard. Anna tried to imagine Marie in this city, wondering what she would make of it and how scared and alone she must feel. As they walked to Joanna's office on the upper floor surrounding the square courtyard, she peered around every corner and snuck a look in every window of every room they passed, hoping for a glimpse that would change everything. But she didn't see her. Hope and disappointment ebbed and flowed in familiar waves. *This was a waste of time.* She'd spoken to Mama Judy the previous night and had told her that they were coming here, but she'd been hard to read, preoccupied. 'Well, you let me know how it goes, dear. Call me straight away.' She still had hundreds of other children to deal with and a busy centre to run.

Heidi pushed the door open to Joanna's office, letting out a glut of muggy air, and exchanged greetings. 'Joanna is our child welfare manager.'

'Pleased to meet you, Anna.'

'And you.'

Joanna, a fellow Brit with a well-to-do home counties accent, indicated the chair opposite her desk. 'Why don't you pull up a chair?'

'I'll leave you to it,' said Heidi.

The room went silent for a moment while Anna thought of how she could frame the conversation. 'I'm a friend of Sarah's. I don't know if she mentioned me or that I wanted to drop in.' *Drop in* – so casual an expression for what was such a momentous task.

Joanna paused to think, a puzzled expression crossing her face. 'No. I don't recall.'

Anna wrung her hands together under the desk. What was going to say? *Have you got our adopted child who ran away before we had a chance to take her home?*

'I know you take in vulnerable children and young people off the streets. There's one girl in particular who may have passed through your doors: a girl called Marie. Marie Uwimana.'

'How old is the girl?' Joanna rifled through papers in a bulky lever-arch folder, perspiring slightly on her temples. The air was unmoving, stifling.

'Thirteen,' said Anna.

So young. Marie was still just a child.

'We don't have anyone here by the name of Marie Uwimana, I'm afraid.'

Anna's heart plunged. She took out the photo she'd shown to every police officer and passer-by who would look.

Joanna peered down at it for a few seconds, her puzzled expression unwavering. 'We have had girls of that age brought in recently. Is it possible that she would go by another name?'

'I guess so. If she … didn't want to be found.' Anna shifted in the hard, wooden chair. She could never get comfortable.

'Why would she not want to be found?' Joanna's voice had a harder edge to it now. 'What is your

The Shadow Beyond the Hills

relationship with the child?'

What *was* her relationship with Marie? She'd barely established one. 'We, my husband and I, are her adoptive parents. She hadn't yet come to live with us. Just before she was due to move into our home, she went missing from the children's foundation she was living in.' She forced the faltering words out.

Joanna narrowed her eyes. 'We have a duty to protect the children in our care. Details of the children here are confidential, you understand?'

'Of course.'

'Do you have any form of ID with you and confirmation of your adoption status?'

Why did she feel like she was being interrogated? A wave of irrationality crested in her.

'Please give me a minute. I need to make a couple of phone calls.' Anna walked outside and gripped the balcony railing. Thick, grey clouds hung stolidly over the city, a canopy of bleakness that Anna wanted to break through, surfacing for real air.

Children were shuffling out of rooms and filling the courtyard below, their excited chatter reaching a crescendo through the clammy air. Tim would surely call soon to ask how she was getting on. He should do, anyway. Was he in an urgent meeting still? Or was he enjoying talking to someone who had 'missed their long chats, xx'? How had she reduced their relationship to salacious snippets, like something out of a trashy morning TV show?

Anna glanced at the bustling scene below, trying to bat away thoughts of Tim and a woman she didn't know but vehemently disliked. It was then that she saw it: the unhurried, loping gait. The faint, faraway look. Every fragment of hope, every grain of faith, collected and held together in unmistakeable form: Marie. Anna soared. She broke through the canopy and breathed in real air. *My God. Thank you.*

The ground was beginning to feel solid again, the sensation of endless free-falling coming to a stop. She needed to call Tim. Each ring of the phone whipped her feelings into a frenzy.

'I saw her! Just a minute ago, it was her!'

Tim breathed heavily into the phone. A sigh of the vastest relief. 'I'm on my way.'

'Don't forget to bring our passports, ID and adoption papers.'

'Will do. I love you.'

'See you soon,' said Anna, breathless and lightheaded again.

Anna had wanted to jump the balcony railing and run to Marie. She'd wanted to hold her and tell her everything was okay now. That she would be fine. They would be fine. She bridged a gulf and fast-forwarded into the relationship she dreamed they would have years from now, when they would go on mother–daughter shopping trips and coffee dates. Anna wouldn't have to ask how her studies were going because Marie would freely tell her. They would talk about everything. Anna dared to hope again. Anything was possible.

Anna had watched Marie disappear out of the courtyard and into the dining hall. She couldn't bear seeing her walk out of sight again. But she wouldn't unload her joy on her all at once. This was going to be

The Shadow Beyond the Hills

as much of a shock to Marie as it had been to her, and she needed to put her feelings and needs aside.

Anna bounded back into Joanna's office. 'She's here! I saw her!'

'Okay.' Joanna's voice was laced with subtle scepticism. 'You need to speak to Linde. She's the centre director.'

Joanna took her down the polished concrete steps and around the side of the courtyard with its bright red railings draped in passionflowers. Anna tried to bring her stride back under control and steady her breathing.

'Sorry to interrupt, Linde. This lady needs to speak with you.' Joanna raised her eyebrows and threw a sideways glance at Linde as she walked out of the office. A fan rotated on the desk, circulating the muggy air.

'I don't think we've met before. I'm Linde.'

Yes, yes, let's cut the pleasantries.

'Anna.'

'How can I help you?'

'I've just seen our adopted daughter. She ran away from the Beauty from Ashes Children's Foundation in Ruhengeri before coming to us and we've been looking for her ever since. It's definitely her, I'm sure of it. I just saw her in the courtyard.' Anna showed her a photo of Marie.

'Ruhengeri? That's quite a way to come ... What's her name?'

'Marie Uwimana. I know you don't have anyone here by that name, Joanna told me, but she must've given you a different name.' Anna tried to slow down, but the words came speeding out.

'I see.' Linde began pacing the short space in front of her desk. 'I expect Joanna informed you that we need to see your identification details.'

'My husband's on his way with them now.'

Anna tried to call Mama Judy, but there was no answer. She wanted Mama to confirm that Anna was who she said she was.

She forced herself to sit down, feeling dizzy and unsteady on her feet. How had Marie been getting on here? They weren't that far from Kevine's college. What had made her stay rather than find her sister? Surely that's why she'd ended up in Kigali? It didn't make sense, running from one institution to another, but it was all she'd ever known, so maybe it did. In a way, Anna was grateful that Marie had found her way to Kigali, where finding her didn't seem impossible, unlike in the endless hills of the countryside.

Anna tried to contain her nerves and excitement as she surveyed the artwork and decoration in her office. A photo of Linde and her family stood tall on her desk, her husband and children all smiles and good looks.

The door swooshed open and Tim burst into the room clutching their folder of adoption papers and ID. He greeted Linde and set them down on her desk, then planted a heavy kiss on Anna's cheek as he pulled up a chair next to hers.

'The traffic downtown wasn't too bad,' said Tim, always finding a way to bring the banal into life's greatest moments.

Anna indulged him with a smile and a hand squeeze. A squeeze that was perhaps a little harder than she intended as the name Celia sat heavily on her tongue.

Linde scanned the documents Tim had brought in and said she'd bring Marie to the office to see them.

They sat in the swollen stillness of the room, tense

The Shadow Beyond the Hills

and expectant.

Linde finally breezed into the room.

'We need to establish Ennistine's identity,' said Linde.

'Ennistine?' said Tim.

'Where is she?' asked Anna.

'She's just outside,' replied Linde, her voice steely and unflinching.

Who was Linde to keep them all waiting like this? Why was she acting like some self-appointed gatekeeper? Granted, this was her organisation, but Marie wasn't her child. She didn't even know who Marie really was.

Tim made for the door.

'Please, wait a minute. This may be incredibly overwhelming for her, too.'

Did she think they didn't know that? While she treated time in units she could control, monitoring the minutes with rigid precision, had she any idea of the time *they* had spent agonising over Marie?

'The problem is that she has no formal means of identification …' Linde looked again at their ID and adoption paperwork.

'It's her! Can't you see?' Tim thrust the photo of Marie under her face.

Linde didn't answer. 'Okay, I'll bring her in.'

Marie walked in, her steps calm and measured. She was smartly dressed, as she had been at Beauty from Ashes, wearing a plaid, pleated black and yellow skirt with a white turtle-neck top. She stood in front of them, holding Anna's gaze for a moment before staring at the floor. No fireworks. No flicker of recognition even.

Anna stared at her, a flame that had been snuffed

out and left to smoulder in the silence.

'Marie.' Anna had to say her name out loud. Hearing it would surely wake Marie up out of whatever this was.

She and Tim stood in front of Marie. Tim held his arms open, loaded with unmet expectation.

Marie didn't move.

'We've been so worried about you,' said Tim. 'We're glad you're okay.'

Anna took a step towards Marie and reached out her hand, a token offering. The distance between them loomed larger than before.

Why wasn't she saying anything?

Marie stepped forward and took Anna's hand, finally looking at her. Her eyes were unreadable. She'd been found, but she still looked lost.

'I'm sorry,' said Marie.

Was it guilt, shame even, being carried on those words? Did she feel like she'd failed them somehow?

'Sweetie, you don't have anything to be sorry for,' said Anna. But as soon as she said it, she knew it wasn't entirely true. She couldn't deny that Marie had let them down. She'd put them through hell. Which could have been redeemed in that moment with a simple, heartfelt hug, a few tears, just some expression of emotion.

Holding both of Marie's hands in hers, Anna pulled her close and held her. 'You don't have to tell us everything that happened.' Anna released Marie from her gentle grip. 'There'll be time for that.'

Marie didn't look quite the same as she did in the photo they'd shown people. Her face had narrowed out slightly, framed by hair that was longer and styled differently.

Linde stood by the door, observing them. 'Are you

okay, Ennistine? Or should that be ... Marie?' She teased the question out in her softest, most non-accusatory Dutch voice. It sounded contrived.

'Yes, I'm fine, thank you.'

Linde nodded, unconvinced.

'Would you offer some refreshments to our guests?' Linde indicated the bottles of Coke on a table at the end of the room.

We aren't just guests, and this isn't Marie's home.

Marie opened a couple of bottles and brought them over with straws. She could have been a waitress and Tim and Anna could have been anyone. Maybe that's all they were to her: anyone. It hit her with icy clarity – Marie meant more to them than they did to Marie. Had she been foolish to ever think otherwise?

CHAPTER SEVENTEEN
SISTER

Marie lay on her bed with Anna's bright white face burning in her mind. She'd wanted to give them what they so desperately wanted, and she'd failed them, crushed under the weight of their expectations. She could never be what they wanted. In Linde's office, while sipping their Cokes, Tim had told her that Kevine was coming, and Anna had asked if they'd like some space. Marie realised that this meant talking in private. Anna understood her like that.

Ever since she'd arrived at New Beginnings, she couldn't shake the feeling that Linde was on to her. Did she really believe her name was Ennistine, or believe the story Marie had spun for them? Marie had fed snippets of information to Brenda, telling her about the man she'd met at the bar who'd touched her under the table. How her belly ached with hunger every day, and how she felt so ashamed and alone. Brenda had filled in the gaps, writing 'sex worker' on her clipboard. But Linde eyed her with suspicion, as if she didn't buy that story.

The Shadow Beyond the Hills

So, when she'd called Marie out of class, she'd felt a lurch of fear. It hadn't helped that Linde was silent as she led Marie to her office and asked her to wait outside, not giving anything away. Tim and Anna had stood inside, waiting, their faces shining as Marie felt herself crumbling.

A burst of rain lashed the window as a flash of lightning lit the room. The afternoon storms were becoming more regular now. *The farmers will be happy*, Mama would say. She thought of Mama at evening devotions, perched on the edge of a bed, reading from the Bible. Even Mama's face was fading now, paling like something left out in the sun.

Marie flicked open her maths workbook and started the assignment they'd begun in class that day – something clear and straightforward that would take her mind off what had happened. On the previous page in red writing were the words 'Excellent work, Ennistine! You show so much promise.' Tim and Anna's desire to have her in their life, her fears, the future, leaving Mama and Beauty from Ashes – those were equations she didn't know how to balance.

She finished solving the first problem set by Mr Nkurunziza when a couple of soft knocks at the door broke her concentration. She walked to the door, her legs suddenly feeling heavy.

'My sister!' Kevine clasped her tight and knocked the wind out of her. She held her for what felt like minutes.

They sat side by side on Marie's bed. Kevine's hair was different to how it had been the last time she'd seen her. It was straight at the top with loose waves tapering down past her shoulders. She must have put some relaxant in it. Her lips were a shock of bright red, contrasting starkly with the long black dress she was wearing, which was embroidered with Indian-style patterns in semi-circles of yellow. She looked like she was at home in her college life in the city.

Marie smiled at her. 'You look amazing. How is life for you here?'

'Good. I'm making new friends and I'm learning a lot from classes. My tutor is a professional textile designer.' Kevine looked proud. Marie was proud of her too, if not a little jealous. She was still the star of every show, just getting on with things in her confident way. She would never have run away and let anyone down like this.

Kevine must have read her mind, because her expression darkened.

'Sister, what happened?'

Marie felt a look of disapproval bear down on her. 'Let me make you some tea—'

'No. I don't want any. I want you to tell me why you're here.'

Marie pulled at a loose fibre on her bedsheet, trying to weave its frayed ends back together. Where would she start? Her night with Paul, one of her sister's favourite topics for jokes? She couldn't decide where everything began, or if there even was a single point at which things began to come undone. How would she tell her about the life that had grown inside her, or the blood that flowed not long after? It was too shameful. There were some things she was just never going to tell anyone, not even her sister.

Kevine took her hand and held it on her lap. 'Mama's been worried sick about you. We all have. You don't know the tears we've cried for you, Marie.'

But she did. She'd drowned in them, spluttering for air like she had when she'd fallen from the bridge into a freezing black torrent near Mugisha's house. If she listened, she could still hear the thud of Papa Mugisha's heavy, drunken steps chasing her through the maize field.

'Talk to me, Marie!' Kevine's voice turned from concern to anger. 'Why would you run away from the good things you had in your life? And why do this to Tim and Anna? They're good people. Kind people. And they'll give you opportunities to go far in life. Look at me: in just a few years, I'll graduate and open my own fashion boutique here in Kigali. Tell me, what will you do, eh? I thought you wanted to study medicine?'

She had. She did. Marie burned with shame and remorse; not for running away, which had seemed like the only thing she could do at the time, but for letting everyone down. For failing them. She got up and looked out the window. The city was a smudged painting of greys and browns bleeding into one another.

'Don't ignore me, Marie. You've ignored us all for too long.'

Marie slowly turned to face her. 'I got scared. I was scared of the change that was coming – living with Tim and Anna, and you ... you wouldn't be there for me, like you always have been. You're all I have.'

A solitary tear slipped down Kevine's cheek, smudging her mascara and leaving what looked like a faint trail of charcoal down the side of her face. She stared down at the circular rug in the middle of the room.

'I'm always here for you,' said Kevine, wiping away

another tear. 'I wasn't going to abandon you.'

'But you weren't going to live with us. You'd be in college, living with your new friends. It wouldn't be the same.'

Silence swelled the room. She'd told Kevine the truth. Part of it.

'I would have come to visit,' said Kevine. Even she sounded unconvinced by this small concession. 'So, what now? Are you just going to stay here?'

Marie shrugged, wishing there was a way she could please everyone at once.

'Don't you want to be with Tim and Anna?'

Marie didn't know what she wanted.

Kevine sighed. 'I really thought things were going well for us.'

'They are for you.'

'And they could be for you. Look, come with me. We can't hide out here forever.'

They walked in awkward silence, Marie leading the way to Linde's office and Kevine following closely behind.

Tim and Anna stood up when they walked in. Tim looked tired, his eyes puffy and red. Anna looked flustered, like she was trying to hold herself together.

'Good chat?' asked Tim. He tried to sound cheery and upbeat, but his voice was flat and washed-out.

'Marie, would you like to pack your things?' said Anna.

Linde, who'd been looking through some files, turned on her heels towards Tim and Anna and sharpened her gaze. 'I don't think that's a good idea.'

'I don't think anyone asked your opinion,' muttered Anna.

The Shadow Beyond the Hills

Tim looked at her, vying for her attention, as if asking her not to go any further.

'Excuse me?' Linde slapped the files back down on her desk.

'How do you presume what's best for Marie? We're her legally adopted parents,' said Anna, emphasising the last word.

'That may be true, but there are protocols to follow. We have to show due diligence – we can't release her into your care when we've had no confirmation of her identity from the police or district officials concerned with her adoption.'

'But you have the adoption papers right here!' Anna's raised voice seemed to shake the room. Maybe it just shook Marie.

Anna held her face with milky-white hands and rubbed her forehead. Marie thought she was crying, but instead Anna took a deep breath and gave Linde a fierce look. 'You people come here with your Master's degrees and your impressive titles and drive around in your Toyota Prados thinking you own the place. But you can't use your privilege to call the shots on people's lives.'

Linde let out a short, withering laugh. 'I think we *all* benefit from our privilege.'

Anna's face turned a deeper shade of red than Marie had ever seen it. 'What the hell is that supposed to mean?'

Tim murmured to Anna under his breath. 'Anna, let's not do this in front of the girls.'

'Are you the girl's mother? Biological, I mean?' said Linde.

'Of course not! She doesn't bloody have one, does

she?'

'Anna, stop.' Tim tried to hold her arm, but she shrugged him off.

Anna took another deep breath and turned to look at Marie and Kevine, her face softening and showing traces of regret.

Marie didn't know where to look. She'd never seen Anna lose her composure like this.

'Marie, what do *you* want to do? Would you prefer to stay here for a few more days?' asked Tim.

Marie stalled. She hadn't expected to be asked. Seeing the drained look on his face, she answered. She didn't want to be uprooted again, not yet.

'That's fine. Isn't it, Anna?'

Anna looked lost in thought. 'Yes, sorry ... of course it is.'

Linde looked satisfied.

They said their goodbyes to Marie and Kevine and left just before dinner.

Kevine picked up her big leather bag to leave too, but Marie pulled on her arm. 'Wait. Please stay, just for this evening.'

They ate dinner together in the hall. Her sudden need for Kevine's presence was overwhelming. She felt empty without her, almost like she'd turn into a ghost if she left. Kevine was the only person who gave her any substance, any solidity.

'Have they treated you well here?' asked Kevine.

'Yes, very well. The teachers are good too. I've been put on the gifted and able programme. They're linked with some universities around Africa who offer scholarship schemes.'

'You can't leave them like this for too long. Tim and

The Shadow Beyond the Hills

Anna, I mean. You know that, don't you? It's not fair.'

Marie knew it wasn't, but it still helped to have Kevine guiding her again. She'd missed that. She'd needed it.

They ate dinner and walked outside to the courtyard balcony. The clouds had cleared, and the air was fresh. Kevine shivered, pulling a long silk shawl around her shoulders. Marie pictured Anna's face when she'd said she wanted to spend a few more days at New Beginnings. The idea of going back to their house now was too much. She needed more time. At least she could remain somewhat anonymous if she stayed here. She hoped she could carry on attending classes, which was the only thing she knew with certainty that she wanted. Was Anna angry with her like she'd been with Linde, when the veins had shown through her crimson face? Marie stood closer to Kevine, who pulled her in for a side-hug that warmed her through to her bones.

Kevine talked about her future boutique: what it would look like and what designs and styles she would have in store. She talked about hosting a fashion show one day, with catwalks and models, like the ones they had in Paris and New York. She talked, and Marie listened, just pleased to hear her sister's voice again – her sister, who'd read stories to her before bed and had taught her how to bake and shown her what colours and patterns went together when she got dressed. She didn't want her to leave, but she knew she had to let her go. She watched as Kevine sped off to college on the back of a moto, her silk scarf billowing out behind her.

CHAPTER EIGHTEEN
SCAR

Anna wandered the cold tiles of their house. It was midnight, and she still hadn't managed any sleep, despite the tablets she'd washed down with a liberal glass of wine. She'd still not gotten hold of Mama Judy, who she'd wanted to share her frustrations about Linde with. Her and Mama Judy weren't exactly close, but she felt like they'd become allies in some strange turf war. Mama Judy would have fumed about it too and made Anna feel like she'd been justified in her rant. Tim had tried to be understanding on the drive home, but he, too, lost the energy for it in the end. They'd sat in silence the rest of the way, their faces bathed in the glaring light of streetlamps, but their minds darkened by Marie's continued withdrawal.

She pulled her dressing gown tighter, sprayed some mosquito repellent on her ankles and went to sit on the veranda. A radio played from over the compound wall. *There may be some attachment issues*, Mama Judy had told them in what seemed like an age ago. At the time, Anna had processed this the way a junior doctor might have done while being instructed by a consultant: eager, keen to learn, but ultimately detached. Now, as she recalled Marie's indifference to her in Linde's office – her limp hold when Anna had pulled her in for a hug and her blank expression when she first saw them – she was wounded by it. A book on adoption and child psychology was still open and folded down on its front on the coffee table, both a silent reproach and a mockery.

She sat there for hours, drifting in and out of sleep, woken only by dogs barking in the street or in a nearby compound, until the sun broke over the hills and splashed its first golden rays over the city.

Tim handed her a croissant and a coffee, resting his hand her on shoulder as he surveyed the sunrise. 'Even when things are difficult, beauty smacks you in the face and tells you everything's going to be alright.'

Yes, it did. It also reminded Anna of how inconsequential they were – her, Tim, everyone waking up and starting their day in this city and in cities everywhere. As if the natural world could quite happily go on being stunning and magnificent even if the human race was to disappear, or if they'd just never been here in the first place. Trees would still grow; tides still ebb and flow. God had never seemed as distant to her as he did now.

'We need to go to Beauty from Ashes. We have to tell Mama Judy,' said Anna.

Tim rubbed his eyes. 'You mean she still hasn't

called?'

'No.'

'I just need to fit in a couple hour's work. Luckily, I don't have any meetings today.'

'Yeah. Lucky,' said Anna. It was Sunday and he still needed to be glued to a screen.

Tim removed his hand from her shoulder. 'Hey, it's not just you that's finding this a little overwhelming, okay?'

Anna stared into the distance. 'Got a lot on your plate, have you?'

'In actual fact—'

'Right, best get on with it then, hey?' Anna placed her coffee on the table and left Tim on the veranda, incredulous.

She took a cold shower, having forgotten to set a timer for the water heater again after it had broken a few days ago, and then pulled on some clothes. If Mama Judy wasn't going to answer the phone, Anna was going to tell her in person. No bags would be packed. There was nothing to stay at Beauty from Ashes for this time. Then again, was there anything worth coming back home for? Would Marie want to see them any more today or tomorrow than she had yesterday?

Tim worked on his laptop for a couple of hours, then they set off, navigating the morning traffic past the bus park and taking the familiar right turn leading to the steep, meandering road out to the north of the country. They were slowed down as always by a truck that chugged up in first gear all the way to the top, belching thick black smoke.

Anna broke the silence. 'Who's Celia?'

'Celia?'

'I saw you had a message from her on your phone the other day.' Anna kept her voice level and calm.

Tim narrowed his eyes at the road ahead and gripped the steering wheel tighter. 'You remember her, don't you? At uni? Law student, shouted her mouth off at parties when she was a bit tipsy but was really quiet the rest of the time.'

Anna teased out the silence, waiting for him to fill in the gaps.

'I haven't really kept in touch with her since then, apart from the odd message on the alumni forum.' He cleared his throat. 'She got in touch a few weeks ago.'

Anna tried to catch any waver in his voice, but he wasn't giving anything away.

'I think she's going through a rough patch. Her divorce came through earlier this year. Why?'

Why was he still not mentioning meeting up with her on his work trip? 'I just didn't think you kept in touch with any uni friends.' She didn't press any further, Tim didn't go into any more detail, and they sat in silence for the remainder of the journey.

When they pulled up the drive at Beauty from Ashes, Emmanuel was the first to greet them. He gave them a broad, toothy smile, opened the gates and waved them through. They pulled to a stop under the flame tree, which was no longer adorned with deep-red flower buds. A few toddlers were being entertained on the lawn, giggling over a ball that a staff member was trying to wrest from the branch of a jacaranda tree. The compound was humming with the life she'd known it to possess before Marie left, when it had whispered hope and happiness – the promise of a new start.

Alphonsine managed to prise the ball from the

jacaranda tree with a long stick and threw it to a chubby-cheeked little girl of around two years old and made her way over to Tim and Anna. 'Mwaramutse! Amakuru?'

Although she was anything but fine, it never went down well when she said this. People looked at her askance. 'I'm fine, thank you. Do you know where Mama Judy is? We'd like to see her.' She knew she should ask about family before getting down to business – she would seem curt if she didn't – but every conversation was tiresome, a heavy load of words pushed up a mountain of etiquette to get to the point. The only person she wanted to speak to was Mama Judy.

'Yes, she's in her office. Come with me,' said Alphonsine, her floral dress dancing around her stocky legs as she led the way.

They didn't need a chaperone, but Anna didn't have the energy to suggest otherwise. Children wended their way to class in the distance, treading well-worn paths of routine in pockets of animated chatter. As they drew nearer to the entrance of Mama Judy's cottage, those sounds were drowned out by something heated and clamorous. One of the voices was definitely Mama Judy. Anna hesitated before going into the cottage.

'Should we wait?' said Tim, looking to Alphonsine for a cue.

'No. This can't wait.' Anna strode ahead of them, walking down the corridor and opening Mama Judy's office door. Mama Judy stood behind her desk, looking small and strained. Her face hung open in shock when she saw Anna. In front of her desk sat a woman wearing a kitenge skirt wrapped around an old-looking green t-shirt. Her shaking hands rattled the papers she was holding, and Anna could see streams of tears trickling down her cheeks. She got up from her chair, dropping papers with the Beauty from Ashes logo at the top and signatures scribbled at the bottom, and knelt in front of Anna. She held her hands up to Anna, begging before a god.

'Ndashaka abana banje!'

'Stop this!' Something in Mama Judy shattered. She looked broken, undone.

'Ndabakunda!' The woman sank to the floor, pleading and hysterical. She gripped Anna's legs and anchored her down.

Anna was suddenly aware of Tim's tall presence beside her. 'What's going on here?'

Mama Judy looked straight past them to Alphonsine, who was standing at the back of the room. 'Why didn't you let me know they were here first? How dare you march them straight into my office without informing me.' Her voice was tremulous with the effort of containing her rage.

Alphonsine stared at the floor.

'Silly girl,' said Mama Judy under her breath. 'Just go. And take *her* with you.'

Her head hung low in humiliation, Alphonsine walked the manic woman out of the room. As the woman limped past, she shot a fraught look at Anna, which made the long scar just below her hairline disappear into deep lines etched on her brow. She clenched Anna's arm with urgency. 'Don't take. I beg. Don't take.' Pure fear possessed her. Her haunting wailing trailed down the corridor.

'Why was she … why was she begging for her children?' Each strained syllable pierced her in new, raw places. 'Why was she begging *me*, for her children?'

'Do you want to tell us what's going on here?' Tim's voice shook with quiet anger. 'Who was that woman? She was beside herself.'

'If you don't start talking to us right now, I'm going to call the police,' said Anna. Her chest was impossibly tight.

Mama Judy shrank in front of them, hunched over and stricken, hands placed squarely on her desk for support, as if she'd collapse without it there. 'I've only ever tried to protect them … give them the best life possible. I love all of the children under my care like they're my own. They are … until God gives them to someone else.' Tears pooled in her eyes and threatened to drop, but she blinked them back.

'What are you trying to say?' Tim stiffened.

'Do you think it's easy, doing what I do? Taking these kids from the bleakest, poorest places and giving them hope and a shot at a future? Heck, even just a daily wash and food to eat?' Judy's voice cracked as she gripped the edge of the desk. 'That woman you saw there … do you think she could buy even one bar of soap a month to wash her lice-riddled children? Do you think she could cope when their father was found guilty in the gacaca courts, drinking himself half to death and beating them all to a pulp? I did what I thought was right, and I stand by that.'

'I wouldn't have any idea, would I?' said Anna. 'Not a fucking clue.'

Tim recoiled beside her. 'Sorry, let me just process this: you mean to tell me that while we were applying to adopt those girls, they've had a mother the whole time?' He spanned the length of his forehead with his thumb

The Shadow Beyond the Hills

and index finger. 'You've been lying the entire time?'

Judy stood tall now, an animal ready for the fight. 'The only lie I see is that these kids don't deserve a better life. That they're better off in homes where they're abused, hungry and malnourished, and deprived of everything that could free them from that. They deserve better. And I give them that opportunity. I give them a life they would never have had.'

'You're a mad woman ... You're actually deluded!' said Anna. 'You need to tell them. You owe them that dignity.'

'Dignity? I gave them a life free from indignity. They've had everything a child could possibly need.'

'Except the truth! And the choice to decide what *they* wanted. You deprived them of that freedom!' If she didn't leave now, she feared she would do something terrible.

CHAPTER NINETEEN
COWARD

Anna kept feeling strong hands gripping her, holding her down. It was a nightmare she couldn't wake from. The hills rolled by in a swirl of sickening green as Tim drove back to Kigali, gripping the steering wheel hard and keeping his eyes on the road.

The house had a stale smell to it when she opened the front door and headed straight to the kitchen for a strong gin and tonic – though tonic wasn't a deal breaker. Looking around at their traditional woven bowl mural on the wall and elegantly carved wooden statues and Congolese masks dotting the décor, she thought of how futile, how silly it all was to have made a home here. To think they could ever have made a life for themselves in this city, this country. As if by running from their old life, a new and better one could be forged in the heat and pressure of another. The words from Jo's most recent message lay in a mangled heap in her mind: *Be glad, Anna, when trials come your way. Your faith and your strength are being tested – as fire tests and purifies*

The Shadow Beyond the Hills

precious metal. It was a biblical allusion, somewhere from the New Testament. But Anna didn't feel like she was being refined into gold or silver. Her life had burned away, and she was the impurity, the dross that was left, poured out and left to cool and harden into a dull lump.

Cheap gin burned her throat on the way down. She was leaning against the counter as Tim joined her in the kitchen.

'Are we going to talk about what happened back there? You've barely spoken a word all week, and now you've clammed up completely.' He drummed his fingers on the counter and gave her a cutting look.

'What is there to talk about, Tim?' Another swig of gin, banging the tumbler down on the counter. 'It's over, isn't it?' She gestured with outstretched arms at their house. 'This. Them. *Our* girls.' A snigger escaped from her dry, cracked lips.

Tim shook his head in disbelief and fixed his eyes on her. 'Just like that? We're done with them, are we?'

Anna turned her back to him as she walked into the living room, not caring if he followed her or not.

'Don't walk away from this, Anna. Aren't you upset? Aren't you going to fight for them?' His voice boomed off the walls of the house.

After her outburst at Judy and everything that had gone before that, Anna thought she was done with searching, hoping, fighting. There was nothing left now. But at Tim's suggestion of not caring about the girls, fury consumed her. She turned to face him.

'You're fucking unbelievable, you know that?' she shouted.

'Can you stop swearing and have a rational conversation?'

Anna snorted into her gin. 'Oh! You want to talk rationally do you?'

Tim held her gaze, a steely glint to it now. 'That would be helpful, yes.'

'How about the fact that they already have parents! Actual parents of flesh and blood, Tim, not some pathetic foreign couple on the brink of collapse …'

Tim's shoulders slumped in defeat. 'Is that what our relationship is to you? Our marriage – on the brink of collapse?'

Silence filled the room, thick as smoke.

Tim's eyes begged for resolution. 'Well?'

'You always have to do the right thing, don't you? That's why we're here, isn't it? That's why you signed away our chance to have babies of our own with the swish of a pen. "Embryos aren't disposable," you said. "Precious humans made in the image of God aren't collateral damage."'

Tim's eyes widened in surprise. Her grief at this had only just hit him. 'I thought we were in agreement about that?'

'You never asked.'

Tim looked stung by this revelation.

'You have to do the right thing, or your conscience be damned, but you don't see a problem with going ahead with this? Are you serious?'

'I didn't say there wasn't a problem … but maybe there's a bigger problem in leaving them in that situation,' said Tim. 'I just can't help but think Mama Judy—'

'Can we *stop* calling her that?' Whatever pedestal Judy had stood on in Anna's mind had now been firmly kicked from underneath her. She'd been dethroned, disgraced.

'... had a point. Where is their father? In prison on crimes of genocidal murder. And their mother? Like Mama ... like Judy said, she was and is destitute, with no means of providing for those girls or changing her situation. She might want us to give her daughters opportunities she could never give—'

'Oh yeah, Tim, it looked like that didn't it? Was that the part where she was on her knees begging for her daughters, or when she was wailing down the corridor in abject misery?' Wailing ripped through the room again and sucked the breath out of her lungs. Hands gripped her legs and tugged at her arm.

'Look, all I'm suggesting is that we open up these conversations together rather than shut them down. Is Marie going to run straight into the arms of a woman she's not known the existence of, and who doesn't have the capacity to raise her? Would she want to live with her mother after the life she's had at Beauty from Ashes? I'm not saying that this doesn't raise major issues for the adoption—'

'Oh good, Tim. But while I'm glad you recognise at least that there are "major issues" at stake here, I think total shit storm would be a more accurate description of this situation.'

'Please, Anna, language.'

'So, it's not enough that you want to censor my body and biological urges; you want to censor my language now, is that right?'

Tim took a deep breath and shook his head. 'I can't do this with you anymore. I'm going out, and I'll be back when you're ready to talk properly ... maybe with less gin in your system. I'm done for the day.'

Emma Lawson

A thousand city lights blinked at Anna as she sped through narrow streets on the back of a moto taxi, hair flying round her face underneath the helmet tied loosely to her head. The evening air was fresh after the brief storm and felt like balm on her skin. Maybe she had drunk too much gin in a short space of time, but it hadn't clouded her judgement enough to see that Tim was wrong in seeing any sense in Judy's decision. How could he not see that? Poverty and abuse were awful, despicable realities, but they weren't despicable enough to cancel out truth, surely?

They passed the prison at Nyarugenge and rounded the corner to the mosque. Was the girls' father in that prison? She remembered reading an article about this prison receiving thousands of genocidaires when the RPF had won the civil war and stopped the genocide in 1994. He probably wasn't sentenced then if he was found out through the gacaca courts. Perhaps it was a few years later. Would he ever be released? *Damn Judy.* Why did she have to learn these details from her now? The enormity of reconciliation and releasing thousands of civilians who'd participated in genocide struck her afresh.

The moto went down a steep, rutted drive and spluttered to a stop. 'Murakoze,' said Anna, handing the driver a note. She recognised the lime green walls of the building and the stark logo above the entrance. A yellow cog, or an emblem of the sun? Anna couldn't work it out, but she read the words 'THE FUTURE BEGINS HERE' in navy-blue letters underneath. She took a deep

The Shadow Beyond the Hills

breath, steeling herself for the task that lay ahead, and walked through to the reception area to sign herself in. Her hands were shaking as she tried to grip the pen and move it in familiar strokes. She remembered which floor and room she needed to go to, the memories of her last visit still fresh in her mind. She'd felt hopeful then. Happy, even.

It took a little while for Kevine to come to the door. She beckoned Anna in and pulled up a chair for her. Piles of fabric were strewn over a small table in the corner of the room along with a few pages of pencil drawings. Large books displaying various African textile designs were laid out on another desk. Her bulky laptop rested in the middle of the desk, its fan whirring away. They'd bought it for her as a gift for getting a place at the college.

'How've you been, Kevine?'

Kevine's hands were folded in her lap as she gave Anna a smile that didn't quite reach her eyes. 'Fine, thank you. I saw Marie today and brought her some cake and chocolate. I don't think they have that there, and she needs some meat on her bones.' She attempted another smile.

'That's kind of you. You're a good sister. She's lucky to have you.' *Lucky to have you ... Just tell her. Tell her that she isn't all Marie has.*

'Have you spoken to Ju ... Mama Judy recently?'

Something had shifted in Kevine. She was tense, guarded. Anna had never given anyone news of this magnitude, and she felt totally inadequate being the bearer. She shouldn't have been the one to have to do it. But she had to. Seeing their anguished mother on the floor of Judy's office had changed everything.

'No, not since last week.'

How was she going to break this to her? Kevine had such a bright, sunny spirit. She was definitely the more extroverted of the two girls. She'd always been easier to reach than her dreamy, distant younger sister.

'Kevine, there's something I have to tell you. It's going to be a shock, and I want you to know how much Tim and I care for you and your sister. You're such special, wonderful girls ...' Anna's throat grew tight and itched with buried sobs.

Kevine tensed in her chair, her eyes searching Anna's for meaning. A look – was it fear? – shadowed her face, making what Anna was about to say all the more difficult.

'I'm afraid we can't go ahead with the adoption. We will of course continue to sponsor your tuition fees and living costs, if you'd like us to. But we can't adopt you and your sister.' She tried to force out the next lot of words, but they sat on her tongue, thick and stodgy, like lumps of ugali.

Kevine's fixed stare was unnerving. Anna was so used to not being looked in the eye by young people.

'The reason, Kevine ... is that we discovered that your mother is ... there. In Ruhengeri. We saw her yesterday in Mama Judy's office. I am so, so sorry that this has been kept from you both for so long. I can't imagine how you must be feeling, but I'm here for you.' It was forced, contrived. As though she was going through a mental checklist and ticking off all the right things to say.

Kevine averted her gaze from Anna, tensing in her seat even more.

Anna had no idea what to expect, especially after her

reunion with Marie ... Tears? Anger? Indifference? Some combination of the three? Anna waited, leaning into the loaded silence in the knowledge that sometimes there was nothing you could say, but that sitting with someone through whatever they were going through was the most compassionate response.

Finally, Kevine spoke, her voice inflected with a stony hardness that sent an electrifying jolt through Anna. 'That woman is *not* my mother. She's a coward. She's weak. And you are never to tell Marie about her. Do you understand me?'

CHAPTER TWENTY
LONDON

A wall of bracing, autumnal air hit Anna as she stepped off the nimble cityhopper plane she'd taken from Amsterdam to London. She'd always liked airports. She could sit for hours and people-watch, wondering where people were coming from and going to, what stories their embraces at arrivals told. Now, as her boots clicked along Heathrow's polished floors, it wasn't because she was on her way to something exciting, something worth travelling to. She'd reached a terminus in her life, and the allure of travel, holidays in the tropics and weekends at high-end hotels by the pool dispersed and rippled out into nothing. More than that, she was a fool – the naïve white girl, now mid-thirties woman, running from Africa, way in over her head, caught up in layers of deceit she couldn't begin to fathom. She'd been burnt by something she'd tried to hold and had been left raw and blistering. A fool, but not a fraud. Mama Judy could keep that mantle to herself.

She took a taxi to their house in Highgate, passing

giant posters of London beefeaters, black cabs, the London Eye and Madame Tussauds. She hadn't told Jo or her parents when she was coming back exactly. She didn't want a welcome party at Arrivals. All she wanted was to get back to their home on Talbot Road, just far away enough from the city centre to have a village feel to it, but close enough that she could take the tube to Camden Town station in just under twenty minutes to get to the market for some Dutch pancakes, French pastries and artisanal food at one of the grocers.

Everything she saw through the windows on the drive back was familiar, yet somehow alien. It had been her and Tim's upmarket playground when they'd moved from the cheap – London cheap – flat they'd rented in Bexley in their mid-twenties to this Georgian-style townhouse with its sash windows and ivy-laced portico. They'd dined at restaurants every weekend, trying out every flavour of food on offer, from Vietnamese Pho Ga, to Indonesian Gulai. They'd gotten up late at weekends and had coffee in bed, reading the papers or reading books, only getting up to stroll around Hampstead Heath and then try out a newly opened café. Tim had a respectable salary in the commercial sector back then, but they would never have been able to buy the house had they not come into some money from Tim's grandparents. She'd looked out onto their leaf-lined street the day after moving in, feeling like their happiness was unshakable. As the neighbours kept to themselves and passers-by stared straight past her on the street, the familiar pangs of loneliness crept in again. How could people be so close and distant at the same time? Why had she expected Highgate to be any different to Bexley?

Emma Lawson

The taxi drew to a stop outside her drive. The fiery azalea by their front door had long since lost its flame, but swathes of ivy were still creeping indomitably up the brickwork. The agent had assured her that the house had been left in immaculate condition. Some previous tenants of theirs had left it in such a state while they were abroad that she'd considered never leaving it again. Wine stains marked the upstairs carpets, the oven was burnt out, and the burnished hardwood floors in the downstairs living room were bashed in and scratched. It was all so pedestrian now.

Anna flung her coat on the hallway table and dumped her bags on the floor. A pile of mail lay on the mat, but she'd deal with it later. The house was cold and empty, a shell of what it was when they'd spent lazy weekends by the wood burner, drinking wine and talking about the future – always the future, never the present. With no food or milk in the kitchen for a cup of tea, she walked back down the street to the petrol station shop to pick up some essentials. Even there, there was so much choice; not just the one brand of bread or soap. It was always bewildering, having spent so many months abroad. Her head was dizzy with options, so she left with the bare minimum and made her way back home.

She took her cup of tea into the living room. The agent was true to his word – it was immaculate. The white-washed wooden furniture was gleaming and spotless; the potted plants trailed to the floor in lush vitality; the textured cushions and duck-egg blue throws draped over the sofas were bright and stainless. The blend of modern and farmhouse chic was still styled into every feature of the room, just as they'd left it. In the cold light of the autumnal sun streaming through the windows, with Tim still in Kigali tying up his project and selling the Toyota as well as the last few things in their rented house, she saw all of this pretentious crap for what it was. Or what it wasn't.

How had she engaged in entire conversations about which shade of curtain they would go for, or whether the colour palette for the other floors of the house should always match exactly? And yet she had: with Jo, with her work colleagues, with her mum. Why had she measured her life in that way? Just before they'd left for Rwanda, she'd become a small, snobbish version of herself, but she ached to truly come alive again. She'd hoped that bringing Marie and Kevine into their lives would be the impetus for some kind of re-birth. She'd hoped that it would spur her on to be the sort of human she really wanted to be. She'd even failed at that. Everything shouted failure: from the doctor who had declared her cervix *incompetent* and her womb *inhospitable*, to the doctor who had repeatedly told her that she *failed* to ovulate. She came into the clinics feeling like a failure and left feeling no different, every diagnosis a condemnation.

She cupped the lapsang souchong in her hands, its bitter aftertaste lingering in her throat. Tim was due to come back in a couple of weeks. She'd gone ahead of him after several nights of silence, punctuated by the odd argument, their bodies turned away from each other in bed night after night. There was nothing left for her in Kigali anymore. She had to leave. Her job at Cubs Montessori was easily filled by another expat. Marie had made it abundantly clear that she didn't care for them, Kevine was intent on making them keep up this lie of a life that Marie inhabited, and Judy insisted on her rightness. Her self-righteousness. How many others had she duped at Beauty from Ashes? How long would she and Kevine weave this web of falsehood for Marie? Anna wanted to tell Marie. But she also wanted to retreat. She was way out her depth, and so was Tim, and they both knew it.

He'd taken up a job offer at a London Head Office with another non-profit. The post was for a programme manager, which was a paygrade higher than his previous job. He was to manage a portfolio of corporate donors to improve access to water and sanitation across the developing world, for an extra ten grand a year. 'Not bad', he'd said during one of their stilted, passive-aggressive conversations. What exactly was he living for? Would he be content to sit behind a desk from a comfortable office all his life, waiting for the next holiday, the next mobile phone upgrade, or car? Would their life be separated into segments of when they would next work on the house, and which part of it they would redecorate?

Maybe she'd tell Beth about Mama Judy's cover-up. Beth could write an article for the *New Internationalist* or one of the newspapers. Beth would relish the scandal. This would be Anna's way of exonerating herself and appeasing her guilt. She couldn't get Marie and Kevine to love her, but she could expose the injustice. Maybe she'd get in touch with one of her old Camden Market artisan shopping buddies and they'd talk about starting an advocacy campaign over some Peruvian street food from one of the market vendors. Maybe there'd be an outcry in liberal circles.

She ran a bath in the stand-alone Victorian-style

bath that she'd spent hours deliberating over when they'd decided to redecorate. She stepped out of her clothes, leaving them on the black and white tiled floor, and slipped into the steaming water, its vapour coiling towards the ceiling. Her ankles were pockmarked with scars from the mosquito bite scabs she'd picked, and tan lines ran along her upper arms and above her breasts. She dried her hands with a towel and gathered up the post that she decided could be looked at only in the soothing solace of a warm bath. Of course, it was mostly takeaway menus and bills for the previous tenants who hadn't yet changed their address. The odd letter concerned them. The address on one of the envelopes was handwritten in sophisticated, flowing cursive, addressed to Tim. Suspicion snuck up on her. It wouldn't normally have done.

She tore it open and took out the letter inside.

Dear Tim,

I hope this finds you well. I wasn't sure if you'd want to meet up again when you're back in London, so I've thought about how I would say this to you. I haven't stopped thinking about our last evening together. It's brought so much clarity at a time when I'm hurting so much, but what hurts more is how much you love your wife and would do anything for her. She's your world, not me. I know I never will be.

I'm so sorry that she couldn't give you what you wanted. And I know that I can't give you what you want either, because what you want is her, not me. I know that I had my chance. We had our moment, and it's in the past.

Sometimes, in quiet moments, I lie in bed thinking about us. About what we had. I think about what she would have been like. Whether she'd have looked more like me or more like you. What she'd have wanted to be when she grew up. Maybe she would have wanted to make the world a better place, like her dad. I'm so proud of you, Tim – of what you've become, the person you are. I'd be proud to journey with you and be your partner. You're one of those rare people in life: honest, principled, dedicated.

I think about how unfair I was to you back then. I just went ahead and did it. I was scared. I was in my final year, the stakes were high, and I was just an immature girl whose parents had such high expectations of her. But you never had the chance to be involved and be part of that decision. I'm so very sorry. Such trite words, I know. If we ever have the chance to meet up again, I'd really love that. But if you don't, I completely understand, even if it pains me to do so.

With love,
Celia x

Anna dabbed the letter in the bathwater so that the ink smudged and bled into the page, and then hung it over the side of the bath, where it fell apart in small, sodden strands on the bathroom tiles. She plunged her body beneath the rippling water and closed her eyes, letting the warmth envelop her. She let it cover her eyes, nose and mouth, her life held in liquid suspension, until unspent breath burned in her lungs, and all she could see was darkness.

PART TWO

CHAPTER TWENTY-ONE
MAKERERE

Marie was used to life in Kampala now. She was proud to be studying at Makerere University. It made her feel part of something special – a heritage and legacy that she'd stepped into and had now become hers. The memory of her first day, which began with her walking out of the bus park into the hot, throbbing centre of the city, still glowed in her mind. The city pulsed with frenzied energy that both astonished and exhausted her. The streets were a riot of noise and colour, with thumping music blaring from every loudspeaker. She'd had to weave through packs of boda-bodas and matatus moving in thick blocks of traffic. It wasn't clear where the road ended, and the pavement began. Her stomach had growled, and she'd looked for a place to eat, but was bombarded by street sellers hawking peanuts in small plastic bags, sambusas wrapped in greasy paper and muchomo piled atop woven bowls. Why were people eating outside? This was the first of many questions that Marie would come to ask.

Emma Lawson

It was strange and scandalous to be eating her sambusa in the open, her first taste of freedom. This would have gotten her barbed looks and comments in Rwanda, where how much food you had and what kind of food you ate was confined to restaurants or hidden behind closed doors. She'd navigated her way past throngs of people, stray dogs and stinking piles of rubbish. She'd never realised just how clean and organised Kigali was until then. There were a multitude of stalls across the road selling bundles of clothes, Nike and Adidas trainers, leather bags, school bags and watches. The sellers had even followed people down the street in pursuit of a sale. Beggars had stretched out their worn-looking hands in hopes of a few shillings, while gleaming Landcruisers and Nissans drove past.

Because of the insane traffic, it had taken a couple of hours in a matatu to get to the main university campus off Makerere Hill Road. She'd been humbled by its grandeur. Should she really have been there? Her grades on the scholarship programme had said yes, but the needles of nervousness starting to pierce her had screamed no. The rectangular creamy-white building reared up from a wide lawn, its rows of blue shutters matching the sky on a cloudless day. A clock tower jutted out from the top. It looked like everything Marie had imagined. She'd envisaged herself sitting on the lawn with her medical books laid out in front of her, surrounded by a fortress of giant note-filled folders. The nerves had subsided and given way to a glorious, giddy feeling. Everything that had shut down in her began to open again, petals of promise unfurling before her. Everything about the hallway as she walked in was prestigious. Polished wood panels flanked her on her

The Shadow Beyond the Hills

way to visitor reception and a spiral staircase to her left had promised new levels of grandness. She joined a parade of people with a remarkable history. People who were respected and admired. A lady on reception with impeccable English had told her to take the left turn on the roundabout to Tennis Court Road to get to her halls of residence.

She'd thought about hailing a boda-boda and somehow hauling her suitcase onto it but decided to walk. Not everything was that different from Rwanda: women walked past in colourful igitenge, some carrying plastic buckets of mangoes, passion fruits, tomatoes, cassava and sweet potato. Others pulled goats along on a rope or waved sticks at pigs to get them to walk where they wanted. Women carried babies on their backs, shrouded in thin white blankets or shielded from the sun by umbrellas.

Her halls, a grey tower block lined with row upon row of imposing balconies, had risen above the other buildings. She'd heaved her suitcase past black metal gates and a sign mounted on a blue pole that read 'Mary Stuart Hall: Train a Woman, a Nation Trained'. What would the women here be like? She pulled the question apart and other interwoven questions started unravelling with it. What was expected of women here, and how did their men treat them? Would there be mixed classes, or would they be segregated, as they were in halls? Did a good woman mean a silent woman, as in the villages around Beauty from Ashes?

She'd climbed several sets of stairs, seeing various posters welcoming the 'boxers', and finally reached her room. It was like her room in the student centre at New Beginnings International – small and plain, but decent enough – with a sturdy-looking desk by a window that looked out past the mottled landscape of the surrounding city. She'd flicked through the welcome pack on the desk, the words 'Bachelor of Medicine and Bachelor of Surgery' shimmering from the front page. They'd reached out and pulled her into the prospect of a fresh start. When tiredness overcame her, she fell asleep to the sounds of the city and fading images of a graduation gown and a huge, panelled hall. Her mother had stood at the back, pale and weak as a ghost.

They'd broken her in gently to the rigours of studying medicine in her first year, but it wasn't long before things ratcheted up a level in her second year. She walked to her lecture now without the lightness of step she had before. It was a fair distance from her halls to the School of Public Health on Mulago Hill Road. She steadied herself and the bulging bag of books she carried as she walked towards the large white building with its odd wave-like ripple near the roof. It didn't quite have the colonial look of the main university campus.

Marie took her seat next to Sanyu as Dr Kagiso began his lecture. She'd taken an instant liking to Sanyu. There was something about him that reminded her of Paul. He'd looked out for her in their first year, and she'd wondered if maybe his interest went beyond pure friendship. He'd never made a move though, and there'd been plenty of chances. He was more like a big brother – or what she imagined a big brother to be – even though he wasn't any older than her.

The Shadow Beyond the Hills

'Welcome, class,' said Dr Kagiso. 'I'm sure you've all heard the English idiom, *gut feeling.*' Dr Kagiso paced the floor with his hands clasped behind his back, his well-spoken South African accent lending gravitas to his appearance. 'This morning, we will see that there is some truth in that expression, as we turn our attention to the enteric nervous system in the gastrointestinal tract.'

She tried and failed to focus on his diagrams and bulleted lists on the board. She wanted them to distract her from the most glaring gut feeling she'd ever had. Mama Judy's voice rang in her head: *your mother.* Those two words had plucked her from the world she knew and placed her in an alien one, where everything she thought she knew shifted and turned in on itself. She'd felt it deep in her gut when Mama had uttered those two words, her head hung low and her lips pursed tightly after she spoke. Marie had summoned the image of the woman who'd stared blankly at her so many times. The woman who'd sometimes stopped to watch as Marie had walked past on her way to class, her eyes peering out from beneath a bandana as she dug a patch of the vegetable gardens. Marie had once checked to see if she looked at any other children the same way. She'd supposed that perhaps this woman wished she'd the chance to go to school, like her, and that her looks were simply ones of longing and regret. Now she realised that perhaps they were. Her mother's eyes had stared straight at her, devoid of emotion. Laughter had echoed around her, her own joining in with that of her Beauty from Ashes classmates as they stood around squealing piglets. Pierre heaving that bloodied sack. *No one asked for sausages for dinner, Beatrice*, Calixte had jeered.

Emma Lawson

When Mama walked away in defeat, knowing that Marie wasn't going to come back to Beauty from Ashes with her, shame had burned a deep hole through her, leaving in its place a cavernous emptiness. Marie had known from that moment that she could never see her mother, a stranger from an unknown life.

Dr Kagiso delivered the rest of the lecture in his hypnotic singsong voice. He had a way of sending Marie to sleep, until Sanyu gave her a nudge.

'Wake up, girl!' he said in a jokey, hushed voice.

Her arm panged with pain. He'd nudged her on bruised skin, which he obviously hadn't seen. She didn't say anything. She knew he wouldn't let it go if she did, and he'd start lecturing her again, telling her that she shouldn't let herself get knocked about by any man. That she should take care of herself. The blush of a bruise on her skin hissed menace to everyone but her. What did it matter if things got a bit rough? It was meaningless.

Once Dr Kagiso had concluded the lecture and set their weekly questions, Marie and Sanyu headed to the canteen and chatted over plates of posho and steamed Nile perch wrapped in banana leaves. The delicate white meat melted in her mouth.

'Are you coming to the club tonight?' Sanyu leaned forward on the table, eyebrows raised and eyes gleaming. 'Me and a few friends from halls are thinking about going to Vibe.'

'I should probably study for the mid-terms ... and you probably should too.' Marie smiled at him.

'Come on, it's Friday! We all need a break. We've been working like dogs.'

She settled on a tight black dress with white frills on the shoulders, and heels that made her feet ache. She'd learnt how to apply make-up by copying other girls as they'd squinted in mirrors and painted their eyes and lips various shades of blue, green, pink or red. She could be anyone she wanted now, hiding behind layers of cream, gel and powder. Tonight, she would bring out the brightest shade of red lipstick she owned. She wanted her lips to be full and sensual. An invitation.

The queue to get into Vibe was heaving, thick with the overpowering fragrance of perfume and aftershave. She could barely breathe. Sanyu and a few of their course mates joined her in the queue, trying to make themselves heard over the uproar. Bathed in sultry red light, Marie sashayed straight to the bar and ordered a couple of shots of Tequila for her and a bottle of Tusker for Sanyu. They clinked their glasses. Marie knocked back her shot, barely pausing for breath before downing the other. She'd skipped dinner so that it would go straight to her head.

They sloped onto the dance floor amid a mass of bodies and she danced until her toes and ankles throbbed. Countless backsides bumped against her. Hard crotches brushed her from behind. She buzzed in the vibration of relentless bass, the room spinning in a mad helix of heat and light.

It all got too much for a moment, so Marie sauntered over to the seats near the bar, her body swaying and legs wobbling. She was clocked by a girl on her course, who came and perched next to her. Miremba was one of those towering personalities in the face of which Marie shrank. Her hair bounced around her face in neat curls as she talked, and she wore her dress with grace and elegance. Her grades were intimidating, even by Marie's standards. Lots of her course mates' grades were intimidating. She'd gone from being the top of her classes at Beauty from Ashes and New Beginnings to fading into obscurity, her talent levelled out on a flat line. However, Miremba was also one of those likeable people whose kindness and modesty made it impossible for even the smallest seed of envy to sprout up. She was also impossibly attractive, and for the first time, Marie felt something stir in her that she'd never felt before. Maybe it was the alcohol. Maybe she was confusing her feelings for admiration. She looked away, embarrassed.

'You seem like you're having a good time,' said Miremba.

Marie wasn't sure if she was being serious or making a joke, but she smiled and nodded in agreement, her head feeling loose on her shoulders.

'I think you've got an admirer over there.' Miremba looked over at Sanyu. 'He hasn't stopped looking at you all night.'

Marie raised her eyebrows. 'Sanyu? He's like a brother. He looks out for me, nothing more.'

A dubious smile spread from her lips to her eyes. 'That's what I thought about a guy once. He'll be my husband after graduation.'

The jealousy surprised her.

Miremba took a comb out of her bag and ran it through her hair. As she did, notes of sweet fruit and coconut drifted over to Marie. She breathed it in for a moment and relaxed into her seat. Feeling both

The Shadow Beyond the Hills

spellbound and silly, she couldn't help but let a short burst of laughter escape her lips. It woke something in her that had lain dormant, and she wanted more of it.

'That's more like it!' said Miremba. 'I never see you smile. It looks good on you. You should do it more often.' She looked Marie in the eye, and Marie found herself drawn into them more deeply than ever before.

'What are you having to drink? The cocktails here are lush. I'm going for Sex on the Beach. Do you want the same?'

Miremba came back, drinks in hand, and motioned for Marie to join her on the dancefloor. Even with the all the alcohol surging through her body, now that Miremba was dancing with her, Marie felt awkward. She did her best to hide it and took a generous swig of her drink.

Miremba eventually danced with other friends and left Marie alone under the hot glare of red light, and the emptiness yawned open once more, threatening to swallow her up. Someone knocked her on the arm, sending the double vodka Miremba had bought for her splashing silently to the floor.

'Oh, I'm sorry, baby,' came a throaty voice.

A familiar body rubbed against her. Though they'd met a few times in bars and clubs, she couldn't remember his name. He hadn't told her, and she hadn't needed to know, nor be known. She knew him by his hands only. The marks he left. When he decided that he wanted her, she reckoned with him for a moment, testing his resolve, provoking him. Then he claimed her, a lion going in for his kill. He stole her away in a plume of white smoke emerging from the dance floor. Marie knew where he'd take her – the curtained booth with the semi-circular spread of plush purple seats inside. She dragged her heels as he took her by the wrist. She feebly resisted every stride, but it was all an act. All part of their choreographed routine.

By the time Sanyu pulled back the curtain, he'd bent her over the seat with her dress pulled up around her waist. He held her down. His hands clenched and covered hers. Marie had always thought she could release them if she wanted to. She looked around at Sanyu and laughter tumbled out of her in uncontrollable swells. She almost choked on it.

'Get your hands off her!' Sanyu lunged at him and pulled him off Marie, both of them falling to the floor in a clumsy tangle of limbs.

Marie had never seen such ferocity in Sanyu. Still, he took several sharp punches to the stomach and face. Her midnight man scarpered. Sanyu was silent as they hobbled out of the club. Neither of them spoke as they took a taxi back to her halls, even when they had to pull over so she could void herself of all the drink she'd imbibed. Only as he stopped outside the hall gates did he look at her. He would never be seen taking an inebriated girl back to her room.

'We've been here before. When is this going to stop?' said Sanyu, his voice hard and unflinching.

Marie fixed her gaze on the Rosewood tree by the gates, trying to pull everything into focus to stop it from spinning.

'Look at you. You're a mess. A beautiful mess.' Sanyu's voice began to thaw. 'Why do you do this to yourself? Why do you let a man touch you like that?'

Marie staggered and gripped the iron gates, righting herself. 'You're overreacting, Sanyu. Like you said, it's

Friday night and we all just need a break.' Nausea threatened her again. She bent over, ready.

Sanyu's voice hardened. 'You call that a good time? If you're having such a good time, why drink yourself sick?'

She looked up at him and only now saw what a beating he'd taken: his swollen eye, the bulge on his temple, a dribble of blood on his cheek. She wanted to reach out and wipe it away. She wanted to take it all back so that he'd never gotten hurt.

'You're worth more than this, Marie. So much more.'

CHAPTER TWENTY-TWO
GULU

While the sun rose over Kampala and cast a rosy blush across the city, Miremba's sweet voice sang in her head, tempered only by visions of Sanyu's bulging temple and bloodied cheek. He would forgive her – he always did. Her initial anger at him presiding over her like those old village fathers she'd heard people talking about had fizzled out, giving way to relief that he'd stopped something that she was too intoxicated to stop herself. As for Miremba, her only hope was that she hadn't seen what a complete fool Marie had made of herself.

She ate breakfast alone in the canteen, deciding on a large bowl of katogo. The mixture of fried plantains, beans, vegetables and soup would sustain her on a journey that would take them most of the day, until they reached the rural village in the north of the country. She'd been looking forward to this trip for weeks. It was a chance to finally put some of the skills and knowledge she'd attained into practice and get out of lecture halls. It was highlighted in luminous yellow in her diary: two weeks blocked out for 'mobile outreach elective, Gulu.'

She sidled up to Sanyu outside the Public Health building. They were waiting for their driver, Godfrey, who would take them and two other students to one of the most remote areas in Uganda. She gave Sanyu a coy look, but he melted her stiff embarrassment with a knowing grin. His face was drawn and tired, but it brightened when she looked at him.

'I'm sorry for what happened to you … It was my fault,' said Marie.

'What that beast did to you is not your fault, Marie. And let's say you did brew the tea? No one has to take it like that. You didn't have to take it.'

'Well … I hope you can forget about it.'

'Forget what?'

She smiled. Normality had been restored.

They waited for a couple of hours, Sanyu supplementing her ample breakfast by bringing her a mandazi while they waited. Godfrey, a small and cheerful man dressed in a baggy suit, showed up in a ragged-looking Nissan. The larger buildings thinned out in the rear-view mirror as they drove over the bypass and left the city centre behind them. Tired already, Marie looked at the blur of houses, people and animals out the window and tried to focus her mind on the task ahead of her. With the help of some medics travelling up in another car, they would need to have the clinic up and ready to receive patients by 9 a.m. the next day at the latest. The boot of their car was chock full of boxes of latex gloves, hygiene supplies, condoms and vaccination kits. She couldn't wait to see what they would achieve through the clinic. Her stomach was swamped with nervous excitement. She didn't know who she really was or what she was born for, but this felt natural and right – as though she'd slipped into new skin that held her together in perfect tension.

They'd driven for several hours when Godfrey pulled the car over to buy a jackfruit from a woman selling them by the sack-load from her ramshackle shed. He cut it up with a knife from the glovebox and shared it out. It wasn't long before they were back on the road. Godfrey insisted they made it to Gulu by nightfall, his eyes hinting at something dark and dangerous if they didn't.

The Nissan rocked and jolted with every speed bump. There was no time to stop as they drove on the outer rim of Murchison Falls National Park, but that didn't stop some of the local wildlife making an appearance. Baboons sat staring at them with penetrating yellow eyes as they crossed the Nalubaale Bridge over the Victoria Nile, its mad waters churning with white spray and rampant power. She'd never seen so large a river. It made Mukungwa and even Nyaborongo seem like tepid streams by comparison. As they drove further north, the vegetation thinned out into sparse scrubland and villages were fewer and more far between.

Dusk draped over them like a warm cloak by the time they reached Gulu. They shared a simple dinner at a Catholic-run guesthouse, where they'd be staying for the duration of their elective. Godfrey slurped down his fish stew and looked at each of them in turn.

'So, what are you going to be doing here?' He directed his question at Sanyu.

'We're seeing how a lack of resources affects primary healthcare delivery.' Sanyu spoke with quiet

The Shadow Beyond the Hills

authority, aware of the immense privilege he had in studying one of the most respected professions there was. His chest was broad and puffed up as he talked.

'But you know what happened here, don't you?' Godfrey's eyes glinted; an old man telling a tale around a fire.

Marie knew this region harboured something rotten. She'd heard some Ugandans murmuring things about Joseph Kony and the Lord's Resistance Army and was learning that this part of the country had been the heartland of vicious forces, still a raw and open wound, and that it wasn't just Rwanda that had borne the scars of violence. She'd had to learn the roots of those scars too, not being old enough to remember the genocide that had touched the lives of everyone she knew.

Dickson, a fellow medical student in their group, leaned forward on the table, his arms folded and face stoic. 'Museveni's government is pumping all this money into the urban centres and forgetting that people in the rural areas can't send their kids to school, buy maize or get vaccinated. Decent health clinics here are non-existent.'

It struck her just how open Ugandans were. How could they speak so freely and critically of their president? No one in Rwanda spoke like this. The people were like an obedient wife to their President husband. Even Mama Judy spoke in hushed tones about certain things, aware of the weight of politics and history sitting on everyone's shoulders.

Marie headed back to her room. All she had to refresh herself with was a bucket and a leaky tap that let out a pathetic trickle of muddy water. She fell into a bed shrouded in ripped mosquito netting and tried to guard her dreams from children with AK47s and women held down by men in khaki uniform behind locked doors.

The Nissan jerked and rolled along a rutted track the next morning as they ventured into a rural village, sending up huge clouds of swirling orange dust in their wake. Godfrey pulled the car to a stop under a tall palm tree, letting the dust settle. They were surrounded by large, circular houses with thatched roofs. Some of them still had the look of freshly baked mud, while others were rendered in grey cement. The ground was hard beneath her feet as Marie stepped out into the dry air. Sanyu, Dickson, and Zawadi, a Kenyan woman who brought their number to four, all gathered in a line to greet Dr Lukwago and a few of the village elders. A gaggle of young children ran up and chatted in excited voices around them.

Marie had never seen houses like these before. They were nowhere to be found in the rural villages in Rwanda. There, it was all rectangular mud brick houses rendered in cement and either corrugated iron or tiled roofs. People lived in gated compounds, or compounds demarcated with neatly kept hedges and bamboo fences. How little she knew of the Africa beyond her own small country. She tried to imagine a large family crowding inside one of these houses, although when they went inside one, there was ample room. Also, family members lived in different houses around the same family camp.

They drank extra sweet tea and then set up the mobile clinic, which they wanted to do before the worst

The Shadow Beyond the Hills

of the morning heat burned down on them. The other car had yet to arrive, so Marie and Sanyu unloaded the one gazebo frame and parasol they had from the roof of the car. Dickson and Zawadi joined them and set up a row of tables and fold-out chairs. The other group of medics and students arrived in a dirty white Toyota mini-van and unloaded the rest of the medical supplies, one of them putting up a banner that read, 'Makerere–Gulu partnership, Mobile Outreach Clinic.' Marie worked until her sweat-drenched body demanded rest.

She revelled in seeing rolls of clean white bandages and gauze, containers of antibiotics and penicillin, sterile needles and testing kits. She felt as she did when volunteers at Beauty from Ashes had brought over boxes of new stationary. She used to love opening them and unwrapping cartons of pens and crayons and reams of coloured card and craft materials. She would make stacks of new books in her classroom. Previous volunteers had brought over dog-eared books and tired-looking stationary. Mama soon put an end to such gestures. *We don't want your second-hand junk, thank you very much! Our kids deserve more than your rejects – they deserve the same as kids everywhere!*

A spasm of anger gripped her. She looked down at her Makerere University Medics polo shirt, reminding herself of where she was, and who she was, or could be. Mama Judy, who was supposed to have been her guardian, had guarded her from her own mother. And yet the anger always cooled into indifference. How was she supposed to feel anything for her mother – a woman she'd never truly known – or her father, who was in prison for murdering his neighbours? She wanted to feel something for her mother, but she couldn't. And

Kevine… supposed to be her sister, the only family she thought she had. A liar.

Marie was beginning to feel sick and dizzy. She had to sit down.

'Marie, are you alright? You look awful.' Sanyu got on his knees and looked up at her with concerned eyes.

'I'm fine.' Marie took the bottle of water he gave her and knocked back several large gulps, which came straight back up as her body choked and spluttered in protest.

'Come now, we must take you back to the guesthouse. You can't work like this.'

She sat under the gazebo and had her temperature taken, and then felt a sharp prick on her arm as Sanyu tested her for malaria. It came back negative, but Godfrey still drove her back to the guesthouse where she spent the rest of the day on a hard, lumpy bed in her room, trying to sleep off whatever malaise had settled in her. Desperate to get to work, but overcome and exhausted, she drifted in and out of delirium.

It was pitch black in her room. A knock at the door startled her. Sanyu poked his head around it. Zawadi was with him, her hair wrapped in an avocado-green, sequined head covering.

'How are you doing?' asked Zawadi in her delicate Kenyan accent.

'Just really tired, but I'll be fine, honestly.'

Sanyu turned the light on and walked in holding a small tray of mandazi and chapatis. 'No bananas. Can you believe it?'

The Shadow Beyond the Hills

Bananas grew in abundance in the south of the country.

She took the tray from him and attempted mandazi, its sweet, fried goodness sticking in her mouth and giving her a little energy boost. 'Thanks.'

'If you need anything else, you know where we are,' said Zawadi.

'Sleep well, my friend. Tomorrow is a new day, and we have lots of work to do. I hope you're well for it.' Sanyu smiled at her.

'See you in the morning.' Marie returned a faint smile as they left.

They clicked the door behind them, sending a small piece of plaster to the floor where the wall was cracked.

The prospect of the work ahead buoyed her. She knew how to give people their shots. She knew how to wrap and tie up a bandage so that it didn't slip. When the children cried for their mamas as she injected them, she didn't wince inside. Everything was a procedure, clean and simple. Whatever the pain involved, if it needed to be done, she got it done. Some of her other course mates had struggled to get over their trepidation in dealing with younger patients and their tears. Not Marie. She was made for this.

The call to prayer from Gulu town curled through the air. Perhaps they would get a chance to explore the area after work. There was so much to explore and discover. She wanted to do it all. But first, sleep.

She found herself on the back of a bicycle the next morning. A surprisingly decent sleep and some breakfast had revived her, and a morning wash with the bucket of water that Zawadi had brought over had cleared her head. The bicycle taxi took her past palm trees and traditional houses flanking the mud track to the mobile clinic. When she arrived at the clinic, Dr Lukwago assigned their small team various tasks to deal with the hundred or so patients already queuing outside. Marie would deal with vaccinations, Sanyu would test for Malaria, Hepatitis B, HIV/AIDS, and Pneumonia, and Zawadi would tackle sexual and reproductive health.

Each of the patients was to take an exercise book where their diagnosis would be recorded, and then present it to Dickson, who would give them their prescriptions. It was a simple system, but it was going to work. Marie had the biggest queue waiting for her, lining up mostly for the Hepatitis B vaccine, which was the biggest threat the community faced. Mothers brought their babies for routine vaccinations against polio, measles and rubella.

Her first patient was a father of two who'd ridden his bicycle from a village a couple of hours away. He could only have been in his early thirties, but he looked at her with an already wizened face, his eyes searching hungrily for hope in a needle. Usually it was the mothers who brought their children in for medical care. Marie assumed she'd died, leaving him to care for their children. He propped his youngest on his lap as she prepared the shots, a look of terror spreading across the little boy's face when he saw the needle. He couldn't speak any English, nor could she speak his regional dialect, so she said as much as she could through a warm smile, gentle eyes, and deftness of touch. Taking the

The Shadow Beyond the Hills

boy's slight, unyielding arm, she placed it softly on the edge of the table. He began to cry. His father cupped the boy's face in his hands and cooed to him, while Marie pierced his fragile skin and pushed down on the plunger of the syringe.

She continued seeing patients all morning, stopping only for brief respite – a few sips of bottled water – around midday. The team finished their duties by 6 p.m. when the queue finally petered out. By that time, swarms of mosquitos were feasting on her. There were far more here than there had ever been in the cool, mountainous region where she'd lived in the Northern Province in Rwanda.

Dr Lukwago congratulated them on an excellent first day of work and reeled off a tally of numbers: 76 mothers seen for postnatal care; 105 girls seen for sexual health services; 100 Hepatitis B immunisations given. Marie swelled with contentment. There was gratifying ease in reading out numbers. But there was still far more to do. The numbers needed to increase over the next couple of weeks, but Marie felt certain they would achieve this.

The queue of patients waiting for the clinic to open was even longer the next day. Marie took one last gulp of extra sweet tea and received her first patient. Her name was Juma. She sat on a plastic fold-out chair in front of Marie, wringing her pale hands. She couldn't have been older than twelve years, and her white hair was pulled into short braids that jiggled about her scalp when she spoke.

Marie had a translator with her this morning – a kind lady called Abothi. The language barrier had made it hard to diagnose and treat patients and she needed help.

It was important not just to treat patients, but also to listen to them.

'They call me ghost girl,' said Juma in a timid voice. 'And I am a ghost, because they don't see me.' The white of her skin was spotted with irregular blotches of brown.

Marie looked her in the eye and summoned all the sensitivity and empathy she had. She'd seen very few people like this in Rwanda, but they did exist.

'My parents make me hide when we have guests. I can't go to school. I don't learn anything … other than how to avoid people.' She wrapped her arms together, holding herself in, and took a deep breath. 'When the guests leave, they send me outside again to face the sun, even at midday.' She looked at the patches of brown skin on her arm. 'My mother says it's working.'

Marie hadn't gone into any great depth yet in oncology, but she could tell from a fleeting glance that the weeping, crusty lesions on her face and neck were turning cancerous, if they weren't already. She also knew that there was only one clinic in the whole of the country that could treat certain cancers, and it was miles away from this district. If her community shunned her, it was unlikely that anyone would care enough to get her the treatment she needed. And even if someone did, how likely was it that they could?

All the excitement and energy she'd felt about this trip – about her decision to study medicine, even – drained out of her. She peered over the edge of her expectations and saw the vast drop to the hard reality below. She could diagnose and treat patients with whatever equipment and provisions she had available, but she'd never be able to bridge the vast gulf between this level of care and the restoration of a whole, complex person. She'd never be able to conjure up robust healthcare infrastructure for an entire nation.

'I'm afraid,' said Juma.

Marie shuddered to think what exactly she was afraid of but sat and listened for as long as Juma cared to talk, despite the growing queue awaiting treatment. She could, at the very least, give her the gift of presence in a village where she was invisible. She gave her the Hepatitis B shot and sent her to Dickson, who would prescribe some antibiotics for her infected-looking lesions. Marie marshalled all her strength and worked until dusk. Her muscles ached. Her spirit felt like it was giving out. She had to do better than this. This was her first experience of practising medicine in the real world and she was stumbling already.

Marie and the team finally ate dinner in Gulu town. They sat around plates of steamed bananas, cassava, sweet potatoes and yams soaked in peanut sauce, with generous slabs of posho squeezed in. She hadn't eaten anything since breakfast and was shaking from low blood-sugar.

'I treated an albino patient today.' Marie dropped this into a pause in conversation, ready to confront her newfound feelings of inadequacy.

'Did everything go okay?' asked Zawadi, dipping a wodge of posho in her sauce.

'Fairly routine, I guess. She did have some nasty-looking lesions though.' Marie lowered her voice. 'She said she was … afraid. I didn't know how to help her.'

Sanyu put a consoling arm around her. 'You can't help every person in every way. You're training to be a doctor, not God.' He stabbed a piece of sweet potato and forked it into his mouth.

Marie stared at her plate.

'Listen to me: you'll make a fine doctor, even if you're not a miracle-maker.' Sanyu's voice brimmed with sincerity.

She chose to believe him.

'It might be to do with what's been happening in Tanzania,' said Zawadi. 'Witchdoctors spreading stupid lies about the potency of albino body parts. Children have been kidnapped and hacked to pieces so that some Congolese businessman can sell them on to a fool who believes he'll inherit riches, get cured from a disease or please his wife in the bedroom.'

'Like the Chinese and their appetite for rhino horn,' added Dickson.

Zawadi pushed her covering back from her forehead. 'Perhaps she's afraid that madness will cross the border. It's incredible how madness spreads.'

'That superstitious bullshit needs to remain in the past.'

Sanyu leaned in closer. 'Witchcraft is real for those who believe it, Dickson. And whether we like it or not, both the uneducated and the educated still hold those beliefs.' His contribution raised eyebrows around the table. 'It's going to take time to change mindsets. And denying its power – the power of belief – is a futile strategy.'

'Well, when can you say enough is enough? As if people here don't have enough to deal with after seeing their loved ones butchered by Kony and his rebels.'

'That's the problem,' offered Zawadi. 'Unless people see their needs met in a universe they can control, they'll seek the supernatural to account for misfortune. To make sense of the evil actions of others. It's easier to placate spirits than to accept and confront our own darkness.'

'And these things don't operate in a socio-political vacuum,' said Sanyu. 'They thrive among displaced peoples and spread as rumours in refugee camps.'

'Do you think your God will stop this ... madness, as you call it?' Dickson looked at Zawadi.

'Inshallah.' Zawadi pronounced every syllable with melodic reverence.

Marie tried to hold these abstract thoughts in balance, but they kept slipping through her fingers. *They call me ghost girl.* A community where some still believed in ghosts had made a ghost of one of their own. The tragic irony of it floored her. She had tried to deal with people in parts, but, somehow, they always ended up stubbornly refusing to stay as disparate pieces, instead fusing into faces she couldn't forget and voices that wouldn't be silenced. *They make me hide when guests come.*

Back in the dim light of her room, she pulled out a letter from her bag. It had arrived just before she'd left for Gulu.

Dear Marie,

I hope you're okay and are doing well with your studies. Kevine told me you're studying medicine at a university in Kampala. That's wonderful! I don't really know what to say, other than I wish you well in all that you do. You're such a special person, Marie.

I know I've said it before, but I'm sorry the

adoption didn't work out. I'm sorry if you feel we let you down, but you must know that that decision was the hardest one I've ever had to make. I'll never forget you. If you need any help with school fees or anything else, I'll do all I can. Please don't feel awkward about it, because I don't.

Wishing you the very best,
Anna

Marie folded the letter and placed it back in her bag. She'd keep it for when she was back in her room in Kampala. She'd place it in a carved box made from the wood of a jacaranda tree on top of all the letters.

CHAPTER TWENTY-THREE
CIRCLES

Damn. She was right again. Anna and Jo had huddled over chocolate-dusted cappuccinos in a coffee shop in Covent Garden as rain lashed its enormous windows, while Jo had drawn a messy black mark in the middle of a page from her jotter pad. 'This is how it will feel,' Jo had said. 'A dark, intractable mess that will never go away, never heal. It's all you'll be able to see, and nothing will get rid of it.' She'd then taken other pens in different colours from her bag and had drawn successively larger circles around it. 'Do you see what's happening?' All Anna had seen was Jo's eagerness to share what she'd been learning from her latest lecture. With all her children in school, Jo was using her newfound freedom, albeit bracketed between school runs, to re-train as a counsellor. Now, as she sat polishing glasses behind a bar, Anna saw the circles shimmer into view again, along with Jo's neat handwriting in arcs between each circle: *new friends, work accomplishments, new experiences.* It wasn't that the messy black mark in the middle had gone away or had even shrunk. It was still there, implacable and unmoving, but so were the bigger, brighter circles that overshadowed it. *With time, more will be added.* Six years had added plenty more circles.

The pub she worked at on Bethnal Green Road kept her busier than ever. It began as a stopgap waitressing gig and turned into a management position. She enjoyed the hurried simplicity of it. There wasn't time to think. And any children that were there during daytime shifts weren't hers to manage. It was a pub that toyed with trendiness, with its industrial black pipe lights hanging from the ceiling and bare brick walls. As she got up to write the day's specials on the board, she considered those other circles in her life: the friends she'd met at her weekly groups – Zumba class on a Monday, Pilates on a Wednesday, book club on a Thursday, steel drum classes on a Friday. She was taking evening classes in business management and supplementing it with online learning modules. It wasn't the life she'd imagined, but it was the one she was living, and there were small joys and victories to be found.

Anna finished her shift and walked home in the sickly glow of the streetlights. This pocket of Shoreditch was surprisingly subdued for a Friday night. When she stepped inside, Beth's flat reverberated with typing.

'I can't believe you're still awake,' said Anna, crashing down on the corner sofa.

'143 years ago, he could've been a white man's slave. Now it looks like he's going to win the election.' Beth's tawny hair hung down in curly wisps from her loose top-knot bun. 'How did it take so long to get there?'

Anna kicked off her shoes and rested her feet against the coffee table. 'Give it another 143 years and perhaps they'll have a female president.' A yawn escaped from her lips. 'You only got back from Chicago this afternoon. How are you still up?'

'Same reason you are – work to do. Bills to pay. Plus, I'm going to Kabul next week.'

The flat was poky and claustrophobic. The row of small circular windows high up on the white brick wall didn't let in enough natural light during the day. It made her feel like she was in a ship cabin on some desolate sea. It suited Beth, who was barely there most of the time as she worked on foreign assignments. With Anna to share the mortgage, it suited her even better. She hadn't done much with the place other than hang a few potted plants around the room and frame photos of her travels and art noveau posters. It didn't matter. It was infinitely better than living in an empty shell of a house, no matter how white-washed and homely it had once been. Anna left Beth at her desk and turned in for the night.

No, not again, please. Something gripped her legs with urgent ferocity. Pain shot through them and up into her arms, where frantic hands grabbed at her, pulling her down. Howling sounds ripped through the room. A couple of cats squalled in the street below as Anna woke in a sticky sweat. Those sounds and sensations had lessened over the years, occasionally coming back to haunt her in her sleep. When they did, circles were flung out into the void. She was once again swallowed up in a black mess in the centre of an empty page.

The coffee grinder buzzed through the wall of her room, which was still cloaked in early morning darkness. Beth left the flat for a gym session before work. Anna's shift wasn't due to start until eleven, so there was still time to laze in bed with a book before going for a jog around Weavers Fields. Her shift patterns spun everything into disarray, so she made sure to get some sort of routine into her day – it anchored her in reality. As she returned to bed with an espresso, her phone buzzed with a new message. 'Meet me this morning at 9. You choose where, I don't mind, but don't be late. I have a meeting at 10.' Every time she got a message from Tim, something in her dropped. Everything would be fine, and then he upended it all. She'd picked her way through the debris of their separation, stumbling on the jagged edges of each piece of their broken marriage. She tried to gather the sharp fragments and meld them into something new and solid – something that would hold together.

The park opened up before her as she rounded the corner from Hague Street. The morning air had a bitter edge to it, a foretaste of winter, and the Aspen leaves were a montage of gold and blood red as she jogged past, some of them dancing to their death on the wind. She stretched her legs on a bench by a metal sculpture.

Tim approached her, looking gaunt in a grey suit, a takeaway coffee in one hand and a Prêt-A-Manger wrap in the other. His cheekbones were more pronounced than they'd been the last time she'd seen him.

'You okay?' he panted.

'Why are you panting? I'm the one who jogged here.' She shot him a wry look.

The Shadow Beyond the Hills

A small smile crossed his face. 'Busy morning, that's all. And an even busier day ahead.' He took a bite out of his wrap and wiped the edge of his mouth with the back of his hand.

'Still working too hard then,' said Anna, in equal parts jest and truth.

He stared up at the crows resting on the sculpture. 'It was good of you to share the story with Beth. She still writes a sharp article.'

She'd become largely blind to the shadows cast by her brilliant sisters. All it took was a comment, a look of admiration, to remind her. 'I wasn't going to. I didn't think it was my story to tell.'

It created a minor ripple in the media when it was published a few weeks back, as other orphanage scandals were coming to light in Uganda and Kenya, but it didn't take long for another African girl who'd been lied to about her identity and family history to fade into the background – to be swallowed up in small print and then shoved off the page by other stories. If Anna had been honest with herself, she knew this would turn out to be the case. Still, she'd entertained images of being interviewed on BBC Breakfast, Channel 4 news, Newsnight, Panorama. She'd speak up for Marie and expose Judy, and in doing so would find absolution, release, freedom.

'Well, it needed to be told.' He sat down on the bench and beckoned her to join him. 'Nothing ever happened with Celia while we were married. I've told you that, but it's like you still don't believe me.'

Anna found herself in the bath again in their house on Talbot Street, reading flowing cursive words and trying to make sense of them. She'd tried to assemble them into an arrangement that hurt less.

'Nothing sexual.' He stared at the rows of houses fringing the park.

'Just a deeply emotional connection then, was that it?' She tried to restrain the sarcasm in her voice. They'd argued enough over the years.

'Not even that. Not to her … To what could have been, I guess.'

She still ached deeply, sickeningly, to think of Tim and this other woman creating a baby together. Again, her body screamed failure. It was her all along who'd failed to nurture the seeds of life that entered her. This was why she hated meeting Tim. He dredged up those feelings and she got stuck in them all over again. Yet, there was a tiny part of her that wanted to defend him.

'You weren't responsible for what happened, Tim. Not that, anyway.'

'Wasn't I? Because from where I was standing, the life I helped create ended up in pieces on a petri dish. Forgotten in hazardous waste.' He put his coffee and wrap down on the bench and rubbed his face with sinewy hands. 'If I could have just … given someone else a chance in life …'

'Then what? It wouldn't have undone what happened.' She knew now why it had been so hard to love him in the end. It was hard to love someone filled with such guilt and self-loathing.

'After we broke up in second year, she was just there. And I wasn't sure if you'd ever want me back. I know that doesn't magically make it all better for you. I was an idiot back then … still am … I was never a more thankful and blessed man than when you said yes, even though I couldn't even manage to pull off a successful proposal.'

Silence settled and filled the space between them. The scene unfurled before her: him leaving a series of clues around their leafy campus, a trail of memories of their first year together – where they had their first kiss, where he'd first told her that he loved her – all leading to him kneeling on one knee, having lost the engagement ring but offering her a cheap substitute until he either found the original or bought a better one. He was hopeless, but she'd been hopelessly in love.

Joggers puffed past and mothers pushed prams with one hand and steaming takeaway cups in the other.

Tim raked a hand through his hair and sighed. 'What are you thinking, Anna?'

She tried to gather her thoughts into some semblance of order. 'I'm thinking that you're a conflicted man. You need to work out what you want and stop living with this unbearable guilt. It's what broke us in the end.' Their life was past tense now. 'That, and I was afraid you wouldn't be enough.'

He looked stricken as her words reached him, her breath condensing and curling in the air around them. 'I tried to be everything to you. To give you everything.'

'I think that was part of the problem... You couldn't. No one could.'

He sipped his coffee and held up a bunch of thick papers. 'This came through this morning.'

Even though she knew it was coming, it hadn't stopped the bottom falling out of her world all over again.

'I assumed you would've gotten them, too.'

Anna shook her head.

'It doesn't have to be this way, Anna.' He reached

out a faltering hand.

Despite herself, she interlocked her fingers with his – more as an experiment to see how she would feel if she did.

He let go of her and reached in his bag, taking out a large envelope.

She'd had enough of envelopes and letters. He could tear it up and leave it to the wind.

Reluctantly, she took it from him and tore open the seal. Inside was a prospectus for King's College London. Behind that, a print-out from their website about an MSc in Psychology and Neuroscience.

'I checked and there are plenty of spaces for the next academic year. You'd have to start with the post-grad diploma, but that wouldn't be a problem for you.'

A note of suppressed excitement bloomed in his voice, lighting up his eyes. 'I knew you were never finished with academia, and academia wasn't finished with you.'

Her head splintered in confusion. Why was he doing this now?

'Tim, I'm pulling as many shifts as I can and I can barely help Beth with her mortgage, let alone find both the time and the money to somehow study for a Master's degree.'

'Look again. You missed something.'

Anna tried to hold the cheque with numb hands, the wind stepping up a gear with biting malevolence.

'It's the first year's tuition fees, ready to cash. If you want it. They have a part-time, distance learning option as well.'

She froze in her seat.

'This isn't about buying your affection, Anna. This

comes with no strings attached. You don't have to see me again if you don't want to. I just want to do one more thing to make you happy. To try, at least.'

Tim said goodbye and headed to his meeting, stealing another look at her as he walked away, smiling.

Later that night, when she got home from her shift at the pub, Beth motioned to a large box on the kitchen table. Inside was a sizeable stack of books. Lying on top of them a piece of paper read 'MSc Psychology and Neuroscience, First Year Reading List', and underneath that, another piece of paper: 'Missed books for the missed years. Yours, Tim.'

CHAPTER TWENTY-FOUR
LETTERS

'You may begin,' said an officious voice from the front. A rustle of papers filled the hall, and then silence. Marie glanced at the large clock leering over her from the centre of the wall. A rush of adrenaline focused her mind on the vast list of multiple-choice questions she had in front of her. She now had to prove her knowledge of anatomy, physiology, surgery and medical conditions. She had to prove that she could be a doctor. She'd been studying for her finals late into the night for months, her eyes bleary like a drunk's by the time she finally allowed herself a few hours' sleep. Sanyu had brought her endless cups of coffee. They'd clocked up as many hours in the library studying as they could. It had been a long, hard slog and drained every last ounce of strength and stamina she had. But the end was in sight. Or rather, the beginning. She answered question after question until her mind was eviscerated from five years of medical school being emptied out on paper.

Nearly two hours into her exam, her hand was

The Shadow Beyond the Hills

cramping. Another look at the clock: five minutes left.

> A thirty-year-old man has had weakness in his left arm and leg for three days. He is HIV positive with a CD4 count of 50 cells/mm3. He is not taking anti-retroviral therapy. His BP is 140/90 mmHg, pulse of 95 bpm and temperature 37.5°C. He has power of 3/5 in his arm and 4/5 in his left leg but no other neurological signs. A CT brain scan shows ring enhancing lesions with surrounding oedema.

What's the most appropriate antimicrobial therapy to prescribe?
  A) Amphotericin and ceftazidime
  B) Dexamethasone and acyclovir
  C) Ganciclovir and ceftazidime
  D) Isoniazid and rifampicin
  E) Pyrimethamine and sulphadiazine

Pyrimethamine and sulphadiazine, surely. It had to be, because time was up.

'Please put down your pens and close your papers.' The exam invigilator scanned the hall with narrow eyes.

There was a deep collective sigh as everyone shifted in their seats and shuffled their papers, signalling the culmination of years of hard work. This was their last exam out of a three-part schedule comprising the oral and clinical role play exam and a statistical data interpretation exam. Marie stepped out into fresh air cleansed by an early afternoon storm. Her steps were lighter again, and she could think without swarms of statistics and letters ordering themselves in her head.

Sanyu ran up to her, lifted her off her feet and swung her in the air. 'We've done it! We. Are. Done!'

He planted her back on the ground with an unceremonious thud. They held each other tight for a few moments. His huge arms squeezed any niggling doubts out of her. It was done. She loosened in relief.

Marie still felt as though she were swirling around in the air, her head light and giddy, when Miremba bounded out of the hall. Marie felt the impossible urge to run up and kiss her. Instead, she watched as Miremba's bright yellow dress flowed out behind her, tucked in at the top by a faded blue denim jacket. She glided with gracefulness.

'Marie, what are you staring at? Let's start drinking!' Sanyu took her by the hand, looking over his shoulder and laughing with her as they headed to a nearby bar off campus for celebratory drinks.

Marie headed back to her room and sank onto the bed, heavy with happiness. This life was all hers.

Late afternoon sun slanted through the window. There was still enough time for a sundown swim if she went now, so she gathered her swimming kit and waited for a boda-boda to drive past and take her to the university swimming pool. She stood on the edge of the road outside the gates to her hall. Her skin was cold and tingling. Was someone watching her? She looked up and down the road, seeing only the usual sights. She flagged down the first boda-boda she saw.

She'd decided to face her fear of water in her first year at Makerere. A group of girls from her halls were part of a swimming group and they'd asked her to join them. She'd ended up on her back, panicked and paralysed beside the pool. It'd felt like a huge man was

The Shadow Beyond the Hills

sitting on her chest, strangling her, the compound walls closing in, shutting out all the light. One of her new friends took her to see the university counsellor. After several attempts of standing in the shallow end of the pool, she no longer saw the water as something she could only drown in. She was no longer chased by heavy footsteps, crunching stalks of maize. She wasn't overcome by raging swells and furious currents.

It came easy now as she lowered herself in and pushed off with her feet, parting the water with the palms of her hands as she'd been taught. She practised her strokes and made her body as streamlined as possible, ducking her head underwater and putting the world on mute. Dappled pockets of sunlight played on the surface as she swam up for air at the shallow end of the pool, beads of cool water trickling down her back.

A slender figure in tight jeans, high heels and a light pink turtle-neck jumper was standing at the poolside, staring down at her with horrified eyes.

Marie's legs almost gave way. The water threatened to pull her under. What she'd tried to ignore for so long could no longer be ignored. There was nowhere to run or hide; she had to confront this tortured face.

They sat in a deserted canteen, unsure of how to be with each other. Marie hadn't been able to think of where to take Kevine, who'd made it clear she wasn't going anywhere without her. A bar? Too loud and too busy. Her room? Too intimate and personal. She needed a neutral space, but all she could think of was the canteen in her halls. They'd travelled back to Marie's halls in the dark on boda-bodas. Her stomach had roiled the whole way.

Kevine's face looked drawn. 'Did you ever read *any* of my letters, Marie?'

Marie stared at her hands clasped tightly together on the table. She'd held the first letter to a candle flame. The rest had simply gone straight into the bin. Scrunched up balls of lost words for a lost, severed relationship.

'Well? I've come all this way. Please, let's talk.'

Marie forced herself to look at Kevine. 'How did you know I was here when you wrote to me in first year? And how long have you been watching me?'

'Not long. I've been on the Kigali–Kampala bus all day. It wasn't hard to find you. I spoke to someone who knew you from New Beginnings. They said you'd secured a place on the scholarship programme for Makerere Medical School.' Kevine took short, shallow breaths. 'I couldn't put it off any longer, you're my sister for God's sake, we're blood!'

'I don't know what we are … Who *you* are, anymore.'

'I can understand why you're angry. How hurt and confused you must have been.'

'You have no idea what I felt, Kevine! None! This is my life now. I won't let you turn up and ruin it.' Marie straightened up, seething, defiant. 'Somehow, I'm here, and I'm making something of my life – one that I've had to rebuild from what you and Mama took away from me. I won't let you take it away from me again. How dare you follow me here and assume you can interrupt my life now!' Marie doubled down on her anger. She would make Kevine feel the full force of it. She pushed

The Shadow Beyond the Hills

back her chair to leave.

'Marie, wait, please!'

Every fibre of her wanted to leave Kevine in the empty canteen, abandoned, as she'd felt. As she felt now. She stood to face her, gripping the back of the chair with strained knuckles.

'I thought that time would help you come around … Help you see why I did what I had to do,' said Kevine.

Marie snorted a sour laugh. 'You didn't have to do anything. You could've just cared for me.' She tried to push down the guilt that surfaced – Kevine had always been there for her, looked out for her and doted on her with the only motherly love Marie had known.

'I wish I could've forgotten. I wish I could've fallen off that moto with you and mother. But, unlike you, I can't forget the past. You don't know, but I'll always remember what he did to you … to us.' Kevine's voice split into shivering sobs, her body almost convulsing, racked with grief.

The sight of her capable, wise sister – the one she'd previously looked up to – breaking down in a mucous mess was an ugly, undignified sight. It threatened to break something in Marie that, until now, she'd thought unbreakable.

'I trusted you,' said Marie. 'How can I ever trust anyone again?'

Kevine tried to stifle her cries. 'I know.'

Marie looked away as Kevine wept. She shook as if an evil spirit was being exorcised from her.

'Come on then, let's have it. What happened to us?' Marie felt the need to twist the knife into her sister. To punish her. 'What was so bad that you felt you had to

Emma Lawson

lie about the first seven years of my life? And years of your own life.' She would let Kevine have that small mercy at least – an admission that what had happened before Beauty from Ashes, whatever it was, hadn't just happened to her.

Kevine looked up at her through red, broken eyes.

'Well? Like you said, you came all this way. Now talk.'

'He was a DJ on a local radio station.' It wasn't just Marie who couldn't bring herself to say *father*. 'When the civil war started, he just got ... madder. He came home stinking of alcohol, muttering things about Hutu Power, and cockroaches coming to take back our country and make us their servants again.' She looked up at the rafters and sucked in a tense breath. 'The beatings began. He started with mother. She never cried. She never tried to run. She just ... stood there and took it. A black eye. A bleeding lip. Sometimes I saw her walking around holding her side, as if she'd broken a rib. She probably had.'

Marie saw her mother in the driveway at Beauty from Ashes again. How she'd looked vacant as Mama told her about her duties, piglets dashing and scurrying about their feet. How she'd looked so blankly at Marie as Marie had laughed along with the others. It was almost as if she'd looked straight through her, unwilling or incapable of anything else. Her eyes had been empty. What had she emptied herself of?

'When the RPF crossed the border, he got even madder. He didn't stop with mother; he turned on us, too. Beating us with belts. Kicking us in the stomach until we couldn't breathe. Punching us until our whole bodies were bruised. I was so terrified I wet the bed at

The Shadow Beyond the Hills

night. Then he'd beat me for that.' Kevine's voice cracked again and her mouth twisted, tears pooling in her eyes.

Darkness was closing in on Marie, suffocating her.

'I came home from collecting wood one morning and he was holding your head down ... in a huge cooking pot. I screamed. I thought it was boiling porridge.' She choked on her sobs for a moment. 'I ran up and saw that it was water. He was holding your head in that water for so long. I thought he'd killed you, because you went limp. I tried to grab his arms. I clawed at him, but he was too strong—'

'Didn't mother try to stop him?' Marie felt stupid as soon as the words left her mouth. She just wanted to say something, anything, to make Kevine stop.

'Of course not. She just stood by and watched it all. And I despised her for it. I was too young to understand, and I was too stubborn to try to understand for years. Now I see that she didn't have a choice.' Kevine wiped her eyes and nose, blinking back tears. 'What could she have done? She didn't have the chances we've had since then.'

Marie felt her mother's eyes on her again – walking from classes in her Beauty from Ashes uniform.

'When the President's plane got shot down, he was out all day with the other killers. At roadblocks. In bars. In a way, it was a relief for me. I knew he'd be too busy killing our neighbours and hunting people down in the village to hurt us. Everyone saw him. It was only a matter of time before he got found out. Years too late, but his past caught up with him eventually.'

Marie tried to understand how she'd lived through a genocide that had been blotted from her memory.

While everyone else had had to live with the horror.

'When you woke up in hospital after the accident and didn't recognise anyone but me ... And didn't ask for mother, or talk of our home, I—'

'Lied about everything.'

Kevine buried her face in her hands and wept again. 'I saw a way that I could erase the past. I couldn't forget, but you could. You did. Who wouldn't want to forget? Why would I make you re-live our miserable lives? I saw what Mama Judy could offer us and the new lives we could live.' Kevine stared at the empty serving containers in the canteen bar, her eyes brimming and bloodshot.

'And mother? She couldn't forget. How did you protect her?'

'At the time, I didn't care. In my eyes she'd allowed it to happen, so I shut her out. I didn't want to know. All I cared about was that I didn't end up like her. Weak, used, useless.'

'So, you ignored her?'

'I had to. I never wanted her to come anywhere near Beauty from Ashes, but Mama ... she couldn't leave her to starve.'

At Beauty from Ashes, they'd never missed a meal. She only knew that others did when Mama gave thanks and said grace, asking the Lord to fill hungry bellies and rain down his mercy upon his children.

Looking again at Kevine, Marie couldn't see any bags with her. 'Where are you staying tonight?'

'I was just going to find a guesthouse.'

'At this hour?' Marie was still reeling, but the intense heat of her anger had cooled enough for her to see that Kevine was alone and vulnerable in an unfamiliar city at night.

'Come with me. You're not going to walk the streets alone now,' said Marie, her voice hard and gritty.

Wordlessly, Kevine followed her to the university guesthouse. Marie could feel Kevine's eyes on her as she trailed behind. She was assaulted by fresh thoughts of her father, who'd been nothing but a dark outline of menace. Now, she pictured him holding her head down in a cooking pot full of water. She tried to remember, searching her mind for any scrap, any trace of recollection, but it was like grasping air. She couldn't get any purchase on a past before Beauty from Ashes. Even her earliest memories there were obscure.

Once in the lobby of the guesthouse she wrote hers and Kevine's names on a piece of paper and left it on the front desk, along with the little money she had on her. She turned and walked back out into the cloying warmth of night without saying a word.

Marie woke up with a wet cheek, her pillow damp with tears she'd cried in her sleep. When a knock startled her, she knew who would be standing outside her door. Kevine was never going to jump straight back on a bus to Kigali the next morning. Not when she'd won a small victory the previous night, despite taking the full brunt of Marie's pain and anger.

'Why are you still here? Why can't you leave me alone? Don't you have business back in Kigali?'

Kevine smiled weakly. 'My business runs itself when I want it to.' She handed her the money that Marie had left on the front desk of the guesthouse. 'You walked away before I could give this back to you. I wanted to thank you and tell you that I didn't need it.'

Marie left Kevine's outstretched arm dangling in the space between them. She didn't need it either.

Kevine shrugged and placed the money back in her handbag. 'I run a fashion boutique in the city now.'

Marie remained silent, determined not to give away any more of herself. She'd already given away too much.

'I'm working with a new in-house designer, Analise. She's brilliant – just what the business needs.'

'Good for you,' replied Marie.

'Marie, please. Don't be like this. Let us make peace,' Kevine pleaded.

'Peace?' Marie swallowed back the bile in her throat. 'Peace comes from telling the truth.'

'I did—'

'Five years later. And only because you had to. And now you expect healing to come from one night of conversation?'

Kevine shifted on her sequined shoes. 'Marie, you shut me out for years. How could I have had more than that one conversation with you? You tell me.' The tears had dried from her eyes now and her face was resolute. There was none of the unhinged emotion from the previous night, and this gave Marie a small sense of ease. There was a safer distance between them.

'Can you at least tell me where I can get a decent breakfast around here? Kampala is mad, and I'm lost.'

Marie took her to a café on Makerere Hill Road, where she ordered a couple of omelettes wrapped in chapatis and sat stoic before her.

'They know how to make a good rolex here,' said Kevine.

They ate in silence for a while. Just being with Kevine had left her feeling raw and exposed – something she'd only felt on her trip to Gulu.

Kevine tried again to get Marie to talk. Marie threw back piecemeal bites of conversation, and this only to show her sister that she'd done well without her: what exams she'd taken; where she'd done her electives; how long it would take to get her certificate from the university and her licence from the medical council; what she intended to specialise in. It used to feel so natural and effortless talking to her sister, when they'd giggled over Paul's awkward adolescent advances, analysed the latest crop of volunteers to the centre or dissected the newest teacher at the school. A rush of yearning broke through and consumed her. She ached for that affection now.

Kevine sipped her tea and stole tentative looks at her sister. 'Our mother would be proud of you, Marie. She's pretty sick, you know. That's also why I came here.'

Marie had never wondered what her mother thought of her. She hadn't let herself.

Kevine cocked her head to one side. 'Come visit her with me.' Her bracelets jangled on her wrist as she lay her hands palm upward on the table.

Marie bristled. 'I don't know her. I never have.'

'Doesn't mean to say you can't.'

CHAPTER TWENTY-FIVE
REMEMBRANCE

Marie stared out of the bus window watching the Ugandan countryside race by. Like water circling a drain, she'd been pulled in by the whirlpool Kevine had stirred. It was unstoppable now – a force she could no longer resist. They were on their way to Kigali. With lectures and exams over, there was a brief lull before graduation and applications to hospitals for an internship. *There is a time for everything*, Mama had often quoted. Now was the time.

They took the early morning bus. Kevine looked across at her as the hours passed with a hopeful look on her face. Marie silently registered each look but kept her focus on the rolling patchwork of farmland and the towns they drove through. The road was hemmed in by hills on either side of them as they approached the Gatuna border crossing. Her stomach lurched. She hadn't been in Rwanda for the five years that she'd been studying at Makerere. Her course sponsors had always met her in Kampala.

The Shadow Beyond the Hills

A line of people queued up outside the immigration office, while a group of abazungu sat on benches holding passports and immigration documents, red-faced and sweaty. The bus jerked to a stop, allowing everyone to join the queue to immigration. The sun was directly above them now. Marie wilted in its blistering heat.

'Have you got your ID card?' ventured Kevine.

'Of course I have. Do you think I'd come this far without it?' Marie knew Kevine was treading carefully. She'd already crossed a border there was no going back from. Kevine had got what she'd wanted.

They presented their ID cards, walked around the border gate and got back on the bus, which then took them on the main road to Kigali. The hills banked more steeply as they meandered through lush green valleys. Swollen storm clouds closed in on them as they reached the city. It had changed so much in five years: new hotels reared up from the hills and Kigali City Tower stood tall and proud over them all. The traffic moved in more or less regular, unhurried rhythms, and palms lined the roads, unsullied by mounds of rubbish.

'They banned minibuses and trucks from the city centre. Only cars, official city buses and motos are allowed now,' said Kevine.

There were fewer slum areas than there were before she'd left for Kampala. 'Looks like they're trying to clean up the city.'

'Yes. They can't have it looking shabby for visitors.' Kevine let out a circumspect laugh.

The bus rolled into Nyabugogo bus park, where bands of men held up baskets of bananas, bread rolls and roasted peanuts. Travellers made their purchases through the bus windows. Marie bought a bag of peanuts and let their salty taste linger on her tongue as they wandered off to find motos to take them to Kevine's apartment. Kevine looked at her as she shoved another handful of peanuts in her mouth. Marie tied up the end of the bag and placed it in her backpack for later.

Kevine's apartment in Kiyovu was bright and well kept, every wall decorated with a lively spread of fabrics, bowl murals, and imigongo paintings. Kevine offered her a Fanta and showed her to her room, where Marie slept for the rest of the day, her body and mind shattered.

She was woken by a sharp crack of thunder. She got out of bed and gazed at the winking lights of the city. It was such a colossal, intimidating place when she'd first set foot here as a child on a trip with volunteers at Beauty from Ashes, before she'd encountered the crazy urban sprawl that was Kampala.

So much had changed since then. *She* had changed. She'd lived life at New Beginnings constantly on the edge, a grenade ready to blow. She didn't care who got caught in the shrapnel. Mama Judy didn't dare visit. She'd cut Kevine out of her life like cancer. Linde had broached the subject of her biological mother numerous times to discuss the possibility of reintegrating into the community again and being rehabilitated with her mother. She'd had several rounds of medical, psychological and emotional assessments with social workers and a provisional resettlement care plan had been put in place. Marie had shut it down each

The Shadow Beyond the Hills

time. All she'd wanted was to focus on her studies and get out, get away. She'd stared at the shiny Makerere University prospectus as if it were a portal, and had carefully cut out the Medical School pages, tacking them on the wall above her desk as she studied by candlelight when the power went out. The first year of Medical School both opened her mind to new possibilities and sealed her shut at the same time. No one would get struck by shrapnel because she wouldn't let anyone get close enough to pull the pin.

And now here she was in pieces in Kevine's apartment, on her way to visit her forgotten mother, a shadow beyond the hills. Heavy drops of rain pelted the window now. Feeling neither hungry nor inclined to see Kevine, she got back into bed, tucked her mosquito net under her mattress and pulled the blankets up to her chest. She lay awake the rest of the night, raw and exposed, while the sky split itself open.

'Marie, are you awake? It's 9:30 a.m. I've left some tea outside your door, okay?'

Marie grunted a monosyllabic reply. Bright rays of sunlight poured into the room. Never had she slept in so late. She waited until Kevine padded away and grabbed her mug of tea, draining it in a few greedy gulps that scorched her throat. The heat of the tea mixed with the acid in her stomach. Nausea swept over her. She paced the room, not knowing what to do with herself.

She considered getting on a bus and going back to Kampala but threw on some clothes, ran a comb through her tangled hair and met Kevine in the living room.

'Are you ready?' Kevine looked askance at her slapdash choices. Kevine was dressed for the catwalks she'd always talked about, but Marie had given no thought to the clothes she'd put on. All she'd been able to do was picture her mother's non-descript face, willing it to form into something familiar so she could mentally rehearse the day – how she would greet her and what she would say. But no words came, and no familiar face appeared before her.

'Come on. Let's go,' said Kevine.

They took motos to Nyabugogo bus park, the city flying past her at an alarming speed. Everything was moving too fast. Kevine came back from the ticket office and led her to a clean white bus bound for Ruhengeri.

'You should sit up front. You get sick on these roads,' said Kevine.

Marie ignored her and sat in one of the back seats. A roll of sweet bread kept her nausea at bay as they snaked around the hills, which rose to even greater heights beyond the city. She couldn't sit still the whole way. The last time she'd been on this road had been when she'd been running the opposite way, frightened and alone, her belly swelling with unfolding life and then bleeding out into nothing. How was it that she could remember the cold, hard metal of the trucks she'd held on to, but not her mother's face? Why was her brain failing her again when she needed it most? Her face creased and ached with the effort of remembrance.

Volcanoes loomed before them as the bus drove through Ruhengeri town, its peaks shrouded in mist that looked immovable. The bus dropped them off in a

The Shadow Beyond the Hills

park just off the main street. Marie lost her footing as she stepped onto the hard gravel beneath, but Kevine grabbed her arm and steadied her.

They took motos further out of town, past fields of potatoes and luminous green tea plantations. It began to jog her memory again: Mugisha reading *Harry Potter* to her; the bitter taste of tangawizi and the vile igisura paste his grandmother had ground for her when her body was weak; volunteers teaching her volleyball in the basketball court at Beauty from Ashes; Paul's beautiful body in her dormitory room and how her skin rose to his touch. Memories kept tumbling out in no particular order, falling, echoing around her. They poured out of her now like the marbled beans she'd peeled with Mama Mugisha in their courtyard. Beatrice, her mother, stood in the driveway again, looking straight at her, her face still nebulous. She had a name but no shape. No personality. No meaning.

The motos pulled off the main road and took them down a stony track studded with little boulders which they had to swerve to avoid. Marie nearly bounced off the seat. Every bump jostled her insides, rattled her. They continued on that track and others like it for a while before coming to a stop outside a cluster of compounds walled in by volcanic rock and surrounded by a bountiful crop of carrots and cabbages.

Marie paid her moto driver and watched him chug back up the stony track, wishing for a moment that he could take her back with him. *No – there's a time for everything.* She couldn't imagine how her mother, who Kevine said was expecting them, would react. Why did she care to see a daughter who'd ran away from her and avoided her for the majority of her life? She should be hurt. Angry, even. Maybe Kevine had brought her here to face up to what she rightfully deserved. Perhaps that was her plan.

A clap came from behind her. She turned and saw her mother's hand pressed against her chest, her face split wide open with the biggest smile Marie had ever seen.

'Umukobwa wanje! Imana ishimwe!' She ran up to Marie and pulled her in with bony arms, her leathered skin stretched taut as she held her daughter with the tightest possible grip.

Marie crumpled under the surprising force of it, stunned and confused.

Her mother took her by the hand and led her to a small fenced courtyard, swept to smooth perfection. Marie stole a backward glance at Kevine and saw a look of pure delight spreading over her face. Once in the courtyard, her mother rushed over to a house helper, gave her some instructions for lunch and then showed Marie her livestock. She had several animals but no pigs or piglets. *Good.* Her mother's unabashed smile and wild gesticulations exuded pride. Gone was the vacant emptiness in her eyes. In its place was a delicate, fragile exuberance for life. For her. Blood rushed to her head. She was discovering bizarre, inexplicable layers to a mother she'd never really known.

'Mother's part of a cooperative,' said Kevine, still smiling. 'She's doing well for herself now, as you can see. She saved and bought this piece of land several years ago and then had this house built.'

Marie could see. She was glad. She'd tried not to think about her mother over the years and what her life was like. A deep pang of guilt filled her at the thought

The Shadow Beyond the Hills

of her apathy and indifference, but her mother's elation broke through it like rays of sunshine through thick mist.

'Come with me, my daughters,' her mother said. She couldn't stop smiling. She took Marie and Kevine into the dark interior of her house and motioned for them to take a seat in the living room while she prepared lunch.

'I think she's going to have one of her goats slaughtered now,' said Kevine.

A high-pitched bleat followed by a strangled, guttural sound pierced the air for a moment, confirming Kevine's prediction. Marie knew enough about rural life to know that people typically slaughtered their livestock a few times each year; some only once a year. She shrank in her seat – she didn't deserve this hospitality. This honour. She'd return the honour by graciously receiving it. That had to be the first step in navigating a relationship she didn't have any grounding in. There was no textbook for this. No detailed diagrams or instructions. Her feet felt like they barely touched the ground, and she could still hear blood whooshing around her ears. Bewildered and perplexed, she reached for one of the Cokes that her mother had brought in and placed on the bare wooden table in front of them. Every time her mother brought in a dish for lunch and placed it on the table in steaming bowls, she gushed with delight. Each and every one was a gift to Marie: the cubed, sautéed potatoes she'd cooked in oil, garlic and tomato paste, sliced cabbages and carrots, sweet potato, cassava, roasted maize and beans – all grown and harvested on her own land. Hints of skewered meat sizzling away outside drifted into the house. Marie ached for it. She let herself ache with new thoughts and feelings. For the past and for the future.

Her mother placed the last couple of dishes in front of them: a stack of freshly cooked goat brochettes on one tray, and crispy pieces of rabbit meat on the other. It was too much food. It was all too much. Bowing her head in prayer, her mother intoned loud and laboured shouts of thanks to God – for the food of her harvest and God's mercy and kindness in bringing her daughters to her. She closed the prayer in breathy whispers that Marie couldn't understand, her voice becoming throatier, interrupted by hacking coughs.

Kevine flinched beside her.

As they sat in the bosom of their mother's home, a peculiar and unexpected energy flowed through the room and raised the hair on Marie's skin. She looked at her mother, who was still deep in wordless prayer, and shivered.

Finally, her mother sat with them and spooned out generous helpings of each dish on everyone's plates. Her hands shook with the effort and the feeble flaps of skin under her upper arms jiggled about.

'I thank God you are with us now, Marie,' said her mother. 'God is good.' She coughed again, her face momentarily pinched in pain.

Questions that Marie had stashed inside her over the years spilled out now. 'Why did you let me forget you?'

Kevine went rigid beside her.

Her mother's peaceful expression didn't waver, as Marie expected it to. 'I had no money to raise you. I had nothing. All I had were bruises and broken bones.' Her chest rattled between breaths. 'I tried to manage, but when your father was taken away, I couldn't see a path

The Shadow Beyond the Hills

forward. You were always smiling and laughing when you were in Mama Judy's compound.' Her laugh turned into a coughing fit. They sat in silence while she fought for breath. 'We were on our way there when the moto crashed.'

'I still don't understand. Why didn't you make me remember you? You were still my mother – that hadn't changed.'

Her mother sucked in another strenuous breath. 'She said it was the loving thing to do. She said that to love someone was to let them go, if that's what was best for them. Our children aren't ours – they're on loan to us from God. So, I let you go. I let you forget. I'm sorry, my daughter.' Her eyes watered.

Kevine stared at her plate.

'When Mama Judy talked to me about the abazungu who lived in Kigali, she said they would pay for the school fees. That's why I signed the forms she gave me.' Shame shadowed her features. 'I kept them. I can read them now!' Shame gave way to pride. Her mother darted off to another room and brought the forms back with her, placing them in between Marie and Kevine.

Marie scanned the paper with its Beauty from Ashes logo at the top. Hers and Kevine's names were marked in bold print on the front page, as well as their date of birth, and the names of the district and province they were born in. There were sections about welfare, education and consent. Her mother's signature was scrawled at the end of the page. Marie's head and eyes clouded with heat as the words swam in and out of view and became a muddled mess. She trembled in her seat. *How dare she.*

With a sharp intake of breath, she walked with weak

legs over to her mother, knelt before her, and pulled her so close that all she could see and smell was her mother's musty igitenge dress – the most beautiful thing in the world. Now they would never have to let each other go.

Tears streamed down her mother's smiling face. 'Eh, eh, my child, my precious Marie. It's okay.' Her soft hands stroked Marie's hair.

Marie wept.

Her mother unwrapped Marie's arms from her frail body. She started singing a traditional song, swaying to its rhythm and clapping her hands. She beckoned Marie and Kevine to join her.

Marie pulled herself to her feet and danced with her mother, her appetite sated and her heart full. The weight of years lifted off her like water evaporating in the sun. A slice of peace. Home. Heaven.

CHAPTER TWENTY-SIX
GRADUATION

A heady mixture of heat and happiness filled the marquee. Special honourees, dignitaries and officials walked the red carpet to the front while Marie and her fellow students assembled behind them, all dressed in black caps and gowns with strips of green and red streaked across them. Marie sat next to Sanyu and smiled at the smart length of him as he sat tall in his seat. Further down the row, Miremba glowed in her gown. Marie relaxed into her chair, basking in the joyous result of late nights, early morning starts and five years of study so intense she thought her brain would burst. It had all been worth it.

The University Vice-Chancellor opened the ceremony and gave his opening speech. Marie waited for the preceding students to collect their degrees, her body mellow and still, while others shifted restlessly in their seats. She'd waited a long time for this moment. She wished her mother could be here, but the journey was too long and arduous. She would visit her mother again soon – tomorrow, perhaps. For Marie, the journey to Ruhengeri didn't seem anywhere near as far as it once had – the love she'd uncovered like lost treasure melted the miles between them. And all it had taken was acceptance; more than that – the knowledge that her mother wanted her despite how she'd been treated. Where she'd expected judgement, she'd found only peace. Where she'd expected her mother to turn away from her, she'd been embraced. Marie had been crushed by shame for years, but the weight had been lifted, and she could breathe again. She wasn't just cared for by a guardian; she was loved by a mother.

'Umony, Sanyu, for the degree of Bachelor of Medicine and Bachelor of Surgery,' said the Vice-Chancellor, his voice resonating with gravitas as he surveyed the students.

The Dean of Faculty beckoned Sanyu towards the raised platform to collect his degree certificate.

Sanyu gave Marie's hand a final squeeze and walked up the central aisle to the platform. He held his hands out in front of him, palms together.

The Vice-Chancellor clasped Sanyu's hands. He walked to the opposite end of the platform, collected his certificate and descended the steps.

With Sanyu out of his seat, Marie could see Miremba a little better. Even when tamed under her graduation cap, her hair was a shock of tightly coiled and oiled curls. She'd found out that Miremba had passed her final exams with distinction, achieving over eighty-five per cent. She was brilliant, as well as beautiful.

Marie had passed her exams, but barely. She'd set out to get nothing less than a solid pass, rather than a 'scraping through' pass, but that didn't matter now. It neither added nor removed anything from her. It was entirely outside of her, and, other than being a formality that allowed her to practise medicine, was completely incidental and peripheral. She was loved.

'Uwimana, Marie, for the degree of Bachelor of Medicine and Bachelor of Surgery.'

Startled out of her stupor, Marie rose from her seat and walked the hallowed path down the central aisle, aware of rows of eyes watching her. The Vice-Chancellor looked her warmly in the eyes and clutched her hands in his. She bowed her head and walked down the steps. The degree certificate was light and inconsequential in her hand now that she held it, but what it allowed her to do made her heart quicken.

Marie took her seat next to Sanyu, beaming all the satisfaction and relief she felt in one sideways smile. She was a medical school graduate now. Dr Marie Uwimana MBChB. Known and loved.

The postgraduate students were next up to receive their awards, followed by the doctoral students. The doctoral students' outfits were garish, somehow both ridiculous and spectacular. Finally, the guest speaker gave his speech, his closing words prompting deafening applause. Marie's hands ached from all the clapping. As they got up to leave the marquee, a thunderous rapture of shouting, dancing and drumming blasted her ears. They walked in an orderly procession, certificates in hand, between two rows of singers and dancers, the women dressed in imishanana-style dresses and strappy

Emma Lawson

vests, and the men wearing mint green shirts and black waistcoats and trousers. The dancing was similar to the intore dancers she'd seen in ceremonies in Rwanda. Mama Judy had brought them in to Beauty from Ashes to dance for special occasions, such as the opening of a new school building or training centre within the compound. The dancers had been at a ceremony that Linde had arranged at New Beginnings when she and her cohort of sponsored kids had passed their national exams to get into university. The women dancing them through the graduation ceremony finale made the same elegant swooping motions with their arms and hands. The men bent down and then jumped, their knees reaching up to their chests, swinging their arms in circles either side of their bodies. Some of the men beat ngoma drums with long, thick sticks, and some waved bead-lined shakers.

When they reached the end of the procession, a throng of guests welcomed the new graduates. Hugs and gifts were exchanged. Marie was blinded by white dots flashing in her eyes. Out of the morass of people and colour and noise, came Kevine. She gave a happy shout and ran at Marie with her arms stretched wide, beaming a dazzling a smile at her. Marie was powerless to resist. She let herself become enfolded within Kevine's tight grip. Peace flowed in the channels that had been carved out by her mother. What was the point in holding on to her anger with Kevine? It was just another hard and heavy thing to carry around with her. She was tired of it.

'I had to see my sister graduate medical school! Congratulations, Dr Uwimana,' said Kevine.

A choir started to sing behind them.

The bar was thumping with heavy bass as they walked in. Marie tottered painfully on a pair of high heels that Kevine had given her as a graduation gift. Thin, bejewelled straps cut right into the sides of her ankles, but they were the latest, and most expensive, of Kevine's designs and she'd only just displayed them in her boutique in Kigali. It was like being given a prize cow from a farmer. Kevine had stayed for a few hours after the ceremony but then had to get back to Kigali, leaving Marie to celebrate with Sanyu and several others from her course. She'd decided to give Vibe a miss, so they headed to a mall in the city that was home to a new bar. Marie bought a round of drinks, ordering a minty, lime-tinged mocktail for herself to start the night off slowly. She wanted to be in control. To enjoy the new feelings she was experiencing, rather than drink them away. She also wanted to ensure that if *he* was there, she'd be in possession of herself.

All the tension of pre-exam stress flooded out of her chest, down her legs and out onto the floor. She'd never been this happy. She could take on anything. Miremba joined them on the dancefloor, her lips glistening with red lipstick that made them look like a juicy sliver of watermelon sliced down the middle. Oh, how she wanted to take a bite. She could almost taste the sweetness.

Almost, but not quite.

'If someone wants to drink from a poisoned cup, that's their choice. They know the consequences here,' Natalie, a girl in her halls, had said when they'd been talking late into the night in her room over mugs of Waragi. David Kato had just been bludgeoned outside his house in Kampala, and his name was becoming a byword for what could happen. In Rwanda, it was never talked about. It was the taboo of all taboos. Marie understood that now, as an adult. In Uganda, it was the kiss of death. Those who advocated for equal rights paid in blood, beatings, fines, imprisonment.

'Homosexuality is un-African. It's come from Western culture – the filth of their films, TV, magazines. We don't want it forced on us,' Natalie had added.

'Rubbish,' another girl had retorted. 'That's a myth. It happened before as it happens now. No one can honestly deny that. It was only condemned when the colonisers came, and their missionaries before them.' Marie hadn't made any contribution to these nocturnal ramblings. She didn't feel like she knew anything – other than what she felt. She just listened, drinking Waragi to numb the confusion that fractured her.

A new song came on and more shouts erupted from the crowd. Marie turned away from Miremba and let the punishing pain of her new shoes rein in her thoughts. A few gulps from a glass of Cointreau mixed with fresh tangerine juice instantly numbed the pain. She picked out the sprig of basil leaves floating on a light layer of foam and finished the rest.

'Where'd you go, girl?' Sanyu smiled. His hand hovered for an awkward second over her thigh. He placed it around the rim of his drink. His smile was strained. Their friendship was strained. They were both attracted to what they couldn't have.

'I'm heading back. I'll see you tomorrow, I guess.'

'Okay. See you, Sanyu.' Marie watched him leave,

knowing in all likelihood that their friendship would fizzle out when she left Kampala.

Her phone buzzed in her jean pocket. Kevine's name flashed up on the screen. Marie grabbed her clutch bag and went outside to take the call.

'Marie.' Kevine's voice crackled slightly over the phone.

'Hi. Are you okay?'

'Mother's dead.'

She rested her cheek against the window as the bus rolled into Ruhengeri. It was warm and stuffy inside the bus, but outside Marie saw men, women and children walking the pavements in woolly hats and coats with sweaters underneath. It was one of those rainy season days where no matter how many layers you wore, nothing took away the dank, heavy chill. Even the volcanoes pulled their dense foggy veils tight about their cones.

Kevine sat next to her, her body small and tense in her seat. They'd been silent for much of the journey. Marie noticed a glazed, glassy look in Kevine's eyes. It shouldn't have come as a surprise to either of them. She'd seen how weak her mother was. She'd heard the hacking cough and lungs that rattled as if they were a pair of bone-filled shakers. If, during their visit, Marie had been thinking as a doctor, she would have seen the signs. She would have taken her to King Faisal Hospital in Kigali rather than continue to let her be seen at a poorly staffed local clinic with scant resources. She would have received treatment for pneumonia at King

Faisal, even if it hadn't saved her. They would have tried, and Marie would be able to enter the burial site knowing she'd done all she could. But she hadn't been thinking as a medic. She'd been using all her mental energy to hold herself together.

After Kevine's phone call, she'd had all of one day before taking the Kampala–Kigali bus to meet Kevine and make the journey to Ruhengeri. One day to prepare a goodbye she'd never had the chance to say. One day to prepare herself to see her mother's body. Funerals took place with swift efficiency in rural areas – they had to when each day of decay at the nearest morgue accrued daily fees.

The bus dropped them off in its usual place, where Marie and Kevine made their way on motos to their mother's house. They were her only surviving family, so responsibility lay with them, especially Kevine, to decide the length of time for mourning, burial location and arrangements for the funeral. Marie didn't feel like she had any right to be involved in the decision making. Normally, people would have come to them to pay their respects, but Kevine had felt it right to gather at their mother's house, so that's what they did.

Marie was met by Odette, a small, sprightly woman and neighbour of her mother's, who led them into the house. A wall of stale air hit her. Everything felt static. Oppressive. The vibrancy of life that had been there when they'd eaten lunch, sang and danced together had been sucked out of it, and now all that was left was a vacuous shell. Odette had wrapped the body in a white shawl and laid it on a table, on which Kevine placed the flowers she'd brought with her: a spray of brightly coloured orchids, carnations and dahlias interspersed

The Shadow Beyond the Hills

with white roses. It wasn't enough to brighten the darkness of the room. Marie remembered the elation in her mother's face when they'd seen each other and tried to feel again the sheer force of her embrace. Her mother slipped through her memory now, weightless as air. She was starting to fade already. They'd held each other in this room no more than a week ago. Her mother had been fragile and unwell but nevertheless alive, buzzing with unbridled joy and love. Now, her wiry, lifeless body lay on the table in front of her, wrapped in cloth. A sudden sob wrenched itself free from Marie. Kevine stepped closer and rested her hand on Marie's arm. She leaned into Kevine, who cried with her, the two of them lost in mourning, given to grief.

Marie came back from town with a man wheeling a hulking great stack of firewood on his bike. Kevine had arranged for a crate of Fanta and some food to arrive. When the thick blanket of grey cloud above them was concealed by night and the crickets began their evening song, she and Kevine lit a fire of remembrance in the compound just behind the wall of volcanic rock. Mourners came to pay their respects, sharing stories and sipping Fanta while staring at the flames licking the sky. Marie was surprised by a feeling of envy – envy for the stories they could tell of her mother that she couldn't. Apart from a few sparse images of her at Beauty from Ashes and their reunion last week, all that washed up on the banks of her memory was foam, bubbling and bursting into nothing. She wished she could have stopped her mother from drowning in her own lungs.

She would have given anything to at least have been there so she knew she wasn't alone. The emptiness Marie feared returned.

They prayed and sang traditional mourning songs. Then everyone left. Some would return the next day, others, they wouldn't see again. Marie didn't care. They could all go and not come back.

They slept that night in one of the rooms of their mother's house, huddling together in the one bed to keep warm, a pair of fledgling birds in a threadbare nest. Thick cloud and days of heavy rain in the Northern Province made it hard to keep warm in normal circumstances, let alone in a house where a corpse rested. Marie pulled the thin blanket up to her face and blew her warm breath into it, but nothing brought relief. Deathly cold reached in and froze her through to her bones. She eventually fell asleep to steady drops of rain hitting the roof and a faint whisper of her mother, her prayers hoarse and rasping.

She woke the next morning with stiff and aching joints. Kevine had set the date for the burial, which was to be the next day, so another official day of mourning stretched out before her. The thought of Mama Judy turning up panicked her. Beauty from Ashes would be where it always was, just out of town, on the way into Ruhengeri in the shadow of the volcanoes. Marie hadn't asked Kevine whether she'd visited her. She didn't want to know. She didn't even know if Mama Judy was still in the country or whether she'd gone back to America, but the thought of her visiting their mother's house and

The Shadow Beyond the Hills

seeing them, or bumping into her in town, still panicked Marie. If it weren't for Mama Judy, she'd have had more time with her mother – not peripherally, not skirting around the edges of each other, as they had been at Beauty from Ashes – but actually together. She'd have remembered her after the accident, if she'd been helped to, she was sure of it. She'd re-learnt so many other things. She could have re-learnt the soft lilt in her mother's voice and traced the features of her face like landmarks on a forgotten map. She could have.

Wary and tense, Marie left Kevine to arrange some details for the following day's burial service. She turned out of the compound and saw Odette stoking the fire from the previous night. She wanted to keep it burning throughout the mourning period, but more firewood and coal was needed, so Marie headed to the shop on the corner where the stony track met the main road. It was so pathetic, really – a feeble old fire to remember a life. Marie thought of all the suffering her mother had been through. Was it outweighed in the end by joy? Had it been worth the pain? Her mother had prayed and given thanks like it was. Marie held on tightly to this rope of comfort before it could be pulled away. She was flanked on her right by fields of potatoes, carrots and cabbages. Her mother had laboured over these crops through the years, but nothing would raise her body from the ground once it was buried. The fertility of the volcanic soil wouldn't stretch to saving the hands that tilled it.

The atmosphere was still damp and cold. All it was good for was slowing her mother's decomposition. Marie quickened her pace. As she rounded a bend past some eucalyptus trees, their fresh scent soothing her, a woman called out to her in a happy, booming voice. She followed the direction of the voice and saw a large, stocky woman in a purple and yellow igitenge dress. She rushed toward Marie, her bulky frame wobbling as she tore around some trees and rocks to get closer.

'You're her, aren't you? You're Marie!'

Marie bristled in suspicion, riled at how this stranger knew of her and her name.

'She knew you would come back to her. She came to our church and prayed every day. Imana ishimwe.' She greeted Marie eagerly, holding her upper arms and nearly bowling her over with her strength. 'She said you're a doctor now. She was so proud and happy to have seen you before she left this world. So happy.'

Marie told her how they had lit a fire of remembrance in the compound if she'd like to go, and that there was food and Fanta there. She would be welcome at the burial service tomorrow. Marie wanted her mother to be celebrated, honoured, respected. She wanted these small offerings to give meaning to what seemed meaningless. To make sense of the senseless.

At the shop on the corner, she arranged for a stack of firewood and sack of coal to be taken to the compound and bought bags of mandazi and sambusa to share with Kevine and Odette. She walked home thinking of her mother going out into the surrounding fields and cultivating day after day, always hoping, never giving up. Keeping the fire burning.

Her mother lay in a closed casket with a small window above her face. Enough to see that her soul had gone,

The Shadow Beyond the Hills

and that all that was left was the cold casing of her body. Marie had worked on cadavers as part of her medical training. She was acquainted with the deceased. She knew that upholding her doctorly duty to save and preserve life meant confronting death. But this was different. This wasn't a stranger – this was her mother. The waxy pallor already setting in sickened her.

Kevine was shocked and silent from preparing the body and putting the burial clothes on her mother – an outfit she'd made from the finest materials in Kigali. Marie had made a brief visit to see it at Kevine's boutique before they got the bus together from Nyabugogo. Several people from the village filed in and out during the morning to peer in at her mother's face, which was as still and hard as the mannequins in Kevine's boutique. They continued the ceremony at the burial site in the compound of the church their mother had worshipped in.

There was no music or dancing. The silence was broken only by the reading of scripture. The lady Marie had met on the track the previous day held a Bible open in her large hands and read:

> *'A father to the fatherless, a defender of widows, is God in his holy dwelling. God sets the lonely in families, he leads out the prisoners with singing, but the rebellious live in a sun-scorched land.'*

> *'Those who hope in the Lord will renew their strength. They will soar on wings like eagles; they will run and not grow weary; they will walk and not be faint.'*

They lowered the casket into the ground and

covered it with soil. Marie felt herself sinking deeper. She wanted to believe that she'd see her mother again one day; that their reunion last week wouldn't be their last. She grasped Kevine's hand and held onto the only living hope she had. A simple white cross was laid on the gravesite bearing neat little dates, the span and sum of her mother's life. Marie thought of what she would be reduced to one day, her name, date of birth and date of death inscribed on a cross or concrete headstone. They walked in a procession around the back of the church where a small marquee had been set up for testimonies and ceremonial hand washing. Kevine gave a testimony about her mother's grace, forgiveness and hard-working nature. Marie washed her hands and felt more than just the dirt of the day slide off her skin. She let the water seep into her pores and lathered up the soap, working it into her hands until they were sore. Feeling fresh and cleansed, Marie stayed at her mother's graveside for several hours after the last of the guests had returned to their homes. She even asked Kevine to leave her. She knew that in the years to come, her mother, Beatrice, would be forgotten by her community. People didn't tend to visit the grave unless they were family members and even then, not everyone did. But Marie would. She wouldn't let her mother be forgotten. She would remember.

CHAPTER TWENTY-SEVEN
STRONGER

The life Marie thought she'd lived was birthed in a hospital room in the Northern Province. Now, she found herself in hospital yet again – suturing wounds, checking vital signs, bringing healing to hurting people. There was no artifice or deception in this healing. It was all blood and bone, nerves and neurons. Things you could monitor and measure. She felt full of purpose, sanctified in scrubs and gloved hands, and no one would ever take that away from her. Even her mother's death hadn't taken that away from her. There was hope in healing.

Her alarm woke her just after sunrise. Marie padded down the white tiled stairs of the house she shared with Courtney, an American woman of similar age, who was working with a medical NGO assisting with research in the Paediatric department at King Faisal.

'Would you like a coffee? I picked up these beans from Bourbon yesterday,' said Courtney, throwing her blonde hair over her shoulder. 'It's a lovely light roast. I think these are from …' Her voice trailed off as she looked at the back of the packet. '… yes, a plantation near Muhazi.'

'Thanks,' said Marie, taking the cup Courtney handed to her. Marie hadn't slept much the previous night. Her throat was dry, her head groggy, and she was already thinking about what the day ahead would demand of her. She was provisionally registered as an intern by the Rwanda Medical and Dental Council and needed to complete one year before she'd get her registration and medical licence. But at least she was here, back in Kigali, defying the 'brain drain' she'd been told so much about.

Courtney purred and smacked her lips together. 'Damn, this is good. They don't make 'em like this in Cali. How is it that your country is known only for genocide and gorillas?' A flicker of embarrassment puckered her face, a note of censure creeping into the last few words.

Perhaps it was only her, with her chequered memory, that knew her country for other things. She placed her cup on the counter and smiled at Courtney, trying to ease her discomfort. She may have spoken too quickly and too openly – she would come to learn the culture – but there was something endearing about her too. Marie couldn't help but like her. She spoke as brashly as the Ugandans she knew, but at least Marie knew that when she asked her a question, she'd get a plain answer.

'I think I need to devote a blog solely to Rwandan coffee.' She laughed, her perfect white teeth somehow unstained by all the coffee she drank.

Marie often helped her source food from the market

The Shadow Beyond the Hills

and had showed her that with a bottle of oil, a can of tomato paste, and a Maggi cube, you could make just about any typical national dish, while Courtney had introduced her to the words 'foodie' and 'blogosphere'.

Marie looked at her phone. 6 a.m. 'We should get going. Are you still giving me a lift to the hospital?'

'Sure!'

Marie nearly tripped over one of the sandy-coloured dogs roaming the compound. They would surely amass a whole pack at the rate at which Courtney accepted puppies that had been left outside their gate or thrown over the wall. Courtney's Landcruiser wound effortlessly around the maze of mud tracks to the road through Gasabo district. Marie and Courtney held up their lanyards and badges and were instantly waved through the entrance gate of the hospital. The familiar flurry of nerves and excitement flowed through her. It was still a daunting privilege to do this every day, but Marie knew she was where she was meant to be. The first few months of being thrown into the crucible of clinical medicine were tough but had melted away the doubts that began in a rural outreach clinic in Gulu. Doubts which arose from a scared young girl's pale, mottled face.

Marie was stronger now – until she thought of her mother lying in a grave in Ruhengeri. It started as a dull ache and, if left unchecked by distraction, grew into a knotted mass woven tightly around her chest. Why had it taken Kevine coming to tell her that their mother was ill for her to make the journey and see her? She could have spent so much more time with her. 'It's pointless dwelling on the *what ifs* and *if onlys*. It does you no good,' Courtney had said. 'Don't live your life in regret.' But they could have had more time together if she'd made different choices, and it stung to realise it.

They said their goodbyes for the day as Courtney clicked down the road in her heels and lab coat. Marie pushed through the main entrance of the country's largest hospital, ready to tackle the day. As an intern she had to take on all manner of tasks – tasks that weren't necessarily restricted to her current rotation. They all were all tributaries leading to one river of mission: heal the patient. If there was no one around to change an IV drip, she would do it. If there was no one around to empty a catheter bag, or tourniquet a serious trauma wound, she would do it. Whatever it took to turn a patient from disease and death to healing and life, she would do it – with whatever resources she had.

Dr Luwado, who'd been on call overnight, handed over to Marie.

'There's a new patient on Ward C who requires a blood test, and another in Ward B who requires a physical examination.' He didn't waste time explaining anything, simply turning and walking back down the corridor in his thick-heeled shoes.

Marie was relieved: the morning's duties were lighter than she'd expected. She got the jobs done within a couple of hours, paperwork included, and sent bloods off to the lab. She ate a quick snack in the canteen, signed some discharge letters from the previous week's patients, and then managed a few hours of studying between patients. Studying didn't end at graduation, but she'd known this. The reality was that exams never really ended for doctors who wanted to work their way up to consultant level in their chosen specialism. Though the sky darkened, her day didn't end with

The Shadow Beyond the Hills

dinner in the canteen. She was thinking of going to one of the quiet rooms for a restorative nap before the evening's round of checks on post-operative patients, when a consultant stopped her as she approached the top of the stairs.

'We have an acute referral from A&E on Ward D,' Dr Mpayimana said. 'Please decide if she needs an operation.' His white overcoat brushed the top of each step as he hastened down the stairs.

Marie tensed. She was being asked to make a decision way above her level. Did he know that she was a junior on her internship year? He must have done. So why give her this level of responsibility? She tried to walk the tension out in her steps as her feet pounded the corridor, batting away thoughts of inadequacy and failure.

Marie strode into Ward D and walked past the faded army green walls to the end of the room. When she pulled back the curtain, she stopped dead. Her heart dropped into her stomach. *This can't be happening.* The eyes that met hers widened in pained astonishment.

'Oh, my Lord. Marie … is that really you?' Mama Judy gasped. She raised her trembling hands and placed one back on her chest, grimacing. Her veiny white hands were speckled with sunspots. They were the hands of a much older woman now.

Marie couldn't process this. She wanted to turn and run back down the corridors and out of the hospital. She wanted to run far away and leave this woman in her hospital bed for another doctor to deal with. Anyone but her. But she couldn't. What excuse could she possibly come up with that would wash with her superiors? With the consultant? She tried to formulate some kind of plan, but her brain ceased to function. Again.

'Look at you! Oh my.' Mama Judy laughed, stiff as a sheet of new wax cloth. The laughter turned into a choked splutter. She grimaced again and rested her head on propped up pillows.

Marie peered down at her green scrubs and tried to compose herself. Her pulse still racing, she edged closer to the end of the bed to read the clipboard pegged onto the rails, making note of each of the patient's vital signs on the checklist. *Patient rushed into A&E with severe chest complaints and lethargy. BP: 140/90mmHg. Temperature: 38 °C.*

'Good evening. I'm Dr Uwimana. Can you describe your symptoms for me?' The hideous farce of it made her cringe inside, desperate as she was to reduce Mama Judy to a patient like any other. She had to do her duty. Fulfil her oath.

Mama Judy drew her wrinkled mouth up into an infuriating smile. She was going to play along. 'Well, I had these awful chest pains today. I mean, really bad – worse than it's ever been. I felt sick, faint and dizzy.' Her voice shook with senescence. 'I know my old ticker isn't doing so well these days, but today scared me.' The lines on her face were set into her skin like a cracked eggshell.

Always assume chest pains are cardiac in nature.

'Where is the pain? Can you point to it?'

She held up a doddering hand and made a broad sweep of her neck, chest and arms.

'Any shortness of breath?'

'Yes.'

'Is the pain intermittent or continuous?'

The Shadow Beyond the Hills

'It was intense and intermittent, but now there's a continuous dull ache.'

I know how you feel. 'Are you currently on any medications, and do you have any allergies?'

That maddening smile again. She shook her head, making the loose fold of skin on her neck wobble like a turkey's.

A range of options flew through Marie's head: oxygen therapy, chest X-ray, ECG, a blood test for troponin. First, she would perform another check of her vital signs and record them. She took Mama Judy's shaking upper arm and wrapped the blood pressure cuff around it, suppressing a shudder as their skin touched.

'Oh, sweetheart. Come on. Surely, after all these years, we can talk?'

Marie pressed her lips together. Her head inflamed with heat. 'I don't think here is appropriate. Not in your condition.'

'When is? You never came back to Beauty from Ashes. You refused to see me when you lived in Kigali. Now seems very appropriate to me, since we're in the same room together. I might not get this chance again.'

Not 'might not'. Won't.

'I never stopped thinking about you.' She picked up the silver locket hanging around her neck and rolled it between her frail fingers. 'You and your sister were my first children at Beauty from Ashes.'

'We were never *your* children.'

'No. You weren't. But I took you in, treated you like my own, since your father didn't, and your mother couldn't.' Her hands fumbled to open the locket, revealing a small photo of Marie on one side and some writing too small for her to read inscribed on the other.

'She couldn't provide, but she could still be a mother. She still was my mother.' Marie turned away from her. She couldn't bear to look at her or the locket.

'I know. I see that now. I just ... I saw how I could do something in that situation. It seemed like the right thing to do at the time. I thought I was doing the best by you kids.'

The ward was closing in on her. With her back still turned, Marie recorded Mama Judy's blood pressure on the clipboard at the end of the bed. Marie could hear her struggling for breath. Her blood pressure was still abnormally high. Marie checked her resting respiratory rate and saw that it had climbed. This wasn't right. Still, Marie pressed further. 'Why? Why did you feel like you had the right to make that decision for me?'

'When Jim died, after I'd taken early retirement to look after him, I didn't want to sit around and be someone's g-g-grandma for the rest of my life. Just another Memom ... An afterthought.' She paused for breath. 'In America, when you get old, you're a b-b-burden. It's not like here where you're respected and listened to and valued. To everyone other than your own family, you become invisible. I didn't w-want that. I didn't want to fade away like I was practically dead already. After the Mercy Aid trip in Congo, I knew I had more ... to give to this world.'

Marie checked Mama Judy's pulse again. It had accelerated. Her skin was clammy, colour leaving her face. She was disorientated. Senior staff should be informed immediately. She should call someone.

'When the g-genocide kicked off and left thousands of kids either dead or ... without parents, I knew I had to help. I could mobilise the money easily. That *was* the

The Shadow Beyond the Hills

good thing about being seen as a sss … sassy old Memom. I had the resources. I had the time. I had a heart for it …'

'Did you have a heart for my mother?' Marie needed to call someone. She should be doing it right now. 'She died. Did you know that? She died a few months ago. Did you ever tell her that I found out about her? That you told me? Or did you let her go on thinking that I'd forgotten her? That my own mother wasn't remarkable enough to free my memory?'

Mama Judy squinted a droopy eye at Marie in confusion, as if trying to work out where she was. One side of her mouth was pulled down. Her mouth hung open, twitching slightly, trying to form words.

Marie saw all the signs she needed to make a decision. The life of the old woman in front of her lay in her gloved hands. If she acted now.

'She could have still been a mother to me, and you took that away from us both. What does your white God think about that? You always talked about us needing to be saved by him. In morning assemblies. In evening devotions. The teams you sent – we must have been hopeless if they had to come every summer. Perhaps we just needed saving from you.'

Mama Judy looked as if she'd seen something terrifying. Marie saw it in the eye that wasn't drooping.

'Shh. Rest now, Mama.' Marie pulled her stethoscope back around her neck, pushed the curtain aside and walked out of the ward without looking back.

CHAPTER TWENTY-EIGHT
SOHO

'I propose a toast.' Anna's father raised his flute glass to the small gathering around him. Her mother stood next to him, holding his free hand and smiling up at him as they stood in the humid warmth of the marquee. It had been a wash-out summer, but today's weather had been kind to them. 'To fifty years of marriage so wonderful and beyond everything I could have hoped for. To my wife, who means as much to me as she did on our wedding day. For the children she gave me, and the memories we've made together.' He cleared his throat, eyes narrowing, lost in thought. 'To Carol!' A smile returned to his face.

'To Carol!' the guests echoed. A chorus of whistles and cheers rolled around the marquee.

Her mother looked visibly thin, barely filling out her red and white polka dot dress, but Anna noticed a serene look of contentment about her. It was unusual. Beautiful.

When the pitchers of Pimm's had been emptied and

The Shadow Beyond the Hills

trays of canapé cleared, all that was left of the garden party was immediate family: Jo and her family, Beth and her boyfriend, and Anna and Tim. They piled into the conservatory, looking out on the expansive lawn and beyond to the surrounding rapeseed fields of her parent's thatched cottage home. Anna's mother spooned out the centre of a devilled egg, occasionally looking around and smiling at her family.

'Ella,' she said, laughing. 'You've got to stop growing so tall! I can't keep up with it.'

Ella shifted on her feet and looked over at Jo, who gave a sympathetic nod of the head, as if urging her on.

'How's revision going? It's GCSEs for you this year, isn't it?' asked her mother.

'I passed them. I'm in my second year of uni now. Classics at Bristol,' replied Ella.

Her mother's eyes widened in alarm. 'Gosh. I can't believe how fast you're all ... growing up.'

Ella pressed her lips into a tight smile and slunk away to talk to Lucy, who was staring at her phone.

'Darling? This is Matt, Beth's fella,' said Anna's father.

Matt stepped forward and offered his hand. 'Pleased to meet you, Mrs Blacklock.'

Beth stifled a laugh. 'Very formal, Matthew.'

Her mother squinted at him, inspecting him, scrutinising him.

Poor guy. Anna remembered Beth's last boyfriend: a political aide Beth had met at a press conference. 'You aren't a bedfellow of that awful Blair chap, are you?' her mother had asked at a family gathering. He'd mumbled something about David Cameron and made polite small talk before, no doubt, planning his and Beth's exit as hastily as he could. It didn't matter in the end – Beth broke up with him a few months later. He didn't read enough, apparently, and he left beard trimmings all over her sink.

'Matt's a journalist and writer, Mum, like me,' said Beth. 'We've been dating for around a year now.' She blushed with pride. This was a major milestone for her. 'Matt's up for the British Journalism Award this year … Mum?'

'Oh. That's nice,' said her mother. She picked up the last vol-au-vent and placed it gingerly on her plate.

'Yes, best of luck with it, old chap, best of luck,' cut in her father. 'Maybe you can shake up the industry a bit. Replace the usual dross with some factual reporting for once, hey?'

'Yes, Dad.' Beth rolled her eyes and laughed.

Tim was quiet. He'd tolerated her family at the best of times. Now, with the threat of her mother's mercurial moods, he remained in complete silence unless spoken to.

'How's your course going, Anna?' This from Jo.

'Slowly. It's been hard to find the energy to complete assignments in between shifts. The owner refuses to take on more staff, so I'm left frantically trying to find cover when someone's off sick. Bloody nightmare.'

Jo gave her a consoling look, bordering on patronising.

'I only have the odd evening seminar to go to. It's mainly my dissertation that I'm working on now. Four years later.'

'Well, it's impressive that you've been able to juggle it all. Part-time distance learning can't be easy when you have a full-time job as well.'

Ben tugged on Jo's hand. 'I'm going to see if there's another bottle of Pimm's knocking about, love.' He gave her a wry smile and walked out to the cellar.

Jo tutted and shook her head, smiling, and turned her attention to Anna. 'I couldn't have done what you've done. When I was training to be a counsellor, I couldn't focus on anything else – partly because my brain turned to mush after years of full-time childcare, but also because I just couldn't think about working while studying. I don't multi-task so well!' She tucked strands of highlighted hair behind her ears, large pearl earrings hanging from them both.

'Lucky you! Some of us need to do both,' said Anna, smiling.

'Oh, I didn't mean it like that.' Jo gave her a playful push. 'Now, where's that Pimm's?' She walked off to find Ben.

A message flashed on Anna's phone. 'Hey, Anna. Fancy meeting before next week's seminar? When are you free? Mark.'

'I'll be back in a minute.' Anna left Tim at the mercy of her family and walked along the gravel inset of the front garden.

She texted back: 'I won't be going to the seminar because I'm away on a trip. I'm free Sunday evening, if you're around?'

He responded immediately. 'Perfect. See you then.'

Her stomach tightened. She breathed in the delicious scent of honeysuckle trailing from the nearby pergola, thinking of Mark's persistence. It had been a long time since she'd been pursued like this. She'd forgotten all the rules and etiquette and was transported for a moment back to her awkward schoolgirl self. A wave of excitement rolled through her.

Tim interrupted her thoughts. 'How long do I have to stay here this time? Last year I left after an hour.'

'Yes, but this time it's their fiftieth anniversary, Tim.'

'I don't see why I can't slip out quietly now. Everyone's made their speeches and toasts, everyone's eaten, and now everyone's just milling around. I've been polite.'

'You know why. All I'm asking for is one day. It calms her down to see us all together. You know it would break her if she knew.'

Tim sighed and shoved his hands in his pockets. 'Fine. I'll stay a bit longer.' He looked at her with unexpected tenderness. 'I'm doing this for you, you know.'

Anna stared at the gravel. 'I know.'

Tim started walking back into the house. 'Come on then. If I have to do this …'

A cold, empty feeling ran through and made her shiver, strangling the excitement she'd felt a moment ago. She was asking a lot of him, and he was being gracious about it when he was under no obligation. Anna had freed herself of obligation and expectation years ago. She never took the money he'd offered for her first year at King's College London; she'd wanted to do it off her own back, in her own time. It had taken her longer to get through the course, but that decision had removed one layer of awkwardness between them at least. Still, he'd inspired her to do the course in the first place and for that she was thankful.

She could have spent all evening in the fading late-

The Shadow Beyond the Hills

summer light of her parent's garden, breathing in the scent of the myriad flowers in bloom. Instead, she followed Tim back into the house, which was now an animated hive of shouts and cheers. The family games had commenced. *Great.*

When she walked into the living room, Beth was half straddling Matt in a suggestive game of Twister, while Jo, Ben and the children were battling it out with Bananagrams over in the corner of the room.

'Ah, there you are! Come on you two, who's up for a game of Taboo?' Her mother, who was surprisingly sprightly for this time of the day, hurried towards Anna and Tim, holding the game squarely in her arms.

She should be good at this game. All she had to do was not say the right word, use alternatives and fumble her way through different expressions until someone got there before her. She should be used to that.

'Oh no, not this one.' Her dad scratched his thick grey beard. 'I can't quite remember how to play this game.'

'It's like real life for you, Dad,' said Anna.

'Go on.'

'Well, the person on your team has to guess what the word you have in mind is, i.e., the one on your card, but you can't use certain words to help them. So, say you're thinking of Poland: you might be tempted to say "builder", "foreigner", "migrant worker", or "EU", but you have to be more creative than that.'

Her dad laughed. 'That's about right. You know me too well.'

Anna felt Tim smiling at her. She turned and caught his eye, holding his gaze for a fleeting moment. They'd laughed with youthful smugness like this in the past, when they'd stayed at her parent's house over summer weekends just after they'd wed; in snatched moments in the wine cellar, late night whispers in the guest room – *I can't, Anna. They're next door! It just feels … wrong.* Such a long time ago. So out of reach now.

They played games until the light fell. Her mother was tiring, and her mood was turning sour after a moment of confusion with the final round of games. Beth and Matt were the first to make polite excuses and leave.

Tim started fidgeting and stole a desperate look at Anna. She relented. They said their goodbyes and walked out to the gravel driveway.

'Thanks for coming, you two! And thanks for the gift!' Anna's father waved them out of the drive. Her mother's wispy outline darkened the doorway as she watched them leave.

Anna drove to the end of the lane and pulled into a lay-by, where Tim's car was parked.

'How long are you going to be away for?' Tim asked.

'A week. It's not a long trip, I just need to check out the lay of the land, confirm my interviewees and sources of research. I'll be going out for a few months next time.'

Tim nodded and pushed away a thick tuft of brown hair falling over his forehead. 'When do you leave?'

'Next week.' Why did she feel guilty saying this? This was new and unsettling.

Tim stepped out of the car and stooped down to look at her. 'Well, I hope it all goes well for you.'

'Thanks. And thank you for … you know, today. I appreciate it.'

He didn't say anything. He just shook his head with

The Shadow Beyond the Hills

a weak smile and got into his car. She watched him speed into the distance, round a bend, and disappear.

She met Mark in a microbrewery in Soho that looked like a converted warehouse, with dark-stained hardwood floors and a backlit blue panel running beneath the bar counter. He was standing at the bar when she walked in.

'Can I get you a Punk IPA?' Mark leant on the bar and raised his thick, dark eyebrows at her.

Central London was a pressure cooker of people, noise and heat. 'I'd kill for one. Thanks.'

He ordered a couple of beers and beeped his plastic on the card reader. 'So, have you read the paper Dr Anders emailed? The one on the Neuroscience of Mindfulness?'

'Ha, no. I've just been trying to get my head around my research methodology. Spent the weekend fuelled up on coffee just to get it done. I leave in a couple of days so I couldn't put it off any longer.'

'It's an absolute bastard of a paper. Interesting, granted.' His raised his glass to slightly cleft lips and took a few swigs of beer. 'I always thought the trend towards mindfulness was a load of hippy-dippy bullshit, to be honest. I didn't realise there was a scientific basis for it.'

'The older I get, the more I realise that I don't know half of what I think I know. I'm trying to consider everything with an open mind.'

He drew his mouth up into a wide grin and laughed, putting on a cockney accent for her. 'You talk as if you're a pensioner, love!'

'Well, it's true! I feel like I should be sorted by now. Have it all together. Instead, I still feel totally lost and clueless.'

'Cheers to that.' He clinked his glass against hers. 'Here's to being totally lost and clueless, even if we are grown adults.'

Anna shot him a dry smile and then knocked back a refreshing mouthful of her craft beer.

They talked studies, dissertations, work and relationships. Mark bemoaned his finance job in the City. He couldn't wait to drop it and all its 'insidious temptations and entanglements' and do something more meaningful, more purposeful. Anna remembered feeling like that once. Now, she just wanted intellectually satisfying work she could immerse herself in. She'd work on her garden at the weekends, keep fit and active, and try and get away for a holiday when she could. But there was still a faint ember glowing inside her – a hunger to explore something that had been burning away in her for years – for understanding. To get that, she would need to plan her trip carefully.

They moved on to a livelier bar on the Embankment, where scantily clad young Londoners swayed to salsa rhythms. She was too old for this. She half-expected the staff to turn her away, but Mark was insistent they go for it, having raved about the place on the way there. Dressed in skinny jeans, Gladiator sandals and her prettiest summer blouse, she suddenly felt very overdressed.

'You look fine, babe, don't worry.'

Babe? Where had that come from? She didn't feel like she could ever fit into the category of 'babe'. Nor

The Shadow Beyond the Hills

did she want to.

She downed a couple of mojitos and loosened up. Mark was an attractive guy – of that there was no doubt. He wore his vintage jeans and striped polo shirt well. He could have worn anything, and it would have worked.

She danced and drank for longer than she should have, considering she really needed to pack for her upcoming trip. They had one last dance and slumped down on some chairs.

'I really need to head back. I've got one more day to pack before I leave, so I can't spend most of it in bed sleeping off a hangover.' Anna saw Mark's eyes glistening with want.

'I'll walk you to the station.'

The air was cooler as they walked along the Embankment, all the lights of London twinkling on the Thames.

Mark stopped and stayed her arm. 'I'll miss you, Anna.' He pulled her close, reeking of alcohol and aftershave. His mouth covered hers, kissing her hard with wet lips. This didn't feel like she'd thought it would. Not even a fraction. She wanted to be sick.

She unwrapped his arms from her waist. 'I … I'm sorry, Mark. I can't do this.'

The flash of anger on his face turned to hurt. 'I thought we had—'

'No, we don't. I thought we might, but we really don't.' Anna left him on the Embankment and made her own way to the station.

CHAPTER TWENTY-NINE
HOME

She tried to block out the feeling of his tongue pushing its way into her mouth as she read the departures board in Terminal 5. Still it kept finding her, forcing its way in, just like his humiliated expression. She should have seen it coming. There'd been plenty of signs, beginning with the way he'd looked at her as they'd sat in evening lectures and seminars, his eyes laden with longing. *That*, she had enjoyed, but even those memories were tarnished now, and she didn't know how she was going to face him again.

She bought a magazine she knew she wouldn't read, by which time it was time to queue for boarding. She walked the gangway to the plane and was met by the breezy greetings of the stewards. Only seven and a half hours, and she'd be there. She took some study notes from her bag and scanned the list of people she'd arranged meetings with. A sense of the purpose that had been shrinking inside her over the years was beginning to inflate again. Everything in her course had been

The Shadow Beyond the Hills

leading up to this, from the day of her first seminar to the thesis outline she carried in her bag now.

She worked on her laptop for several hours, re-jigging her research outline for the umpteenth time and going through her literature review. She paused to peer down at the arid land beneath the plane. It was flying somewhere over South Sudan or Ethiopia, neither of which she'd visited before. They looked like forgotten, abandoned places, as if there couldn't possibly be anyone down there. She read through some notes again and fell into an uncomfortable sleep for the remainder of the flight, woken occasionally by the snores of the hefty man next to her.

Eventually, the plane landed with a forceful jolt, coming to a stop outside the odd forked structure of the main airport building. Warm, equatorial air enveloped her as she stepped off the plane, and the city lights blinked into view all over the surrounding hills. She sucked in a mouthful of moist air. A rush of nerves coursed through her.

The visa queue was mercifully short. Through the smudged taxi windows she could tell the city had changed so much since she'd last been here. It would have been unrecognisable if it weren't for the undulating landscape and the fountain roundabout downtown. All the friends she'd made had left, their lives as transient as hers – even Sarah and Matt, who finally did get permission to build a house on some farmland just outside the city and had planned to build ecolodges on the surrounding fields. The buildings they'd painstakingly gotten permission for were no more a sign of their commitment and permanence than their visas. It could all be packed up and dismantled in a matter of weeks. As had happened with her and Tim. She'd left with an already fading tan and a stash of memories, some of them worthy of being blown up and framed; some of them more painful than she could ever have imagined. Aware of just how alone she felt, she wasted no time in checking in and getting into the starchy sheets of her bed. She had a long day ahead of her the next day, and she needed to get an early start.

Bright rays of dawn sliced through her room as she swatted a mosquito away from her ear. Somehow, despite the nets, they always got in. She straightened out her hair and unfolded a trouser suit from her suitcase. Rwandans were smart people with high standards – she'd remembered this. No baggy linen trousers or strappy tops from Primark for her, as she'd been tempted to pack. If she wanted to be taken seriously and get the information she needed from the people she wanted, she'd need to ditch the dowdiness, however comfortable it felt in the heat. Breakfast was a token plate of fruit and a dry croissant. She couldn't handle more – not when her stomach was churning with a virulent mixture of anticipation and trepidation. She tried to focus her mind. Now was as good a time as any to give this mindfulness thing a go. She lingered on the sharp tang of passion fruit and its sweet crunch as she bit down on the seeds; how the light played on her bottle of water and the warmth of her coffee as it poured into her stomach. Which was still churning. *Nope. Not working.*

She gathered her files and folders and headed out

into the city to find a taxi. She knew she was probably paying twice, maybe three times as much as she should have, but she didn't have the energy to haggle. All her energy was being consumed by the fight not to run straight back to the hotel. But she hadn't come here to run away and hide. Not this time. Not again. The taxi took her up out of the city to Mount Kigali. The croissant she'd eaten threatened to make a reappearance as the taxi bumped along winding tracks up the hill. Was she stupid to arrange this? Was it presumptuous? Entitled, even? There was no going back now. When she'd sent the email, she'd set something in motion that had the potential to crush her all over again.

The taxi lurched to a stop in a plume of ochre dust. As it dispersed, a clearer view of the city emerged. It lay sprawled out below a panoramic sweep of spiky trees, terraced farmland and small grey and brown houses. Behind her was the café they'd agreed to meet in.

'Marie.'

She had to say her name out loud before she arrived. It would somehow make it all seem real. Anna walked up to the bar and ordered a Coke, remembering to ask for a cold one – Coke ikonje. She sat down to take the first sip and there was Marie. No warning. No distant view to steel and steady herself. She just appeared, and Anna felt the ground fall away from underneath her. The adolescent girl she remembered had grown into a smart, sophisticated young woman – intimidating, almost, were it not for the gentle smile framing her face. She wore her thick spread of neatly braided hair in a loose ponytail behind her shoulders, and stood tall in black heels, a pencil skirt and sleeveless white blouse.

Anna stood up, not knowing what the most appropriate greeting was. Marie took the awkwardness away instantly, holding the tops of her arms and drawing her into a wholehearted embrace.

'Anna, amakuru?'

'Ni meza cyane.' Anna laughed, lightened by the unexpected ease of their greeting. She offered to buy Marie a drink, but Marie politely declined. She watched the way Marie walked to the bar, her steps no longer shadowed in shyness but exuding a mellow confidence. She came back with a bottle of Krest and sat with Anna in the stillness of the high-altitude air.

'You look amazing, Marie. Kigali life is treating you well.'

'Thank you. You look well too. How's London?'

'Busy as ever,' Anna smiled. 'I'm a post-graduate student now, would you believe.'

'Me too. I'm specialising in cardiac surgery. I'm training to be a consultant,' Marie said with quiet pride.

'You've achieved so much. You have a lot to be proud of.' An outpouring of relief washed over Anna. Marie had thrived. What had happened in the past hadn't hindered her. It confirmed to her that she'd made the right decision.

'I was sorry to hear about your mother.' Another surge of relief. She'd mentioned the thing she was most apprehensive about. It was out there now.

Marie took a deep breath and pulled her mouth into a hard-won smile. 'She's at peace now.'

'And you?' Anna felt herself redden with regret at blurting this out with such little care.

'I'm getting there, buhoro, buhoro. My work helps. I'm helping people every day. I do what I can.'

The Shadow Beyond the Hills

Anna ran what she said next through an internal filter and decided that she hadn't come all this way to skirt around issues. She wanted to be real with Marie. 'You had every right to feel hurt and angry. You don't have to forgive Judy for what she did to your family.'

'It's true, I don't.' Marie bit her lip and toyed with a length of braided hair. 'She had a stroke. I was on duty at the hospital when she was admitted. Did you know?'

'No,' replied Anna. 'I gather she carried on running Beauty from Ashes then?'

Marie smiled. 'She was one of the few who stayed. She would never hand over her baby.'

Anna tried to picture Judy now, still as dogged and tenacious as ever. Age couldn't tame her.

'I left her alone in her cubicle.' Marie swallowed what looked like a hard lump in her throat.

Anna started to feel uneasy. Where was she going with this?

'I didn't have to help her. Except I did,' added Marie. 'I'm a doctor now – it's my duty. I'm my mother's daughter – she taught me how to forgive. I couldn't go on letting her hold power over me any longer. I had every right to forgive and keep on forgiving, so I did. I wasn't going to let her take that away from me too. I came in after her operation to check on the dressing where the surgeon had inserted a mesh tube into her skull.'

'You're an incredible person, Marie. I've always thought that, and I always will.' Anna reached out and took hold of her hand. It was soft and yielding. 'I don't know where you get your strength from.'

'My mother. Her faith. Her hope. Her love.'

Marie shimmered like a mirage in Anna's watering

eyes. She tried her best to regain her composure, remembering why she was there.

'I wanted to ask you something. It would be … your last gift to me, if you like.'

Marie's expression piqued with curiosity.

'I mentioned that I've been studying. Well, I still am, and my last assignment for my Master's programme is my dissertation.'

Anna took a folder from her bag and slid it across the table towards Marie.

Marie read the title printed on the front. 'Memory and Remembrance: An Exploration of the Impact of Trauma on Retrograde Amnesia.'

'I need you, Marie. I need you to help me with my research, and, one day I hope, my doctoral research. To help further understanding. If you'd be willing, of course.' Anna sat heavily in her seat, unsure of the weight of her words on Marie. 'I appreciate that this may dredge things up that you'd rather remain in the past. You can feel free to say no, and even that I'm foolish for having the audacity to—'

'It's fine. Nta kibazo, inshuti wanje. I want to help you if I can. It would be a privilege.'

Anna beamed and wiped away the stray tear that had slipped down her cheek. 'Thank you. Thank you so much.'

Marie had been reunited with her mother before her death. She'd become a doctor. She'd forgiven Kevine and Judy. And she was going to help Anna piece together the puzzle of her research. Anything could happen. Anna marvelled at how these strands of Marie's life had wrapped around each other and were now connected with her own again. Marie set up a meeting for her with the Director of the Neurosurgical Centre, which had proven fruitful. She was able to access their flagship research library containing various case studies, and even confirmed a few patients for interviews. She'd met with the leader of a counselling and support service for genocide survivors, some of whom had suffered serious neurological disorders, and confirmed a sample of interviewees as well as gaining access to their archives. It had been a successful trip, in more ways than one.

She held on to these thoughts as tightly as she did to the bars of the moto she was riding on as it weaved its way round the dirt tracks to her former home. Memories of their beautiful house, still festooned with bougainvillea trailing along the walls, had been blemished by the angst of their last few months in Rwanda. But when the moto stopped and she stood in front of the house, new feelings began to stir inside her. She was filled with boundless energy, her present and future brimming with possibility and potential once again. Yes, her and Tim had made mistakes, and yes, they'd rushed headlong into something they'd had not the faintest idea about – but nothing was beyond redemption. Marie had shown her that. Her memories of the last few months in that house were overshadowed by something greater than her and her disappointment and hurt. Something greater than all of them.

She followed the familiar route she used to take from the house to Cubs Montessori School. Some of the dirt tracks had turned into paved roads since she'd been away. When she'd packed up and left the country, she hadn't cared if she never came back; now she was looking forward to her next trip. It felt good to be looking forward rather than always looking back, remembering painful paths she'd walked. She could plan her next steps now. They came into view with lucid clarity. She knew what she needed to do and where she needed to be. She hailed a moto and returned to the hotel to check out.

She arrived at the airport just as the sun dropped below the hills. Her last sunset in Rwanda. For now. The plane taxied down the runway and rose high above a city she once thought she'd never want to set foot in again but was now coming to love. Life could still surprise her. She could still be surprised by joy.

Anna savoured a smooth shot of cognac to help her switch off and sleep for the flight. She felt Marie's warm embrace once again and pictured her eyes shining with genuine pleasure at seeing her. Whether it was the cognac or the comfort of that memory, she slipped into a deep sleep that carried her across the Sahara, the Mediterranean and into the Netherlands.

A short early morning flight took her across the North Sea to Heathrow. The plane banked sharply to the left, revealing miniaturised London landmarks from her small cabin window. She walked out of arrivals, a sure and steady feeling building inside her with each step. She took the train to the outskirts of London, a taxi to a house that held no memories for her but contained a promise that, despite the years, had never truly been broken.

The door swung open on the first knock.

Anna smiled. 'I think everything's working out. I think it's all going to be okay.'

Tim's face shone.

Anna hauled her bags across the threshold, dumped them on the floor and pushed the door shut with her heel. She was home.

ACKNOWLEDGEMENTS

The beginnings of this story were half baked in the blistering equatorial sunshine of East Africa several years ago, when the image of a frail old white lady lying in a hospital joined by a young black doctor rose in my mind. I wrote the first few chapters and let the story sit for a while as the characters took on form and substance over the years, adding a pinch of plot development here and there.

The experiences I had in Rwanda profoundly shaped my writing and this book. The Rwandan people were good to me. They were gracious, patient and good-humoured, and I'm indebted to those who came alongside us and became our friends while we navigated our way through cross-cultural life. It is them, first and foremost, that I want to acknowledge and thank.

Thanks to the artisans I interviewed, who humoured me in my faltering attempts at Kinyarwanda, and who shared their stories of joy and pain as I sat awkwardly in front of them, listening to them talk about living through a genocide. Michelle, who asked me when I was going to 'write that book', and Claire, who reminded me to keep writing.

Paul for his careful and insightful comments on one of my early drafts. You edited with precision and gave me a good belly laugh along the way. Finally, Sean, for his unwavering belief and support. Thank you for pouring yourself out for our family, and thanks for the adventures!

ABOUT THE AUTHOR

Emma grew up near the windswept tors of Dartmoor, Devon. In her mid-twenties she relocated with her husband and young children to East Africa, where they lived on passion fruits, bucket baths and relentless sunshine. During her time in Rwanda, she worked with Azizi Life (meaning 'precious' life in Swahili), a social enterprise partnering with rural artisans to create fair trade, handcrafted products. In 2019 she left Rwanda and settled in the stunning Wye Valley area of South Wales. She works in the non-profit sector and specialises in writing and communications for faith-based media, having written op-ed pieces and columns for several magazines. She also writes flash fiction and has been published in *Ellipsis*, a literary e-zine. *The Shadow Beyond the Hills* is her debut novel.